HOMICIDE HOUSE

Books by David Frome

Homicide House

MR. PINKERTON RETURNS

by DAVID FROME

WILDSIDE PRESS

Homicide House: A Mr. Pinkerton Mystery

Published by Wildside Press LLC
www.wildsidepress.com

HOMICIDE HOUSE

THE fragrance of burning leaves rose in the quiet golden haze that hung over Godolphin Square. It stirred a mute nostalgia in the heart of the little grey Welshman sitting under the plane trees on the dilapidated bench between a pile of forgotten rubble and the soot-grimed rhododendrons straggling out into the ragged unkempt path. Mr. Evan Pinkerton did not really belong in Godolphin Square. It was still the exclusive West End of London, in spite of the sagging wattle fence that had replaced the iron palings, taken for munitions, and the four bombed-out houses that made a broad gap between the chimney pots on the north side. On the south side the houses were as they had always been, simple and elegant, with only a few of them converted into exclusive service flats.

Mr. Pinkerton had come to one of them—No. 4 Godolphin Square—for two quite simple reasons. The first was that his own house in Golders Green had got an incendiary bomb on the roof. The second was that No. 4 Godolphin Square was part of Pinkerton Estates, and so, curiously enough, was Mr. Pinkerton himself. In fact, Mr. Pinkerton was Pinkerton Estates, although he still did not entirely believe it. It was as incredible to him as it was to everybody else, including Miss Myrtle Grimstead, the lady manager of No. 4 Godolphin Square. She would never, of course, have put him in a maid's room on the third and top story, to share a bath with the chef and the permanent valet, if she had

had any idea of who he was. Miss Grimstead had taken a long look at the estate agent's order for a flat and free maintenance, when Mr. Pinkerton had timidly presented it, and a single very brisk one at the little man. Some impoverished hanger-on, Miss Grimstead had decided; a distant relative no doubt.

But Mr. Pinkerton was happy enough on the third floor. It made him a little more confident that the late Mrs. Pinkerton, from whom he had inherited the Pinkerton Estates, would not suddenly rematerialize, wispy-haired and vinegary-cheeked, by the sheer force of the agony of seeing him squander her substance. Never having allowed him more than a sixpence at a time, even out of his own earnings, she would hardly care to see him rioting away her whole property. Mr. Pinkerton knew very well she would never have left it to him at all if she could have brought herself to lay out sixpence for a will form at the corner stationer's.

But on the whole he was happier outside the house than in it. Down in the square, he was at least out of range of Miss Myrtle Grimstead's managerial eye. The straggling rhododendrons also concealed him from the eternal scrutiny of Miss Caroline Winship, who sat all day at the window of her flat on the first floor, brooding over the ruins of her bombed-out house across the Square. He felt reasonably happy there on the dilapidated bench, and reasonably secure; and when it rained, he could go to the cinema.

That it was not raining today was unusual for several reasons. One was that it had rained all through August. Another was that if it had not just' stopped, Mr. Pinkerton would not have been in the Square to see Daniel McGrath. That was something he would not have liked to miss. Daniel McGrath, coming resolutely, was in search of a dream, and no one in all London knew more about dreams than the little Welshman sitting there on the wooden bench behind the rhododendrons in Godolphin Square. He had two of his own. One was Scotland Yard, in the tawny and stolid person of J. Humphrey Bull, his only friend, his wife's former lodger in Golders Green, and now a chief inspector of the Criminal Investigation Division of the Metropolitan Police. The other was the cinema, where, on rainy days and in the least expensive seat available, Mr. Pinkerton sat with breathless enchantment, not untouched with envy, viewing the life and loves of those strange and fascinating people, the Americans. He knew more about them, their habits and their language, than they did themselves.

In the pale golden haze of the late autumn afternoon, Mr. Pinkerton was unaware that his two dreams were poised, in full bud, ready to burst into the most extraordinary fruition.

Daniel McGrath came swinging along into Godolphin Square. Mr. Pinkerton saw him first as he turned to the left, glancing up at the numbers uniformly inscribed on the broad elliptical fanlights over the painted Adam doorways. The first being, as Mr. Pinkerton knew, illegibly dimmed, it was not until he reached the third house that he made a prompt about-face and set back toward the right and the north side of the Square. Having no business of his own and being inveterately curious about other people's, Mr. Pinkerton watched. A devotee of New Scotland Yard, he liked to make deductions about people, their character and intent, in which he was almost invariably and sometimes notably incorrect, as the time he had mistaken the Bermondsey dog poisoner for the curate's wife and would have helped her catch a miserable little terrier if it had not fortunately bitten him and got away. Now, even at some distance, he recognized that there was something peculiar about the young

9

man in the Square. He was a stranger, obviously, hunting for a particular house. Then, as he came nearer, Mr. Pinkerton straightened up on his bench, his watery grey eyes brightening behind his lozenge-shaped steel-rimmed spectacles. It was no wonder the young man looked peculiar; Mr. Pinkerton recognized the reason for it instantly. He was an American. It stood out all over him. His whole air was quite unmistakable: the free and untrammelled way he swung along, imperturbable and unconcerned, as at ease and at home as if he owned the entire place.

Not that Mr. Pinkerton regarded that as offensive, as some people did. Never having been truly at ease or at home in any part of the constricted universe he had moved in, it was the one thing that could stir a momentary envy in his timorous heart. His childhood had been rigorously regimented by a pair of dour Welsh aunts. The unfortunate interregnum between them and Mrs. Pinkerton had been a nightmare spent as an underfed, underpaid undermaster in a small Welsh school, a nightmare so unforgettable that never without trembling did he see two or more small boys unaccompanied by their parents or keepers. His release from all of it had come too late. Even Mrs. Pinkerton's last and unintended act of grace in leaving him the free and presumably sole arbiter of himself and some £75,000 in cash and property had been too late for him ever to get over what had gone before. Nevertheless, the sight of anybody young and untrod on, serene, calmly sure the world was a friendly and decent place and as much his as anybody else's, had an extraordinary effect on him; it lifted vicariously the colorless load of his inferiority.

He felt it now, watching Daniel McGrath coming along, looking up at the street numbers, and he sat boldly erect, ignoring the fact that the rhododendron branches no longer protected him from Miss Caroline Winship's brooding gaze. The young man had come to an empty hole in the row of houses, two doors from Miss Winship's own. He stopped and looked ahead, then back again, as if shocked; as if a hole where a house had been had not been part of what he had expected to find. Mr. Pinkerton adjusted his spectacles and waited anxiously. The young man went back and looked up again at Number 19, then came on, almost running, it seemed to Mr. Pinkerton, his long legs covered the space so quickly.

"Oh, dear!" Mr. Pinkerton thought suddenly. "The house he's hunting for isn't there any more. It's—it's destroyed. And he didn't know it."

He got up from his bench. The young man had gone back again and was counting up once more, slowly, stopping to look about him, as if in a bewildered daze. If McGrath had been an Englishman—or if he himself had been one—Mr. Pinkerton would never in the world have done what he did do. He scurried across the garden to the flimsy gate in the wattle fence, opened it and hurried along to where the young man was standing, looking over the four-foot wall erected to keep passers-by from plunging down into the ruins of what had been Miss Caroline Winship's basement kitchen area. Ferns and the white silk seed-pods of willow herb grew there now, sprung miraculously out of the brick and rubble of the blast-shredded walls.

Mr. Pinkerton looked over too, glancing anxiously at the young man staring down into the area, his jaw tight, his lean figure motionless as a statue.

"Are—are you—looking for somebody?"

Mr. Pinkerton said it, and then died a sudden trembling agony of apprehension. He was being grossly and inexcusably officious, and maybe by some horrible mischance the man was not an American, but somebody in the disguise of one—or, if he was one, perhaps not a friendly one. He might be different from all the others of his race Mr. Pinkerton had known—there had been two, actually, and in the flesh, not film. He might resent people prying into his personal affairs. Mr. Pinkerton sidled a few steps away along the wall. The young man was turning his head, slowly, like somebody struck a dull blow behind the ear. His frosty blue eyes, curiously light in a lean face sun-tanned the color of juice from a green walnut, were blank and unseeing. Mr. Pinkerton retreated another step along the wall.

"I—I'm very sorry," he said hastily. "I didn't mean to intrude."

"Intrude? You're not intruding."

The young man spoke like a bewildered automaton as his gaze turned back to the ruins of the house in front of him. His eyes travelled slowly up the graceful curve of the stone staircase that swept, fantastically supporting one weather-stained pale grey plastered wall rather than being supported by it, up to the transverse hall on the first floor, curving there at the end of the hall and sweeping on up, its delicate ornamental brass railing still intact, to the open sky. Over the transverse hall a portion of attic roof still remained to make it all look like some forgotten stage set, left standing when the play was ended. A central chimney column stood solidly intact behind it, the fireplaces with their carved roses and baskets of fruit and flowers protected from the weather, the faded peach damask still paneling the overmantel.

The young man turned his head slowly back to the little Welshman standing uncertainly and at a discreet distance from him.

"Is this Number Twenty-two Godolphin Square?"

His voice had a lost, unbelieving tone in it, as if he was awed and stricken, and thoroughly sunk, as Mr. Pinkerton imagined he might put it.

"Yes. This is Number Twenty-two."

The American still spoke out of a bewildered fog. "What happened? Do you know what happened?"

Living at Number 4 Godolphin Square, Mr. Pinkerton knew only too well what had happened. A comparative late-comer, he had been what he believed the Americans would call a natural, to hear the story long after everybody else, each with his own major or minor catastrophe to tell, had heard it, *ad infinitum, ad nauseam,* from both Miss Caroline Winship and her sister Mrs. Scott Winship. If their accounts differed from Miss Myrtle Grimstead's, it was not unreasonable, as they had been there and Miss Grimstead had been safely on the opposite side of the Square, where the bombs did not hit; and if the story improved with the telling and retelling, that was natural enough, as Mr. Pinkerton knew from trying to improve his own sorry tale. There was nothing particularly dramatic, basically, about an incendiary bomb in the attic, especially as he was at Inspector Bull's house in Hampstead that night. But the Winships' story was different, and having heard it so often from the two sisters, and everyone else, he could tell it almost as vividly as he had been there at the top of the hanging staircase himself.

"Miss Caroline Winship's a very determined woman," he ended breathlessly. "She said no Germans would drive her out of the house into a shelter to catch pneumonia. Some people think she ought to have let her sister Mrs. Scott Winship go, even if she didn't care to herself, because Mrs. Winship isn't as strong a character as Miss Caroline. (She married a cousin, that's why the name's the same.) Some people say that sitting up there in that hall all night, with the whole front of the house blasted in, made her even less strong-minded than she was. They didn't get out till morning, and even then Miss Caroline refused to go. She hung on to the bannister, and fought like a harpy, Miss Grimstead says, before the police came and dragged her bodily down and out into the street. Oh, she's a one. She's—really a one."

Mr. Pinkerton blinked his eyes and adjusted his spectacles.

"Of course it was quite extraordinary. The other three houses you can see went completely down. Miss Winship's would have done too, only her father had it shored up with those iron girders when he put central heat in before the last war, Miss Caroline says. They used the hall chimney for the flue, and discovered the back part of the house was sagging, so that's when he had the supports put in."

He paused and looked up anxiously at the young man, whose mind and gaze seemed to have wandered back to the ruined walls, instead of focussing respectfully on the broad iron transverse support that was what had held up the hanging staircase.

"It was—sort of ironical," Mr. Pinkerton ended lamely. "I mean, to have escaped the blitz, and everything, and then get it in 1944, when things were—were almost over."

The young man turned and looked at him then.

"What happened to the—the girl? There was a girl here, wasn't there?"

He did not seem too sure, but Mr. Pinkerton brightened up at once. Of course, he thought. This was it. The films should have taught him.

"Oh, you mean *Mary* Winship!" he said. "Oh, she's all right. She wasn't here. She—"

14

"She's—married, I suppose?"

"Oh, no," Mr. Pinkerton said hastily. "She's not married. I don't think her aunt would ever let—"

He stopped instantly, realizing that that might be hardly a tactful thing for him to be saying.

"I mean, I think her aunt and her mother sort of depend on her—perhaps more than they should, as a matter of fact," he finished hurriedly. But the young man did not seem much concerned with the two elder Winship ladies. A light had kindled somewhere in the depths of his blue eyes, making him seem a little less remote and slightly more tractable.

"You don't happen to know where they are now, do you?" he inquired casually.

"Certainly," Mr. Pinkerton said. "They live just over the Square. At Number Four. They have the first-floor flats. Indeed, if you'll look over, you'll see her aunt, Miss Caroline Winship. She's always at the window. She's supposed to have bribed the gardener to cut off some of the branches so she could see across. It annoyed the other residents of the Square. It's a service flat. I live there too."

He was aware that he could have sounded a little pettish, as if he had a record of omniscience that he did not care to have questioned, which could not have been further from the truth. It was simply that he had been disappointed at the offhand fashion the inquiry had been put in. It was as impersonal and disinterested as if the young American had got an unpaid bill in his pocket and was instituting a routine inquiry as to the debtor's whereabouts. A sudden chill struck Mr. Pinkerton. He swallowed painfully, his heart lurching into the pit of his stomach.

"Oh, dear!" he thought. What if that was the case? What if he was just there to make trouble for everybody? He glanced quickly at the American. He was standing there, fishing about in his pocket. To Mr. Pinkerton's relief it was his pipe he brought out. He looked at it for a moment as if it was something he hadn't himself expected to find there, and put it in his mouth. He was smiling a little, but not very much, as he turned and glanced across the garden in the direction Mr. Pinkerton had pointed when he said the Winships were at Number 4. Then he looked at Mr. Pinkerton again.

"Thanks," he said. He added slowly, "Mary Winship. It's a pretty name. I never knew what it was. All I knew was she lived at Twenty-two Godolphin Square. I came to see her here, a couple of times, but I got cold feet just outside the door. I hung around hoping she'd come out, but she never did. Then my outfit shoved off and I never got back to England again. I guess I'd have gotten up nerve enough if we'd stuck around a little longer, but just an ordinary G. I. punk ringing the bell and asking Can I see the girl with dreamy lashes and curly hair—I guess I figured I'd get booted out on my impertinent behind."

He gave Mr. Pinkerton a quietly amused smile. "So, thanks a lot, pal. I'll shove along now, but I'll be seeing you. McGrath's my name, Dan McGrath."

"Pinkerton's mine," said Mr. Pinkerton.

Dan McGrath turned to go, and turned back. "By the way, Mr. Pinkerton—do you know if her father ever came back?"

"Her *father?*"

Mr. Pinkerton looked at him blankly.

"I—I didn't know she had a father. I mean, I thought her mother was a—a widow. I thought her father had been dead a great many years. In fact, I'm quite sure of it—Miss Caroline Winship told me so herself. You're sure—I mean, we're talking about the same girl, aren't we?"

"I don't know, Mr. Pinkerton." Dan McGrath was pleasant and imperturbable. "All I know is she lived at Twenty-two Godolphin Square. I met her in an air raid shelter. That was in forty-three. She was with her cousin and they'd gotten separated. She wasn't the maid—I know that darn well, because I held her hand all night."

"Oh," Mr. Pinkerton said. His shattered illusions quickly annealed themselves. Dan McGrath was human after all. He could hold a girl's hand. He could also grin. The one he gave Mr. Pinkerton as he set off up the road again was proof of that.

Mr. Pinkerton stood blinking after him for a moment before he turned and scurried happily across the Square, his heart fluttering with excitement like the dun-coloured wings of a moth miller rising from a dusty floor.

2

Inside the door and halfway up the first flight of green-carpeted stairs, Mr. Pinkerton remembered Miss Caroline Winship. Eternally watching from her window, she must have seen him talking to the American in front of her ruined house. He started hastily down again. His impulse had been to hurry back where he could examine and enjoy the romantic potentials of Dan McGrath's return to London over a nice hot cup of weak tea in the privacy of his own room. Halfway up the stairs he realized how mistaken he was. He could not see Miss Winship's door open, or her standing in it like a virulent spider, her web already spun to catch his unsuspecting feet, but he was mortally certain that was the case. He hurried back down again. It was too late. Pegott, the permanent valet, materialized from the shadowy recesses of the lower hall, was blocking his way, his customary insolence more thinly veiled than usual.

"Miss Winship would like to speak to you."

He had dropped the "sir" a few days after he came to Number 4 Godolphin Square and had had an opportunity to inspect Mr. Pinkerton's belongings, which were as meagre and unimpressive as their owner. When he did use it occasionally, it had the effect of cocking a thumb and making a nose, so that Mr. Pinkerton was rather happier when he didn't bother. He had small close-set green-blue eyes that seldom met anybody's directly, but he was able to stare down the little grey man with a superciliousness that Mr. Pinkerton had no defence against.

"I'll see Miss Winship later." It took unusual courage for Mr. Pinkerton to say it, but say it he did. "I'm going out now," he added stoutly. He adjusted his steel-rimmed spectacles and tried to sound as adamant as possible.

"Miss Winship saw you come in," Pegott said carelessly. "I'm going off, and I wouldn't want Miss Winship to think I'd not given you her message. She's ordered up tea especially for you. I'm sure she wouldn't want it wasted."

Mr. Pinkerton blinked. Faced with a personal responsibility for the waste of food when it was so difficult to get, he felt himself weakening miserably.

"Well," he said. ". . . Well, I expect I can go out later."

He turned and trudged unhappily back up the stairs. The permanent valet stood where he was, not attempting to disguise the smirk on his face. And Miss Caroline Winship was waiting in her doorway—determined, imperious, her heavy cheeks raddled with bitterness.

"Come in here." She crooked a bony finger in a peremptory summons. "Close the door. Put your hat on the chair—don't stand there fiddling with it. Who was that man over there at my house? What does he want? Don't try any tricks with me. If he's another of those Town and Country planning people, I'll call my solicitor. Answer me immediately. *Don't* stand there gaping. *Answer* me!"

Mr. Pinkerton was indeed standing there gaping, but his mind was busily at work.

"Oh, dear—she's dreadful," he was thinking rapidly. "She's *really* dreadful." He had never thought of her as particularly pleasant, but she'd always been polite, and if a little condescending, no more than Mr. Pinkerton knew was warranted, considering she was born to wealth and Godolphin Square and he had only accidentally inherited both—which accidental happening, furthermore, Miss Caroline Winship had no conceivable way of knowing about. Whenever she had summoned him into her flat before it had been when she was bored with looking out of the window and irritable with her invalid sister, and wanted someone else to listen to her without interrupting. Mr. Pinkerton had listened. He had listened patiently and interminably, to her reminiscences of the past and her bitterness about the present, to Things in General and her income tax and the socialists in particular. But she had always covered up the corrosive vitriol that was working now like an evil ferment in her thick lips and quivering nostrils. She was frightening. The rouge on her cheeks stood out in dull purple splotches, and her brown eyes flashed under their heavy twitching lids. A heavy-set, large-boned, dominant woman, she always made Mr. Pinkerton feel even smaller and scrawnier than he was. He felt now that he could have stood erect under the oriental carpet on the floor.

"Answer me!" Miss Caroline Winship said.

"He's—he's not. He wasn't at all," Mr. Pinkerton stammered. His hands were trembling. A mild flush of adrenalin, diluted at best, was all that enabled him to answer her without his voice trembling too. "He's not from the Town and Country planning people at all. He's from America. He's just over here on—on a visit."

"A visit? What for? Is he another of their antique dealers trying to buy my staircase and mantel? If he is tell him they're not—"

"No, no," Mr. Pinkerton said hastily. "He's not trying to buy anything. He was—he was just *looking.*"

For some reason that he had not put into words, he would rather have cut his tongue out than tell her what Dan McGrath was really looking for. He hadn't the remotest doubt, born of his previous observation of her relationships with Mary Winship, Mary Winship's mother Mrs. Scott Winship, and her nephew Eric Dalrymple-Hughes, and crystallized by the violence of her present emotion, that she would spoil everything if she knew Dan McGrath had come all the way from America to see Mary again.

"He's really not trying to buy anything at all, Miss Winship."

"I don't believe it." Miss Caroline Winship's heavy lids drooped ominously over her brilliant angry eyes. "He wants something. What is it?"

"—Oh, Caroline . . ."

Mr. Pinkerton started and turned quickly around. Mrs.

Scott Winship, frail and wan, had come from the adjoining room and was there in the doorway, her worn quilted dressing gown huddled about her. Her nostrils were pinched with cold, and the drooping querulous lines of the perpetual invalid robbed her of all the delicate beauty that she may once have had. Looking at her was like looking at an image of her daughter reflected in a tarnished mildewed mirror in a darkened hallway, all the vitality and youthful loveliness faded and withered by the killing frost of years and dependence.

"Please don't be so cross, Caroline. Perhaps Mr. Pinkerton doesn't know. You really mustn't let yourself get so worked up and irritable."

Caroline Winship had never had her sister's beauty, but she had all the concentrated passion and vitality the other lacked.

"I'll deal with this in my own way, Louise," she said shortly. "Go back to your fire. You'll catch cold in here."

She turned to Mr. Pinkerton. *"What* did that man want?"

"He—he wanted to know if Mr. Winship had ever come back."

Mr. Pinkerton had not intended to say it; it had just popped out of his mouth, somehow, as he saw Mrs. Winship draw her robe more tightly around her frail body and start to obey her sister's command to go back to her room. It had just popped out, and in some terrible and inexplicable fashion remained, undissipated, the words as tangible as if they were solidly created objects, visibly formed and frozen.

"Oh, dear!" Mr. Pinkerton thought with a mute and horrified gasp. "What have I done now!"

As well he might. It was as if he had by chance stumbled onto a magic formula that turned everything in the room into stone or lifeless clay. The two women stood motionless, petrified into speechless silence, life suspended. There was something so ghastly about the whole atmosphere of the room and the unutterable quiet of both of the women there, that small beads of icy pricking perspiration broke out all over him.

"He—just asked. That's all," he managed to say. "He just asked me if I knew."

His voice sounded hollow and very loud, as if he was screaming in an empty room.

Then Miss Caroline spoke. "Go to your room, Louise." Her voice was so low and so deathly quiet that Mr. Pinkerton took an involuntary step backward and put his hand out, trying to reach the door.

"Stay where you are, Mr. Pilkington. Don't go. Come over here. Come over and sit down."

Mr. Pinkerton was not sure how he did it. He was aware of Louise Winship somehow fading away and the solid white door filling the place she had stood in. He was aware of himself sitting bolt upright on the extreme edge of the chair that Miss Caroline's thick knotted hand had indicated. And of her hooded brown eyes level with his own, veiled and intent, fixed steadily on him.

"Mr. Pinkerton . . ." Her voice was still low, hardly above a whisper, with none of a whisper's forced or sibilant quality. "Mr. Pinkerton—Scott Winship has not come back. He can't ever come back. Scott Winship is dead. Do you understand that? He's dead. He's been dead for a great many years. He is dead— and his name is never mentioned in this house."

Mr. Pinkerton swallowed. He nodded his head mutely. He was shaking so that he couldn't have spoken if he had wanted to. He nodded again. Miss Winship was rising. He rose too.

"You understand, Mr. Pinkerton?"

Mr. Pinkerton nodded again, hastily. "I do. I—I understand, perfectly." He managed to get control of his voice. "And I'm terribly sorry. I—I didn't mean to upset everybody. And it's— it's none of my business anyway, Miss Winship."

Miss Caroline Winship was moving with him toward the door. He retrieved his hat and clutched it tightly in his trembling hands.

"How very correct you are in saying so." She reached out and opened the door for him. "It is no business of yours whatsoever. I hope you'll remember and not forget it. My sister is an invalid. I have no intention of allowing her to be disturbed. I'd be happy if you'd remember that too. Good afternoon, Mr. Pinkerton. Thank you for coming."

She closed the door. Mr. Pinkerton's knees were as weak as tepid water. He leaned against the wall and pulled at his narrow celluloid collar that was like a constricting iron band round his throat.

"Oh, dear me!" he whispered. "Dear, dear, how dreadful."

He started to close his eyes, and blinked them abruptly open. As he leaned against the wall the angle of his vision brought into view a small segment of the staircase that otherwise he could not have seen—nor would he in all probability have noticed it then if his ears had not caught the clink of a heel on one of the brass rods securing the thick carpet at the base of each riser. It was a stealthy clink, and as Mr. Pinkerton looked quickly he saw the brush of white across the narrow segment of staircase—Arthur Pegott's white shoulder, his head bent forward to conceal his presence as he slipped down the stairs.

Mr. Pinkerton straightened up, his heart curiously still. Pegott had been listening at the door. He knew it as perfectly as if he had seen him there, or seen the imprint of his pointed shoes on the figured carpet. But why? What had he hoped to hear that would make him, after waiting in the lower hall, insolently watching Mr. Pinkerton come up the stairs, nip up behind him and risk his job to listen to? Unless . . . Mr. Pinkerton steadied himself and glanced at the solid ivory-painted door panel. How much had he heard? He listened now himself, to see if Pegott could have heard at all. The sisters would certainly be talking, whether Scott Winship's name was ever mentioned in the house or not.

Miss Caroline Winship's voice was muted but quite distinct. ". . . American must have seen him. That's all I know. You'd better come at once, Sidney. I think he's here. In London."

Mr. Pinkerton heard the faint click of the bell as the telephone was replaced, and the scrape of a chair being pushed back and stopping sharply, as if Miss Caroline Winship had become aware of something. Of him, possibly—of his heart pounding against his ribs. For a paralyzed fraction of an instant Mr. Pinkerton stood rooted there, unable to move. Then an indefinable terror gave his feet a sudden power of speed and silence he did not know they could possess, and he was down the stairs and out the front door into the twilit security of the Square with an almost fantastic sense of relief. It died as quickly as it had come as he looked up at the first-floor window and saw Miss Caroline's solid figure looming darkly against the light behind her.

She was holding the curtain to one side, looking down at him, heavy and motionless. She knew he had been listening to her. The same intuitive awareness that had spoken to him from Pegott's stealthy movements on the stairway told him that. He quickened his steps until at the end of the road he found he was almost running and quite out of breath.

There was something frightening about the whole thing

that was more frightening because it seemed to have an intensity entirely out of rational bounds. Mr. Pinkerton stopped to get his breath and his bearings. Scott Winship was not dead, of course; Miss Caroline Winship knew he was not. But it was more than that. Mr. Pinkerton had not believed he was dead, for the simple reason that she had been so determined to force him to believe it. At least, Scott Winship was not physically dead. Mr. Pinkerton had started to take off his brown bowler to wipe the perspiration off his meagre forehead. He set it down on his head again, blinking. Miss Winship had not said he was physically dead. All she had said was that he was dead, had been dead a long time, and that his name was never mentioned in that house.

As Mr. Pinkerton examined it now, in the cool and peaceful quiet of the evening Square, he breathed a little more freely. There might be nothing so terribly frightening about it, now that he had thought it over. Miss Winship belonged, as he himself did, to a generation that could and frequently did regard its black sheep kinsmen as metaphorically dead. He thought back to her short telephone conversation. ". . . American must have seen him. That's all I know. You'd better come at once, Sidney. I think he's here. In London."

The name Sidney seemed familiar to him, and he remembered, suddenly, the initials on the small car that had frequently stood in front of Number 22 Godolphin Square, and of Number 4, and the quiet and rather austere middle-aged man they belonged to. Mr. Sidney Copeland. And Mr. Pinkerton had heard about him, from Betty the little Welsh chambermaid, when he first came to the flat.

"They have the most frightful rows, the sisters I mean. Miss Caroline wants Mrs. Winship to marry him."

Mr. Pinkerton blinked again. If Scott Winship really was

not dead . . . But it was all coming back to him now, and very clearly: the little Welsh girl, her soiled apron torn and pinned together, leaning on the vacuum telling him about the romance of the shadowy invalid on the first floor.

"Mr. Copeland's a very nice gentleman, sir. He's been after her ever so long, and I know she likes him. I've heard her laugh when he's there, and she doesn't laugh very often. You'd think she'd marry him, just to get away from her sister. Miss Caroline's got a cruel and wicked tongue, sir. I'd marry if it was me. Then maybe she wouldn't be sick all the time like she is now. And Miss Caroline Winship's always at her about it. He's her medical man, so it isn't like he was a stranger or a foreigner, is it, sir?"

And now Caroline Winship was telling Mr. Sidney Copeland, whom she had been trying to get her sister to marry, to come at once because she thought her sister's husband was back in London. Mr. Pinkerton blinked again, in the deepest perplexity—and all because an American back in London to find a girl he had met on one single occasion had asked Mr. Pinkerton a civil and quite simple question.

As he sat at a cramped table in a crowded tea shop eating his compote of game—the seven shillings sixpence it cost failing signally to disguise the fact that it was either rook or starling, call it what they would—he wished very much that he had kept his mouth shut. That not having been effected, he wished very much he had asked Dan McGrath where he was stopping. He would have liked to explain his own part in the unfortunate turn of events, and as quickly as possible. He also wanted to warn the young American. Plainly, for one reason or another, the situation ruled out any polite inquiries about Mary Winship's father. And on the other hand . . .

Mr. Pinkerton was not entirely without some portion of the native Welsh caution, and as he sat there thinking it all over, he came to two sound conclusions. The first was that Dan McGrath was undoubtedly far more capable of managing his own affairs than Mr. Evan Pinkerton was of doing it for him. The second was that whatever family skeleton Mr. Scott Winship, dead or alive, represented, it was clearly the Winships' business, not his. The wisest thing for him to do was to go home and mind his own affairs. It was a resolution that Mr. Pinkerton had made many times before, and kept at least as long—in this case, until he opened the front door of Number 4 Godolphin Square.

3

A PILE of battered luggage stood by the lift. The top piece was a green fabric Army kit with large black initials stencilled on it: "D. J. McG."; and below them in smaller letters was "Baltimore, Maryland, U. S. A." Mr. Pinkerton stopped and blinked, his heart beating a little faster. D. J. McG. Big as the United States were, it was still unlikely that two people with Dan McGrath's initials could show up from them on the same day. In London, perhaps, but not both of them in Godolphin Square.

Mason, the night porter, was coming along from the lighted window of the small office off which, on the right, was Miss Myrtle Grimstead's apartment. He opened the lift door and put the florist's box he was carrying on the leather seat.

"More ruddy flowers for 'er. Bring on another one of 'er attacks, poor lady. 'Ay fever's what it is if you ahsk me."

Mr. Pinkerton looked at the long green box. "Guillaume's," it had painted in flourishing gold script on the cover, and he could see "Mrs. Scott Winship" written on the white envelope tied with orchid ribbon to the orchid ribbon round the box.

"You'll 'ave to walk up," Mason said. He picked up the fabric kit and dumped it onto the floor of the lift. "It's 'er that's the trouble. I've been 'ere twenty-two years and never 'ad no trouble till *she* came."

Mr. Pinkerton blinked for an instant, then understood from Mason's morose glance back at the office. All the servants complained about Miss Myrtle Grimstead, and she about them. That did not matter. And as Mr. Pinkerton always walked up anyway, that made no difference either. But where Dan McGrath, if it was Dan McGrath, was going to sleep did worry him. He knew the flats were all full.

Mason gave the third piece of luggage a heave into the lift. "No vacancies . . ." He raised his voice to imitate Miss Grimstead's coyly ingratiating approach. "Just give me and Betty a 'and 'ere, Mason. We'll just move out all the trunks and the 'ousekeeper's paraphinalia, and make 'im up a bed 'ere in the box room. I'm sure 'e'll be quite comfy till we can do summat better for 'im Monday—and where, Miss Grimstead? I ask—and where I'm still asking."

Where indeed? Mr. Pinkerton wondered. But not for long. Miss Myrtle Grimstead was smiling happily at him through the narrow office window that guarded the approach to the carpeted stairway like a sentry box in an armed camp. Her bright blonde curls under the overhead light were as brassy but not as toothy as her smile.

"Oh, Mr. Pinkerton! A perfectly charming young American, a Mr. Daniel McGrath, has just arrived—he's gone out for a few hours but he'll be back tonight. He simply wouldn't take No for an answer."

Her smile fixed itself intently on the little man.

"You aren't taking holiday beginning Monday morning, are you, Mr. Pinkerton? You have looked so seedy lately, the sea air would do wonders for you. I was telling Mrs. Winship just yesterday you look far sicker than she does. I've got a sister in Bournemouth that I could arrange to make you very comfy indeed. I can just transfer your account and you'll be fit again in no time."

Miss Grimstead waggled her curls at him, and became at once brisk and efficient. "Monday'll do very nicely. I wouldn't want to hurry you at all. Mr. McGrath can manage very comfortably in the box room till Monday, I'm sure."

"—I'm not going on holiday."

Miss Grimstead turned back with a startled jerk of her blonde curls. She was no more startled than Mr. Pinkerton. He stood gaping at her just as she stood gaping at him, at the idea of hearing himself come out and say what was in his mind.

"I mean—I mean Mr. McGrath's a very good friend of mine, and I'm sure—I'm sure he wouldn't like . . ."

"Oh," Miss Grimstead said. "Oh," she repeated. Her pale managerial eyes bored skeptically into his. "He said he had a friend here he wanted to be near. I must say it never occurred to me it was *you*."

Mr. Pinkerton swallowed. He could see her opinion of Dan McGrath take an abysmal dive. He backed toward the door and hurried up.

"Oh, dear," he thought. "When she stops to think she'll know I'm not telling the truth."

In the middle of the second flight, well out of Miss Grimstead's visual range, he stopped to catch his breath, and caught it in fact quite literally. The door of Eric Dalrymple-Hughes's small rear flat on the first floor had opened, and a girl's voice came up the stairs.

". . . be ready, Eric, won't you?" she was saying. "And stop grousing, darling. I promise you I had nothing at all to do with it. I'm just lucky for once, that's all. And *please* don't try to spoil it."

It was Mary Winship. At the sound of her voice the basilisk-eyed Miss Grimstead vanished from Mr. Pinkerton's mind as promptly as if she had never existed, and his face brightened. Mary Winship was the one person at Number 4 Godolphin Street, except of course Betty the little Welsh maid, who ever gave him a friendly smile, or spoke to him as though it was a pleasure and not a duty. He listened to her speaking back through the door to her insufferable cousin. She sounded so gay and excited that Mr. Pinkerton did not for an instant doubt the reason.

"She knows he's here," he thought, himself almost as excited because she did sound so happy about it. He could not have been happier himself, even when he heard her cousin's petulant affected voice answer her.

"I'm not grousing. And don't misunderstand me, Mary. It's not Aunt Caroline personally that I'm objecting to. It's the tyranny of the very old."

"I doubt if she'd like that very much, dear. She's not that old, and if it's tyranny at least you don't have to put up with it. There *are* jobs, you know. You don't have to stick here."

Mr. Pinkerton had started down the stairs again. If he pretended he was going out instead of coming in, he could meet her quite casually. Even if all she said was "Good evening," he would still have the satisfaction of seeing her violet-blue eyes light up—even if Dan McGrath's name was not spoken. But he hesitated now. His device, transparent at best, had become slightly awkward in view of the turn the situation had taken.

"I know you'd like to have me out of the field, even if I am only a soi-disant nephew that's got to sing nicely for his supper if he's to get any. It's not my fault my mother was a cousin instead of a step-daughter like yours. And maybe I shall get out. I'm fed up with fiddling for every kipper I get. I'm on to something that would surprise you, Mary Winship. All I want is a bit of ready cash."

"And all I hope is it's nothing that'll get you in trouble again," Mary Winship retorted cheerfully. "But let's not quarrel. I'm much too excited to quarrel with you now. And *do* be ready. I don't want this spoiled."

As she closed the door, Mr. Pinkerton in his nervous anxiety to get back up the stairs without being heard did precisely what Pegott had done. The toe of his boot hit the brass rod at the foot of the riser. The sharp metallic clink made Mary Winship turn quickly from the door and glance up.

"Oh, hello, Mr. Pinkerton." Her face broke into a sunny smile. She took a quick light step over to the middle of the hall and looked up at him. "Oh, Mr. Pinkerton, the most wonderful thing's happened! You can't ever guess!" Her eyes were dancing, her whole face lighted up. "I can hardly believe it!"

"I—I think it's very nice," Mr. Pinkerton said.

He felt a glow of modest pride because he didn't have to guess. He knew. He thought Mary Winship was a pretty girl, one of the prettiest he'd ever known—in real life, that is, not of course in the films. He also thought she was sweet, an old-fashioned virtue he did not look for in the cinema. At the moment she seemed to be both in an extraordinary degree. Slender and graceful as an osier wand, she had wide-set violet-blue eyes fringed with curling dark lashes so long they would have looked unreal except that her brows were thick and shining and her hair almost blue-black and curly too. She did not always look so radiantly happy as she did just then. Once Mr. Pinkerton had seen her in a tea shop, looking tired and so hopeless, all by herself, that he hadn't spoken to her, thinking perhaps she had just come there to be alone and get a little peace away from her dominant aunt, her invalid mother and her poisonous cousin Eric. But now she was radiant and lovely.

"I'm very pleased about it too," Mr. Pinkerton said. He wished Dan McGrath could see her then.

"Oh, Aunt Caroline told you? I thought she'd just decided. You know, she's really an angel! Just think of it—a whole month in Paris! I knew I was to have a week's holiday, but not now, and here at the flat, not a whole month in Paris. But I've got to rush—I'm going on the night boat. Good-bye, Mr. Pinkerton—take care of yourself. I'll bring you a present!"

She was off, her feet fairly dancing as she waved her hand and ran along the hall to her aunt's apartment, leaving Mr. Pinkerton mute and stricken halfway up the dimly lighted stairs.

"—Paris. She's going to Paris." Some cracked disembodied voice was whispering it in his incredulous ear. "She's not happy about Dan McGrath. She's happy because she's going to Paris. She's happy because she's getting away from here."

Suddenly Mr. Pinkerton caught his breath, standing perfectly still. The truth was brilliantly clear all about him.

"She's not *going* to Paris. They're *sending* her to Paris. To get her away from here. Her aunt's sending her away so she won't see Dan McGrath."

32

Mr. Pinkerton's own voice was telling him that, but he knew it was not the truth. They were sending her away, but it was not on account of Dan McGrath but on account of her father. They were sending her so she would not see Scott Winship. But it was all the same. A month in Paris . . . Miss Grimstead had said a month of sea air in Bournemouth. It was the same month—except that his was to begin on Monday, Dan McGrath's in the box room and Mary's in Paris both began that very night. Mr. Pinkerton's pallid viscera turned over in agonizing protest. It couldn't be, not after Dan McGrath had come all the way from America. Somebody had got to stop it.

He looked around frantically, as if he hoped by some miraculous dispensation Dan McGrath would appear out of the murky depths of the cabbage-scented hallway and put a stop to it then and there. And it was all his fault. If he had never mentioned Scott Winship it would never have happened. And it couldn't happen. It mustn't be allowed to happen. He blinked his watery grey eyes and swallowed. Then he moistened his lips. It had got to be stopped, and he was the one who'd got to stop it.

"Oh, dear!" Mr. Pinkerton said. It was all very easy to say he had got to stop it. The question was how to do it. If only Dan McGrath was there . . . He glanced down into the hall. Eric Dalrymple-Hughes was coming out of his flat. He was whistling under his breath, a jaunty self-satisfied young man, well built and handsome, too handsome for his own good, in Mr. Pinkerton's opinion, and with a weak mouth and petulant voice. He was a feeble reed to lean on, but at the moment he was the only reed there was, and Mr. Pinkerton himself was hardly a sturdy oak.

He straightened his narrow shoulders and made a pathetic

effort to clear his throat and attract Mr. Eric Dalrymple-Hughes's attention as he paused to light a cigarette. He cleared his throat again. It was at least audible this time, but not so audible as to account for the startled jerk of the young man's head as he looked up.

"Oh," he said. "It's you."

He snapped his lighter shut and blew a casual ribbon of smoke upward out of the side of his compressed lips. He started to move along.

"Mr. Dalrymple-Hughes! Wait a moment, will you please?"

Mr. Pinkerton found his voice. He scurried anxiously down the stairs. Eric Dalrymple-Hughes, his cigarette poised with an air of bored distinction, waited for him, his brows raised a little, looking so very down his handsome nose that Mr. Pinkerton would have gone no farther had there been any other way.

"It's—it's about your cousin, Miss Winship—she mustn't go to Paris tonight." He blurted it out breathlessly. "You've got to stop her. She really mustn't go."

That Eric Dalrymple-Hughes thought he had taken leave of his senses was perfectly apparent, even to Mr. Pinkerton. He did not stare at him precisely, but he looked at him a moment as if not quite sure he was actually there. Then he raised his brows.

"And just what business of yours is it whether my cousin goes to Paris or does not go to Paris, Mr.—Mr. Pinkerton, I believe?"

"Yes, I'm Mr. Pinkerton. I live on the third floor. And it's not really any business of mine. But there's an American coming here—to the flats, I mean—"

"An American?" Mr. Eric Dalrymple-Hughes gave another slight start. "I don't understand, I'm afraid," he said briefly.

34

"Oh, I know you don't. But it's quite true. I met him in front of your Aunt's house this afternoon, and he was looking for your cousin. He didn't know where she lived now, and I told him. He's got a room here, the box room, and he wants to see her. So you see she—she mustn't go to Paris just now. Your Aunt thinks he knows her father, Mr. Scott Winship, but I'm sure he doesn't at all. He was just asking if he'd come back. And he never said Mr. Winship was here, or that he'd seen him. He just asked—"

Mr. Dalrymple-Hughes was examining the tip of his cigarette with studied unconcern. "Why should he be interested in my deceased uncle?"

"Oh, no, no!" cried Mr. Pinkerton. "He's not interested in your uncle. It's your cousin Mary. He came all the way from America to see her, so she mustn't go off like this. She's simply—"

He stopped. The young man was regarding him with a skeptical, puzzled, half-amused and half-not-amused-at-all eye that was discouraging in the extreme. It was plain that the idea of anyone so much as crossing the road to see his cousin was too bizarre for him to consider seriously. Mr. Pinkerton almost gave up.

"At least let me speak to Mary Winship before she goes? Do that, will you?"

He was so in earnest that he knew he sounded absurd, pleading this way about such an incomprehensible matter, and knowing that pleading would not be enough he made a sudden desperate gamble. "You said—I heard you tell Mary you needed cash. I can let you have some. I could let you have a hundred pounds—or two hundred. If you'll bring Mary up and let me talk to her, I'll—I'll *give* you the money."

It was not only a gamble. For Mr. Evan Pinkerton, who never spent a sixpence without misgivings or a pound without cold chills, it was more than that; it was fantastic. Eric Dalrymple-Hughes stood looking at him. What he was thinking Mr. Pinkerton had no way of telling. There was nothing on the handsome conceited young face that had any meaning for him, friendly or unfriendly.

He stood simply staring for an instant, said then, quite coolly, "I'll see what I can do," turned on his heel and went back into his own apartment.

Mr. Pinkerton started up stairs. He was not even thinking of the two hundred pounds. He was too numb with a horrible sense of guilt at having ruined Dan McGrath's mission to Godolphin Square, and of defeat at having failed to make Mary Winship's cousin see the truth. If only he had kept out of it, Mr. Pinkerton thought again wretchedly; if only he had let Miss Caroline Winship think it was the Town and Country planning people, and never mentioned the American. But it was too late now.

He took his dejected way up the stairs to the second floor and on up the narrower flight to the third, let himself into the meagre bed-sitting room that was his own, and stood inside the door a moment. Besides being miserable, he was extremely confused. Again he thought, they couldn't be sending Mary Winship away on account of the American they didn't know, so they must be sending her away because they thought her father was coming back, or was back already. Was it only her Aunt Caroline, then, or was it her mother too? He tried to think back, recalling Mrs. Scott Winship standing stone-still by the door when he repeated the ill-starred question. All he could remember was the sudden clap of silence, and the intense motionlessness of the two sisters before Miss Caroline said, "Go to your room, Louise." Then there was Miss Winship's telephone call to Sidney Copeland. Between all that and now—it had been twenty-five minutes past seven when he left the tea shop after his compote of starling—they had decided, or Miss Caroline had decided, to send Mary away and had arranged to send her. And she was going on the night boat—unless he could stop her some way. And *why?* He kept asking it with no possible means of answering.

He tried to think as he stood there in the pleasant darkness of the shabby room. The curtains had not been drawn, and the two French windows that opened out onto the narrow ledge forming a sort of balcony, behind the parapet made by the stone coping to hide the mansard windows of the attic storey and maintain the even classical lines of the Adam square, shone softly silver from the outside light. He went across the room and stepped out on the ledge.

Through the ragged branches of the intervening plane trees he could see the gaunt ruins of Miss Winship's house. The dim orange light from the street lamp threw it into a softly ghostly relief above the black empty spaces where the houses had gone from either side of it. Someone was moving along the street in front. Mr. Pinkerton could make out the dark figure of a man moving slowly along. He passed the house, and a moment later he came back. As he stopped again, Mr. Pinkerton had a fleeting impression that there was something familiar in the outline of his body or the movement of it, as if the man was someone he had seen, and now somehow recognized but could not identify. It was so puzzling that he watched him intently— so intently that he blinked with astonishment when the man was suddenly no longer there. He seemed to have disappeared, quite literally, as if he had dissolved not into the shadows but as a part of them. He had been there, darkly visible; then he was not there, and the space in front of the house, and the whole street, was empty. It was as eerie and uncanny as the shadowy ruin of the house itself.

Mr. Pinkerton leaned forward, peering intently through the murky penumbra cast up through the settling haze by the orange overglow of the street lights. Suddenly he stiffened, every grey fibre of his nervous system quivering, as alert as if he heard again the shrill blast of the midnight siren warning of the approach of terror and death. Someone was in the room behind him. Was it the sound of a stealthy breath drawn or expelled? Or was it the slithering sound of a footstep in the dark room across the worn Brussels carpet? Or a garment brushing against the chair or the table? He could not tell, except that it was something, and something furtive and frightening, and it was there very close, inside the long open window behind him. He tried to swallow, to clear the sudden pounding in his ears, but his throat was dry. His hands were icy as he tried to grip the stone coping, drawing back not to see the street four floors below, paralyzed with a fear so horrible that it curdled everything inside him. When he tried to speak no sound came past his parched lips, and his cry for help was only a hoarse choked breath. As he tried to turn and look into the blackness of the room and cry out, he knew nothing more except a hideous woolly darkness as something thick and soft flashed over his head and a brutal stranglehold fastened about his throat, thrusting back his chin, as he slid down into a vast blinding nauseating abyss, down and down, with the high-pitched echo of something sounding crazily like the hoot of a taxi-horn bursting in his ears before the crash of a thousand lights and the blackness of oblivion. Mr. Pinkerton slumped down on the lead gutter pipe.

Wait. The hooting taxi-horn thrusting in the knife blade of fear stayed the arms of the dark figure standing over him, murderous and intent. *Wait. Wait till it passes and the street is empty again.* But it was not passing. It was stopping at Number 4 Godolphin Square. The dark figure was motionless, arms reached down to lift the body and cast it over the raised coping.

"He *has* seemed seedy lately. I advised him to go to the seashore," Miss Myrtle Grimstead would say with easy tears when they picked him up from the street and brought him in. "I didn't mean to upset him. I never thought he'd take it seriously and try to harm himself this way."

The livid eyes peered secretly down. A sharply drawn breath, again the knife blade of fear. The hands seized the suffocating afghan, thrust it back in its place as the silent feet slipped back through the darkened room and out into the empty hall. The door closed quietly. No one would come. No one ever came. There would be no one until Pegott brought the breakfast tray in the morning—later than to any other room, because the little grey man did not matter. He would stay there, silent and motionless, until it was safe to return. In the morning they would find him down there in the street.

"I never thought he'd do himself harm." Then Miss Grimstead could weep and explain he really had looked ever so seedy lately. It was her constant explanation for tenants who vacated their flats, whether they married, emigrated to South Africa, or died—it made no difference. They had looked very seedy. Miss Grimstead always recalled it vividly.

4

As Dan McGrath's taxi skidded into Godolphin Square the driver stopped talking long enough to sound his horn viciously at a man who had slipped out of the shadowy darkness almost under the wheels.

"Number Four you said, sir?" He drew up at the curb and went round to open the door. "And as I was telling the wife just this morning, you voted for the beggars, I didn't."

He was a voluble man with politico-domestic grievances; Dan McGrath was an American newly arrived and interested.

"—now in America, sir, it's my understanding . . ."

Dan McGrath listened, the two of them smoking his cigarettes, standing together on the curb in front of Number 4 Godolphin Square, four storeys beneath the stone coping overhead. When he finally came in, Mason the night porter opened the iron grille into the lift, and dropped both arms to his sides in impotent frustration as Miss Myrtle Grimstead came trippingly toward them.

"Oh, Mr. McGrath, I can't think what you'll say." Miss Grimstead was at her most ingratiating worst. "I was so sure one of my people was going on holiday. He's looked so very seedy lately I'd quite got it into my head he'd be off to the sea for a bit of rest and fresh air." Her bright toothy smile remained bright, but there was a calculating flicker in her eye that Dan McGrath could hardly miss. "Of course, there may be some mistake. He tells me he's a friend of yours . . ."

"Who—" Dan McGrath caught himself quickly. "Oh, the little—Mr. Pinkerton. Sure, he's my pal. Known him for years."

He smiled at Miss Grimstead with easy assurance. In the

face of her disparaging skepticism he would have claimed Mr. Pinkerton as brother in arms or in nature. "If it's his room you were going to give me, skip it. Any place suits me so long as it's got a bunk in it."

"Oh, thank you, Mr. McGrath." Miss Grimstead covered her disappointment with a shake of her bright curls. "That is kind of you. You mustn't think I was trying to inconvenience dear Mr. Pinkerton. He's such a sweet old thing, so shy and so anxious never to make any trouble. Well, good night, Mr. McGrath. We do like people to be as comfortable as possible, especially the Americans. Poor England . . ."

"Don't worry about me, Miss Grimstead. Good night."

The porter stood aside for him to come into the lift.

"Not tryin' to inconvenience 'im, not 'er she ain't. Not always tryin' to get 'im out because 'e's a poor connection of the owner and likely to peach on 'er, she ain't, poor little blighter."

He stopped the car. " 'Ere you are, sir."

It was a small airless cupboard at the end of the transverse hall opposite Mr. Pinkerton, ventilated by a pull-up oblong of glass set in the sloping roof. It had a bed and washstand with crockery basin and tall blue hot water jug, a chair, and a small table with a lamp on it, attached by a long cord to the single drop light from the ceiling. From Mr. Pinkerton's room probably, Dan McGrath thought with a smile.

"It ain't much," Mason said. "Mr. Pinkerton's opposite, next the bath and w. c. You share it with 'im—'im *and* the chef when 'e sleeps in. Chef's got the best room. Got to mind 'im, sir." He touched his temple significantly. "She'd not ask 'im to move out, not 'er, and 'im not sleeping in more than 'alf the time. Kid gloves is what she 'andles 'im with, 'im and the valet."

Dan glanced along the hall at Mr. Pinkerton's closed door.

"This suits me dandy," he said. "I'm sorry if I've made a lot of trouble." He took a pound note out of his pocket and handed it to Mason. "Good night."

He closed the door, tossed his hat and raincoat on the chair and went over to feel the bed. It was okay. For a moment he had an impulse to drop into it and sleep through the rest of his first night in London. There was no reason why he shouldn't. Twenty-four hours from home in one sense, a lifetime in another, he had reached the first step to his goal more quickly by far than he had hoped when he stepped onto the plane, infinitely more quickly than he had despairingly thought as he stood in front of the ruined house that was the only tangible thread he had to lead him back to her. He hadn't even known her name then, much less how to go about finding her, if she was still alive. Standing in front of the blasted remains of the house she'd lived in, the sudden agony of emptiness that hit him squarely in the pit of the stomach had been almost intolerable. Then the little guy had showed up. Showed up, and almost got kicked out of his room for his pains.

Dan McGrath glanced at his watch. It was almost nine o'clock—not too late, he guessed, to drop in on an old friend. He reached into his pocket to get a cigarette and pulled out a sheet of paper. It was a telegram from his father, delivered to him when the plane landed. He opened it and read it again.

LOOK BEFORE YOU LEAP. BUT IF YOU DECIDE TO LEAP ALL OUR BEST WISHES AND LOVE. DAD.

Something smarted sharply along his upper eyelids for an instant. He knew they'd hoped he'd marry the girl next door, and he would have, probably, if it hadn't been for that night six years ago on the steps of the Underground. It was a long time for an image to hold, the image of a face white and tense at first, in the dreary darkness, crowded with people coming home from work, reeking with antiseptics and the heavy acrid odor of cordite and the pungent smell of human fear. With his arm around her he could feel the bursting beat of her heart, pounding through her blue coat under his hand—just a kid, scared out of her wits. It was a long time to hold the image of the dismayed widening of her blue-black eyes as she realized she was clinging to him and that he had his arm around her, and her sudden crystal peal of laughter when she let go and he did not. He remembered her voice and the warmth of her slight body as they sat close together until the all-clear sounded, the curly tendrils of her clean-smelling hair tickling his flushed cheek. And stumbling home with her after it was all over, to Number 22 Godolphin Square.

It was a long time to hold the image of love that was in his heart that night. There had been times when he thought he had lost it, and times when he no longer believed in its validity as anything but an adolescent dream. It was his twentieth brithday, that night, and he'd come to London from camp to celebrate, and found himself alone and homesick, homesick as hell. It was easy to say that was the reason he thought he'd fallen in love. And he could be all wet, of course. Six years was a long-time period. It was cockeyed to remember a kid's conversation for six years. About her father, for instance. Her father had gone away, but some day he'd come back. She didn't remember him, or wasn't sure; she might only remember her mother telling her about him. But she was sure he'd come back to them—or, if he didn't, she would go and find him when the war was over. And that night, he was going with her. They were going to search the world together.

It was all crazy. If her father had been gone that long without any word, he was dead, or had changed his name and disappeared. But at the time it had seemed a high and noble quest. It was crazy, but he remembered it, practically every word of it. And here he was back in Godolphin Square—twenty-six years old, and she . . . He didn't know. She couldn't have been more than seventeen, that night, sixteen maybe. Here they both were, after six years. She was in the very house, down below, somewhere, in the dreary effluvia of boiled cabbage and brass polish and fresh paint that they hadn't bothered to touch up the box room with. Or the little man had said she was.

Thinking of Mr. Pinkerton again, Dan McGrath went over to the door. There was someone in the hall. He had not heard the lift come up. It was probably the chef, or Mr. Pinkerton, going to the w. c. He opened the door, glanced out and closed it quickly.

It was a woman, coming out of Mr. Pinkerton's room—or going into it, he couldn't tell—dressed in something that looked very much like a wrapper and a nightgown, with a shawl about her shoulders. It was probably Mrs. Pinkerton. Nobody had mentioned a Mrs. Pinkerton, but if she was as pallid and self-effacing as Mr. Pinkerton, they'd probably not have bothered. He thought back suddenly. Miss Grimstead had only mentioned one of her people, not two, as going on holiday. He opened the door again. Whoever it was, he had scared her off. She was disappearing down the stairs, obviously frightened, clutching her shawl about her throat.

He shook his head, wondering a little, started to close his

door again, and stopped. Mr. Pinkerton's door, he saw now, was ajar, but no light shone out. It seemed a little strange. He hesitated, left his own door as it was and went along the hall.

"Mr. Pinkerton?"

He put his head into the room and spoke again. Mr. Pinkerton was not there. He glanced back at the staircase, pushed the door farther open to let in the light from the hall, and crossed the room to the rickety lamp on the table. The bulb was cold as he felt for the switch. He pressed it on and looked about him at a room nearly as bare as his own. A couple of Dresden china shepherdesses and a few photographs on the mantel were the only personal property he could see, together with a red-green woolen throw on the sofa in front of the open French windows. He looked beyond the sofa, through the windows, out onto the balcony ledge, and took two quick strides across the room. The little man was lying inert, crumpled up, his head against the lead drainpipe.

Dan McGrath said, "Good God!" He bent down quickly, picked Mr. Pinkerton up, carried him into the room and laid him on the day bed. He loosened the purple string tie and ripped open the narrow celluloid collar, opened the band of the shoddy grey trousers and looked about. There was no telephone and no bell, no bottle of whisky, no water. He dashed out into the hall, jabbed the call button on the side of the lift half a dozen times and dashed back. The little man's eyes were open. He was staring blindly, his face suffused, trying to struggle upright.

"Take it easy, Mr. Pinkerton."

"She mustn't go," Mr. Pinkerton whispered. He clutched at Dan's sleeve. "Mustn't go. Mustn't go to Paris."

"Okay, okay. Everything's under control. Just take it easy. It's me—Dan McGrath."

As if the word had got through into his dazed semi-conscious mind, the little man sank down on the couch.

"We'll get a doctor right away."

He strode out into the hall, punched the bell violently again and came back. The little man looked pathetically different, lying there, without his brown derby hat. There was something else, Dan thought—his spectacles. The lozenge-shaped steel-rimmed job that made him look like a Dickensian gnome. Without them and the hat he looked indecently nude. Furthermore, he probably couldn't see. Dan went over to the balcony, hoping the spectacles weren't broken in his fall, and glanced along the narrow ledge. The brown derby had rolled along nearly to the drain. He retrieved it and looked about for the spectacles. They were nowhere in sight. He glanced down into the street—they could easily have gone over—and went back into the room.

The little man was shivering, his whole meagre frame trembling.

Shock. You keep them warm and get a doctor. He could hear the lift coming up now. *You get them warm quick.* He picked up the afghan folded over the arm of the sofa, opened it up, threw it over Mr. Pinkerton, and stopped abruptly, staring. A curved metal bow was sticking up through the knitted material. He lifted it quickly and turned it over. Hanging from the coverlet on the inside, the bows caught in the soft woolen stitches, were Mr. Pinkerton's spectacles.

Dan McGrath stared down at them. *Wait a minute, McGrath. Wait just one minute.*

He heard the lift stop and the door clang open, and stood there still staring down at the knitted comforter and the spectacles still hanging to it. He glanced out into the hall as it flashed into his mind that it might be a good idea to have a witness, if this meant what he thought it did. It was not Mason there, it was Miss Myrtle Grimstead; and prompted by a quick impulse he put the afghan back, flattened the bows and bunched the soft material together.

"Oh, Mr. McGrath—is there something?" Miss Grimstead had seen him through the open door and came hurrying along the hall. "Mason had to go out for a taxi. One of my people is going to Paris—"

She came to an abrupt halt in the doorway. "There! I knew it! I told him so not two hours ago. I said, Mr. Pinkerton, you *are*—"

"I know," Dan said. "But let's get a doctor, shall we? Quick?"

Miss Grimstead's triumph transformed itself instantly into brisk and cheerful efficiency. "What a pity," she said. "We'll get him to hospital immediately. He wants rest and care."

"He wants a doctor," Dan said. "My friend Mr. Pinkerton wants a doctor. Right away. And I want the police, Miss Grimstead. I'll settle for a doctor first."

Miss Grimstead, bending down to take the faded cloth cover off Mr. Pinkerton's sagging couch, flashed rigidly erect. "The *police*? Mr. McGrath!" Her blue eyes were bulging, her pink powdered cheeks mottled. "What do you mean? Are you mad?"

"I'm pretty mad, Miss Grimstead. I'm going to be a whole lot madder if there isn't a doctor here in about five minutes."

Miss Grimstead's eyes were sharp points of calculation.

"Very well," she said stiffly. "I'll call a doctor. I'd like to say first you're making a great mistake. I don't know what you're thinking, but this is England. Not America. Mr. Pinkerton wants care. He's got neither family nor friends here—"

"Oh, yes." Dan gave her a frosty smile. "You're forgetting

me. And remember that doctor we were talking about? Isn't there a doctor in the house?"

Miss Grimstead's face was still more mottled. "It happens there is. Not professionally. He's a surgeon, here making a social call. However, I'll ask him if he cares to step up and see Mr. Pinkerton. Mr. Sidney Copeland is a very busy man . . ."

He listened to her departing feet pepper the worn hall carpet. Miss Grimstead was very angry. He looked thoughtfully down at the bunched bit of knitted wool concealing the lozenge-shaped spectacles. If they had been on the outside of the thing, it was conceivable that they could have fallen off as the little guy staggered out into the fresh air. But they were folded up on the inside.

He looked at the grey pinched face. Mr. Pinkerton's eyes were closed. There was pain in the haggard lines about his nose and in the blind naked look about his eyes. Dan bent over him, looking more closely. There was a dark scratch on the left side of his nose. He took out his handkerchief and touched it carefully. The scratch was fresh. He had just put his hand out to touch what looked like a good-sized lump on the side of Mr. Pinkerton's head when he started at the sound of a voice behind him.

"What seems to be the trouble here?"

It was not the voice that was startling but the approach, which had been silent and very prompt, and must have been by foot up the stairs; the lift had not come up. He looked around. Mr. Sidney Copeland was a precise middle-aged man, clean and antiseptic-looking, pleasant on the whole, or looking as if he might be under other circumstances. He seemed tired, but so did almost everyone else Dan had seen. He had good brown eyes and a solid chin and firm mouth, sandy hair greying,

48

slightly stooped shoulders, and wore a neatly brushed threadbare black suit. He glanced at Mr. Pinkerton on the couch, and back. Of the two, he seemed more intently interested in Dan McGrath.

"I found him out on the balcony. It looks to me like somebody's conked him on the bean."

Mr. Copeland put his fingers on Mr. Pinkerton's wrist, passed his hand delicately over the swollen area at the side of his head, lifted up his eyelids and let them close.

"Should he go to the hospital?"

Copeland spoke with composed deliberateness. "Possibly. He seems to have got rather a nasty crack. It's best to leave him here till he regains consciousness. His pulse is retarded, but it's reasonably strong."

Mr. Copeland, Dan thought, was at least reasonably casual.

"You found him out on the balcony?"

"Right."

"And—you think somebody had—er, conked him on the bean. If I understand you, I presume you know what you're saying? Isn't it conceivable he may have fallen and struck his head?"

All right, McGrath. Why don't you show him the spectacles folded up inside *the wool comforter and see what he says to that?* Dan wondered. It was the normal thing to do. But as the surgeon moved over to look out onto the ledge, the rigid lines of his back were even more skeptical, and to Dan even more positively offensive, than the brief smile that had been on his lips.

When he turned back from the window he regarded Dan with open amusement.

"Isn't it simpler to assume he walked up the stairs, and feeling a bit faint went directly out for a breath of air? Had a touch

49

of vertigo, stumbled and struck his head on the pipe? Miss Grimstead tells me he's not been particularly fit recently."

"Seedy, I believe," Dan said.

Copeland glanced at him sharply. "Precisely. I believe in your country, Mr.—McGrath, is it?—it's fairly common to find people conked on the bean, as you put it. You're in England now, Mr. McGrath. However, I was already aware you're a young man who enjoys making mysteries without regard to the feelings of the people they presumably affect."

Dan stared at him. "What—sorry, I don't get it, sir. I don't know what you're—what mysteries am I supposed to have made around here? Except this if you call it a mystery?"

The sudden angry light that kindled in the surgeon's brown eyes was a startling change from his precise and passionless detachment.

"You're the American who was making inquiries of this man," he jerked his hand toward Mr. Pinkerton, on the couch, stirring a little, his breath coming more easily, "over the road this afternoon. Are you not?"

Dan stared with blank incredulity.

"I have no idea what your game is, Mr. McGrath, but if you'll take my advice you'll clear out of here. And if Scott Winship is in London, and has even a shred of decency left in him, Miss Caroline Winship's solicitors will be very glad to hear from him. You may tell him that Miss Winship expressly forbids him to attempt to communicate with his daughter—either in person or through you. She's left London and isn't expected back for some time. If it's money he wants, tell him—"

Dan took a step forward. "Wait a minute."

"We've waited long enough, Mr. McGrath. Tell him that

so far as the family are concerned he is dead and buried. His daughter thinks so, and she is to continue to think so. So far as all of us are concerned, Scott Winship is dead."

He moved abruptly over to his patient. Dan, watching in stupefied silence, saw his long fingers tremble as they rested on the little man's pulse, his eyes, focussed on the watch-face on his own wrist, still burning with suppressed fire. He put Mr. Pinkerton's hand back under the coverlet.

"I know a hospital nurse, Mrs. Beckwith, I can get to come and spend the night with him till his own medical man can make arrangements. If he wakes and complains of a headache, give him some aspirin. Nothing else. Keep him quiet till she gets here."

At the door Sidney Copeland turned back. "Miss Grimstead tells me you plan to call the police. If that's part of your game, by all means do so. You'll find Scott Winship would much prefer the police to be left out of it. Good night, Mr. McGrath."

5

DAN McGRATH stood motionless in the shabby room, listening to the surgeon's footsteps rapidly going down the stairs. He said slowly, "Well, I'll be quadruply damned."

He turned and looked at Mr. Pinkerton. He was lying there, his eyes open, staring blankly up at the ceiling. Dan went over to him. "Hi, there," he said gently. "How're you coming, old-timer?"

"I'm coming all right," Mr. Pinkerton managed to say. He moved his hand up to his scrawny throat.

"They choke you too?"

Mr. Pinkerton tried to nod his head, but the movement made him wince with pain. He closed his eyes to keep the American from seeing the tears in them as he felt feebly at his forehead.

"Did—did they break my spectacles?" he whispered. "I'm afraid I can't see without them. I've only got the one pair."

"Half a minute."

Dan's jaw was tight with hard white ridges along it as he lifted the afghan and released the steel bows from the woolen strands. He polished the lenses with his handkerchief and put them into Mr. Pinkerton's hands.

"There you are. They got caught in this cover thing."

Mr. Pinkerton put them on and blinked up at him. "You—you're very kind," he said. It hurt him to try to move his vocal cords, but something in his heart hurt worse. "I'm—ever so sorry," he whispered. "It's all my fault. I heard what the man said. She's gone, isn't she?"

"I'm beginning to gather so."

"And you—you don't *care?*"

Mr. Pinkerton tried to raise himself, but the effort was too much.

You don't care? No answer sprang immediately to Dan's mind. If by "caring" they meant Why didn't he dash off to stop her from going? it was not the way he felt at the moment. You didn't stay patiently on the track of a star for six years and then go berserk standing on the threshold, especially when you still had to find out if the star was a star or a star-dusted dream that had never truly existed. If you could wait six years, you could wait a little longer. And Dan McGrath was angry. A cold solid rage was burning quietly behind what seemed to the still dazed little Welshman an impassive and deliberate stolidity.

"Mr. Pinkerton," he said quietly, "this happened to you because of me, some way. And they can't push us around like this. I care more about what happened to you, just now. You feel well enough to tell me?"

The idea of anybody's caring what happened to him was a little startling to Mr. Pinkerton. He blinked rapidly. "Oh, it doesn't matter, really," he whispered hastily. "I—I'd just come upstairs. I hadn't meant to make any trouble. I thought Mrs. Winship was a widow. I just thought it would be nice if Mary didn't get sent off to Paris until after you'd seen her."

He tried feebly to think how to put all of it into some understandable form.

"I told the Winships you'd asked if Mary's father had come back, when Miss Caroline wanted to know who you were. They were upset, and I was upset, too, so I came up here and went out on the balcony. Then I heard somebody behind me in the room, and something black was over my head and they were choking me. I thought they were going to throw me over the coping. Then I thought I heard a taxi-horn, and a crash, and that's all I remember till I heard that man telling you about Mary's father. That was Mr. Sidney Copeland, wasn't it? Miss Caroline Winship rang him up as soon as I'd got out of the flat, and told him to come over. She thought you'd seen Mary's father. All I said was you asked if he'd come home."

Dan McGrath listened in silence. He said then, "This is all as clear as—as English coffee, Mr. Pinkerton. But I know enough about one thing. I'm going to call the cops now."

Mr. Pinkerton forgot his aching throat and his nauseatingly throbbing head. "Oh, no!" he cried. He stared wildly up at Dan McGrath, trying to find words. The young American would think he was afraid of the police, that he'd done something—perhaps even that he was an old lag. How could he explain something so very important and so intensely personal? Dan McGrath did not know about J. Humphrey Bull. Or, worse still, Sir Charles Debenham the Assistant Commissioner.

Mr. Pinkerton, shuddering, almost forgot his throbbing head and aching throat. The last time he had got himself mixed up with crime, the Assistant Commissioner had been very severe. Mr. Pinkerton could still hear him. "Now look here, Bull. Mr. Pinkerton's got to stay out of these things. Someday somebody's going to bash him over the head, and I'm going to see they're knighted for it. Ha, ha!" Of course he was shaking Mr. Pinkerton's hand as he said it, because if it had not been for Mr. Pinkerton they would not have got Vincent Delaney by the heels nearly as quickly as they did. But where there was smoke there was potential fire. Mr. Pinkerton glanced sideways up at the mantel at the photograph of Chief Inspector Bull, looking very deceptively mild in his capacity of family man on the front lawn of his semi-detached villa in Hampstead, with Margaret Bull and J. Humphrey Pinkerton Bull, and a liver-and-white spaniel named Dr. Crippen that had been a present to Mr. Pinkerton from the Chief Constable of Bath.

He looked back at Dan. "Please don't call the police," he said earnestly. "Miss Grimstead would be very much put out. It must have been a—a mistake, of some kind. And it—it might make trouble for *you.*"

He did not believe that, but it was a straw to clutch at, after the mistake of saying what he had said about Miss Grimstead, which only made the American's jaw go harder and his eyes fleck an icier blue. "You see, the—the Assistant Commissioner of Scotland Yard is—is sort of a friend of mine, and he told me to—to keep out of trouble."

He trailed lamely off as Dan McGrath looked silently down at him with an expression of concern he could not keep off his face. If ever a little guy had been born that was not likely either to get in trouble or to know an Assistant Commissioner of New Scotland Yard, Mr. Pinkerton was it. Dan wondered, with anxiety, if the blow on the head could have done something to him. Head injuries were tricky.

He nodded reassuringly. "Sure. Anything you say, Mr. Pinkerton."

"Did—did her cousin come?" Mr. Pinkerton forced himself out of a dazed silence. It was relief, not dizziness. He had not expected Dan McGrath to give in so easily.

"Didn't see him."

"I thought he'd come." Mr. Pinkerton shook his head painfully. "He said he wanted cash. I told him I'd let him have two hundred pounds, to—to see if he could stop her from going to Paris. I expect it wasn't enough."

Dan stirred uneasily. The little guy was really bats. He listened through the closed door into the hall, wishing the nurse would come, and drew a breath of relief as he heard the rap on the door. But it was not the nurse. It was Mason, the night porter, with a silver tray in his hand. On the tray was an envelope.

"For you, sir."

He peered around at Mr. Pinkerton, obviously distressed. " 'E's coming round, sir, is 'e? Would 'e like a nice 'ot cup of tea, do you think?"

"I'm sure he would. Bring it, will you?"

Dan tore the envelope open, read the contents without surprise, and turned back to Mr. Pinkerton with a grin on his lean face. "The Manageress presents her compliments to Mr. McGrath and would like him to get the hell out of the storeroom, the sooner the quicker."

The grin disappeared from his face as Mr. Pinkerton drew himself up on the couch, blinking with sudden indignation. "You'll do nothing of the sort," he said heatedly. "I—I won't allow it. I own these flats. I—I won't permit it."

Humor them. Don't let them get excited. Never argue. Head injuries are really tricky.

"Sure," Dan said gravely. "They can't do this to us."

He went over to the day bed, took the cover off, folded it and turned down the blanket.

"We're here, Mr. Pinkerton, and we're going to stay. Now what about you getting your clothes off and climbing in. It's late and you've had a tough night."

Mr. Pinkerton blinked, speechless. "He—he really thinks I'm crazy," he thought hopelessly.

"Where are your pyjamas?"

Dan went to the cupboard. An old-fashioned nightshirt, mended and patched, was hanging on the inside of the door, under a faded but spectacularly extraordinary dressing gown that looked as if it had come from Hollywood and not from Piccadilly as the label alleged. He took it down with a suppressed grin.

"It—it was a gift," Mr. Pinkerton said weakly. "The Duchess of Cleves gave it to me when I admired one the Duke had. After I'd helped Scotland Yard get back the old duchess's emeralds. That was before the War."

"Nice going anyway," Dan said. He knelt down, wishing the nurse would come, unlaced Mr. Pinkerton's solid black boots and took them off. "Come on now. Let's get in bed. Then I'm going to give you some aspirin and you're going to sleep. I'm going to lock the window, and lock the door, and you're going to stay right here till I get back."

Mr. Pinkerton managed to nod. "What—are you going to do? Are you going to—to the boat train?"

"Mr. Pinkerton, I'm going to call the Prime Minister and have him stop the boat train."

He meant it to be mildly funny, and had no way of knowing Mr. Pinkerton would not take it so. He had seen enough motion pictures to know there was nothing too fantastically improbable for an American to do when he set out to get his girl. "Good," he said. "Good." He put his head gingerly down on the pillow and closed his eyes. He did so want the American to see Mary for the first time while she was still radiant with excitement. It might make all the difference.

Dan shut the door. The hospital nurse was coming out of the lift. She looked capable and honest.

"He's quiet now," Dan said. "I've locked the door so he can't get out. Here's the key. Will you sit in the door of my room here till I get back? And don't let anybody in."

Mason was still there with the lift. There was a tray on the leather seat with a pot of tea and a cup and saucer.

"Give it to Mrs. Beckwith here," Dan said. "Mr. Pinkerton's gone to bed." In the lift he said, "Mason, I'm going to catch a train—if I'm not too late." He took two one-pound notes out of his billfold. "Stop right here and tell me which train. You got the taxi for Miss Mary Winship, didn't you?"

The porter stopped the cage midway between the first and ground floors. He shook his head at the notes.

"Put them away, sir. 'E said if you was to enquire, I was to 'ave no idea—but if you was going to France tonight you might fancy the nine o'clock boat train from Waterloo to Southampton. You'd 'ave to 'urry. I've no idea what Miss Mary and 'er cousin did."

"Thanks," Dan said.

He hurried through the hall. Outside, the golden haze of the afternoon, degenerated into a murky mist, was now in actual and permeating precipitation. He yanked his hat on and pulled on his raincoat, and made a dash for a taxi at the corner. "Waterloo. I've got to make the nine o'clock boat train. Step on it, will you?"

They dodged in and out of narrow side streets, crossed Piccadilly, headed down St. James's Street between the Palace and Marlborough House into Pall Mall, and cut through the Park. He sat there looking out on familiar ground without seeing it—on the right the two pelicans asleep on their rock, to the left the Horse Guards Parade and the lighted windows of Whitehall Palace. It was a fool's errand, he was thinking. He felt an almost fatalistic sense that what was to be was to be. If he missed her, he missed her. He could even get to the train on time, he thought suddenly, see her there and not know her. Six years was a long time.

In fact, his best chance, actually, was her cousin. Thanks to Miss Myrtle Grimstead, he could spot him easily enough. It had happened while he was making the deal for the box room with her; she had leaned smiling out of the small office window toward the man in a chalk-stripe blue suit and black homburg hat, adjusting his fancy cravat in the mirror beside the lift as he waited for it, as self-satisfied as Narcissus contemplating himself in the woodland brook.

"Oh, Mr. Dalrymple-Hughes! Miss Winship asked me to tell you to be sure and look in on her before you go out. *Thank* you."

She had given Dan an arch smile before coming back to the business of the room. "He's rather hard to catch before he's off and away. A trial to his aunt rather, I'm afraid . . ."

So, unless there was another cousin . . . Dan settled back in the cab. They were in Parliament Square, with the Thames and Westminster Bridge ahead of them. As they came out on the Bridge he looked back to the left at the flattened turrets of New Scotland Yard rising above the misty plane trees of the Embankment, shadowy in the river fog, and grinned suddenly, thinking of Mr. Pinkerton's friend the Assistant Commissioner. The taxi lurched sharply into the blackened purlieus behind the overhead activity of the Southern Railway terminus. Another swerve to the left and he was there. On a fool's errand, with five minutes to spare.

"Thanks, pal." He thrust a note into the driver's hand. As he made his way quickly into the lighted hall he felt a throb of excitement and a sense of sharpened anxiety that had been absent before. He spotted the gate and went rapidly over to it, thought of an excuse as the guard stopped him, and gave it up. "I haven't got a ticket. I want to say good-bye to a girl."

The guard looked at him with a dour smile. "You've got more time than you think. We're running a bit late. Step along. Tickets, please!"

It was a dingy train, the first-class compartments older and dingier looking than the third-class. He went along the platform, looking for Dalrymple-Hughes, and spotted him, standing at the door of a third-class corridor car, one hand raised as he looked at his wrist watch. He turned and spoke into the vestibule.

She's there inside. All you have to do now is move along opposite the open door and you'll see her. He hesitated, and went instead over to the side of the train and along to the door of the coach in front. Dalrymple-Hughes's petulant voice was clearly audible.

". . . go, if you insist. But don't tell Aunt Caroline I ditched you, will you. Of course it's a perfectly beastly bore seeing people off when you've got to stick at home yourself. But you'll be all right. And I *have* got an important engagement."

When he heard her voice his heart stopped beating for an instant before it began again, thumping hard against his ribs.

"Do go along, Eric. I'll be all right. The train may be hours late starting."

"Well, if you insist . . ."

You've twisted my arm, let me out of here quick. Dan turned his head just in case Dalrymple-Hughes had bothered to notice him at Miss Grimstead's office window.

"Cheer-oh, then. Do try to get Agnes to give you some of Bernard's castoffs for me, even if you won't try for yourself. Thank God I'm not proud. Cheer-oh. I'll push along."

Dalrymple-Hughes moved off. Dan went quickly to where he had been standing. He was too late. All he saw was her back as she disappeared into the corridor. He went quickly along to see her through the windows when she took her seat, and caught his breath sharply.

Mary Winship was running along the corridor. At the door of the third compartment she stopped for an instant, looking back, her body a taut tense line. She flashed into the compartment, pulled her suitcase down from the rack and bent quickly to drag a bulkier one from under the seat. She pushed them into the corridor, caught up the gloves and book on the seat and flashed out. It was then Dan saw her face—small, pointed and intensely pale as she stood there, her breast moving with her quickly drawn breath, her eyes wide.

She raised her hand and pushed her dark hair back from her forehead with a quick nervous gesture before she stooped to gather up her bags. For Dan McGrath standing outside on the damp murky platform it was as vivid an instant as he had ever lived. He was back in the Underground shelter on the dark chilling stairs, the reek of fear and antiseptics in his nostrils, all hell loose in the invisible world above them, his arms tight around her, feeling her pounding heart against him, her breath in staccato tempo cool against his burning cheek. It was the instant he had lived six years to feel again. It was a sharp renascence, an affirmation of a dream that was no star-dusted illusion but brilliant reality, swelling his heart, melting it with sudden warmth and glowing tenderness. He had had a vision, and he had doubted it. There on the platform in the instant his doubts had been swept away.

6

SHE was struggling then in the narrow vestibule with her bags, trying to get them off the train, and he sprang forward to help her.

"Oh, thank you!" she said breathlessly. He lifted the suit-cases off as the guard closed the door of the next carriage. She dropped her handbag and book, caught them up and stepped out onto the platform. "Thanks very much!"

"You—you aren't going to Paris?"

He heard himself speak, his voice unnatural and curiously far away.

Mary Winship raised her head, her lips parted, an instant light springing into her eyes, blue-black under their extraordinary lashes, and dying as instantly as her cheeks flushed with sudden crimson.

"Oh, I'm sorry," she said quickly. "I thought—for a minute you sounded like someone I—I knew a long time ago."

She turned abruptly. "Porter! Will you take these for me, please?"

She remembers. She hasn't forgotten.

"I'd like to leave this one in the parcel room."

The porter picked up her bags. Dan stood as the train slipped quietly past him and the platform miraculously emptied, watching the two of them move toward the gate. Once Mary Winship glanced back, but only for an instant, before she hurried along again.

She remembers but she isn't sure.

He went through the gate. He could see her going along to the parcel room. He waited till she turned away, took the smaller dressing case from the porter, tipped him, glanced quickly about her and hurried over to the telephone kiosk.

Why didn't you carry her bags? Why didn't you tell her then and there?

He knew the answer. In some way that he had no remote understanding of, he stood for danger. There was some connection, fantastic as it seemed, between the attempted murder of a harmless little man on that isolated balcony ledge, Mr. Sidney Copeland's scarcely veiled threats, the taut pale face he had first seen, just now, through the soot-stained windows of the coach. Mary Winship was afraid. It was not the tenseness and pallor of her face that had struck the first sharp chord in his memory. It was her voice. "I'm not afraid, not really. It's just the noise I mind." He could hear her in the shelter, pretending that, and hear her again, speaking to her cousin before he had seen her face: "Do go along, Eric. I'll be all right." She was afraid now, of something. She was covering it up from Dalrymple-Hughes as she sent him away so she could slip off the train.

What was she getting into? All he knew was that it was somehow tied in with an attempt on the life of a frail and inoffensive little man who seemed to have done nothing more than repeat a simple question that he, Dan McGrath, had asked. "Has her father come home?" Dan thought of Mr. Sidney Copeland again. It was apparently not a simple question; it was loaded with dynamite. And if Mary Winship refused to be sent off to Paris, it was dynamite that so far as Dan McGrath knew could as easily go off under her as under the little grey man who could hardly be so intimately connected with it.

He went across the draughty hall. A hand truck loaded with parcels and left near the entrance was between him and the telephone kiosk. He went toward it casually, and came to a halt. The man standing at the end of it, apparently engrossed in his newspaper, was looking intently over the top of it at the door of the kiosk. On Eric Dalrymple-Hughes's too handsome face was a look of such completely transparent triumphant malice that he suddenly seemed to become uncomfortably conscious of it himself. He glanced quickly at a small group of people standing near him and composed his features to their normal bored petulance. He fixed his eyes again over the top of his paper on the kiosk.

The door opened, Mary Winship came out and hurried to the entrance. Dalrymple-Hughes folded his paper, stuck it in the pocket of his trench coat and sauntered after her. Dan Mc-Grath brought up a quiet rear guard, out into the foggy night.

She set off across Waterloo Bridge, walking rapidly without hesitation or a backward glance. Dalrymple-Hughes followed coolly. She turned left into the Strand. Abruptly, in front of the Savoy, Dalrymple-Hughes was no longer to be seen. He had turned off, and Dan, quickening his pace, saw him cross the court and go inside. He cut down the distance between himself and Mary. Was Cousin Eric not following the girl? Did he know he was being followed himself? A third possibility, more likely, came to Dan's mind: he knew where she was going; there was no need to follow her further. After all, there must be a limited number of places she could confidently run to at that time of night, when nobody could call the Strand a crowded thoroughfare pulsing with life.

He quickened his step again. She had turned left, and as he reached the narrow entrance of Adam Street she was hurrying across it to the short block of houses on the opposite side. The street was an intimate *cul de sac* overlooking the Gardens on the Embankment, dimly lighted, and empty so that he could hear the quick echo of her heels on the cobblestones. He looked back to see if Eric had changed his mind, but there was no one in sight.

"Mary!" he called. "Mary Winship!"

It was a sudden impulse as she came into the mist-silvered

light from the street lamp. In a moment she would be gone, thinking they didn't know. Everything else aside, he had to warn her. Hearing her name, she would think it was someone she knew, stop under the light and turn and see him.

It seemed to him she gave a sudden start and hurried faster, not looking back. He called her name again. She broke forward wildly, running blindly. He saw her trip, stagger and catch herself.

"Mary! Wait a minute! It's me—it's Dan McGrath!"

His pounding feet echoed, drowning his voice, as she dropped her bag and book, caught hold of the iron step rail and flashed around, her face white with terror, her mouth open as if she was trying to scream and no sound would come. She was clutching wildly at the rail, her knees sagging. He put his hands out and gripped her arms.

"Don't be afraid, Mary. It's Dan McGrath. In the shelter, Mary—you remember—during the raid! I took you home, to Godolphin Square!"

It was not the way he had planned it, not the way in all his day dreams he had ever thought he was some day going to tell her.

"I love you, Mary. That's why I'm here. I came back to find you."

He had thought he might say that, but he was saying it more violently, with none of the vague nostalgia he'd pictured in his own mind but with an intense and present reality. Nor had he ever dared hope she might do what she did then. She raised her white face to his, her lips parted, her eyes searching his. Then her head drooped forward on his shoulder and she clung to him tightly.

"It *was* you," she whispered. "Oh, I hoped you'd come. I hoped you'd come some day."

Her trembling body was suddenly quiet. He could feel her pounding heart slow down.

"I love you, Mary." He murmured the words, holding her closer, and straightened abruptly as she raised her head, her eyes suddenly sparkling with laughter.

"But isn't this a hell of a way to meet a girl." She shook her hair back from her face and moved away a little. "Do you remember? That's what you said. And you were the first boy that ever kissed me."

"That makes it simple. I'm going to be the next, and the last."

He kissed her, then he said, "I wish we'd both gone to Paris."

As she drew back quickly, dropping her arms to her side, he reached down and picked up her book and bag.

"And I don't know what you thought you were going to do, but what I mean is, I don't know what this is all about—but unless it makes an awful lot of sense you're not going to do it. Your cousin knows you didn't go. He saw you get off the train, and followed you as far as the Savoy."

"Oh, no! He couldn't—"

She looked at him, her eyes widening, not understanding for an instant. She broke off and turned away quickly. "Then I've got to get home. I was—I was going to stay here tonight. In a friend's flat. He's away, and—"

"Why?" Dan said. He added gently, "I mean, what's it all about, Mary? Why were you going to stay here? Why didn't you go on to Paris?"

When she didn't answer he said, "Maybe you think it isn't

any of my business, but it is." He thought of Mr. Pinkerton and his spectacles caught in the inside folds of the red and green wool shawl. "For a couple of reasons. You're one of them." He managed a grin to make it all sound less abysmal. "After all, Mary, when a guy comes three thousand miles to find a gal and take her back home with him, he's got a right to know why she ditches her cousin, ducks off trains and goes zooming down back alleys. Hasn't he?"

"You'd not want to take me back home, probably, if you did know," Mary Winship said slowly. Then alarm sprang up quickly in her eyes. "I've got to get back home. Eric's probably on the phone now, telling my aunt—"

"But—you were on the phone yourself. Not ringing an empty flat—"

"No, I wasn't ringing an empty flat. I was ringing my uncle —my father's brother."

"All right, Mary. But what's it all about?" He tilted her firm pointed chin up and looked down at her. "I can help you if you'll tell me."

The sound of a car coming into a side street made him release her chin and take hold of her arm. "But not here. You're coming home with me."

She shook her head quickly. "My own home. I'm terribly late already."

They started across the road back into the Strand.

"It just happens it's the same place," Dan said. "Number four Godolphin—"

Her arm resting lightly in his was suddenly rigid. She stopped dead in the center of the road, staring at him, her lips parted. "You—you're not the American Miss Grim—"

She caught her breath, still staring at him, without finishing as much as Miss Grimstead's name.

"Sure," Dan said. "That's me." He was as startled as she was. "Or at least it was me. She may have put me out by now. And why not, Mary? I told you I came over to find you."

Her arm, still rigid in his, came to sudden life. She jerked it away and moved quickly a step from him.

"*Dan,*" she said. It was not spoken to him but as if she was speaking to someone else. She looked at him again. "What—what did you say your last name was? I—I'm afraid I was too upset to hear it."

"McGrath," Dan said calmly. After all, he had not known hers either until Mr. Pinkerton had told him.

"Oh," she breathed. "Oh!"

She stood rigidly where she was a moment, then turned and started forward. He had the fantastic impression that she was about to break into a run. He took a step after her and caught her arm.

"Mary! For heaven's sake, what's the matter?"

He turned her sharply about to face him. "What's happened? Why shouldn't I be the American Miss Grimstead told you about? What in hell did she say? You can at least tell me that, can't you?"

Mary Winship's chin shot up, her blue-black eyes were hot as burning pitch in the blank white of her face.

"Nothing at all," she said curtly. "She didn't even tell me your name. All she said was it was too bad I was leaving just when a handsome American had arrived."

The intonation of her voice gave it the quality of devastating scorn. She released her arm from his grasp and moved quickly forward into the Strand.

"I'm sorry I forgot my bag. Give it to me, please."

She held out her hand. "I can get a bus at the next corner."

"Look, Mary!"

"Taxi!" She spotted a cab and held up her hand. As it pulled into the kerb, she reached out and snatched her bag. She stepped quickly forward to the cab and turned.

"You needn't have pretended, Mr. McGrath," she said. Her voice was low and quivering with passionate intensity. "It wouldn't have helped you. My father is *not* a thief. There's no use your trying to find him. You shan't, not ever—not if I can help it."

She got in the cab, pulled the door sharply to behind her and reached out for the lever to draw up the open window. "So now you know why I didn't go to France."

She leaned forward to the waiting driver. "Fifty-three Saint—"

The window snapped shut, cutting off the rest of it. Dan McGrath had not heard enough to tell him where she was going. It was enough to tell him it was not Godolphin Square. The cab pulled away. He stood blankly where he was, blinded for an instant by the after-image of her small vivid face, eyes fixed ahead, chin up.

He pushed his hat up and scratched the back of his head, as completely bewildered as he had ever been in all his life. He looked down at the hand she'd snatched the bag away from. The whole thing was screwy as hell. He reached in his pocket to get a cigarette. It was an automatic gesture he was not aware he was making until he touched her book he had put in his pocket when he picked it up from the street where she'd dropped it.

He took it out and looked at it blindly, as if automatically searching for any kind of clue that might explain what was a fantastic and completely incoherent muddle. Then in spite of himself, he blinked. His own name was on the book. He saw that before he saw the title. "McGrath," it said there. The author was somebody named McGrath. He moved over to the lighted shop window behind him and opened the book.

"Masterpieces They've Never Found," was the title. The author's name under it was Arnold D. McGrath, Former Inspector Metropolitan Police, Boston, Mass., U. S. A.

Dan McGrath looked down at it a long time. Then he turned the pages to see if it had an index. There was none, and a jeweller's show window in the Strand was not a particularly adequate reading room. He closed the book and put it slowly back in his pocket, wondering if perhaps a first dim flicker of light was creeping into his bewildered mind.

He headed for home, trying to figure it out. As he became conscious of the hollow echo of his footsteps in the dreary empty side streets leading from Piccadilly back into Godolphin Square, he was ironically aware that it was the way he felt himself. It reminded him of background music in a movie. It had the same lonely hollow feeling he had, in the form of a curiously empty ache somewhere in the bottom of his stomach. He couldn't quite get rid of it no matter how detached he tried to make himself, even though he could view it with a certain amount of quietly sardonic humor. After all, it was something to come to London to find a girl, and find her, and find he really was in love with her, and lose her, all in less time than he had expected would take him to get settled and start looking for her. It was a record of some sort.

In fact, he thought, the brief period he had been there had seen a series of records new in his experience. He had become the self-appointed guardian of a rabbitty little Welshman obviously touched in the head (that he had got conked on it too was beside the point for the moment, although that was hardly normal in his experience either). He had been accused of being the confederate and finger man of a guy he'd merely inquired about in the most innocent way. He had gotten what could be called a room to stay in and had been asked to get the hell out of it. And finally, he had been mistaken for a Boston-Irish cop who had written a book, and had been left holding the book, as it were, because his girl thought he thought her father was a thief.

As he reviewed it, he could only conclude it was not the sort of thing to happen to a McGrath—at least not to Daniel J. McGrath. McGrath, he reflected, should have stood in bed. His big mouth twisted in a wry grin as he turned into Godolphin Square. Maybe the Savoy *would* be better, he thought. It was lighter, anyway—lighter and noisier. Godolphin Square was dark. The few street lamps seemed frail discouraged candles, their wispy yellow beams chewed off by the hungry shadows of the plane trees in the central garden. The fanlights over the uniform doorways were a shabby phalanx of sleepy single-eyed robots standing at attention around the Square's dark perimeter, broken only when they came to the rude gap where the bombs had fallen.

He looked across. He could see the black empty spaces on either side of Number 22, and the gaunt ruins that were all that was left of it. That was where his trouble had started. He thought of that, still trying to convince himself the whole business was a comedy of errors, easily explained as soon as he could get anybody to stop long enough to listen. But his own mood had changed. There was something curiously fascinating, and at the same time moving, about a house that had been bombed. He had found himself at other places in London stopping to look down into the empty holes at the broken masonry and then going on quickly, a little ashamed, as if he had been caught staring curiously at the open wounds of someone who was poor and naked and without defence. It was all in his own mind, he knew. No one passing in the street cared whether he looked or not. Still, he had found himself turning away, as if somehow the burden of guilt was also partly his. And at this house, he thought now, Mary Winship's mother and her aunt had been there the night it was destroyed.

He thought of the story the little Welshman had told him, as he went across to that side of the Square. It was a vivid picture in his mind—the two terror-stricken women huddled at the top of the fantastic stairway, the whole front of the house torn away, collapsed in a mass of powdered brick and mortar, the two women imprisoned behind it, half-crazed, clinging hysterically to the ornamental rail, refusing rescue when it came. It was his fear that Mary might have been there too, and his relief learning she had not been, that had made it so much more vivid than the little man's telling, he thought as he approached the void that had been the house next door to it. What had happened to the people here? Had they got out, or had they been buried in the debris?

He looked up at the stairway that had held fast to the steel-supported transverse hallway that was now a balcony open to the winds and rain, the wall behind it intact with the supporting column of the chimney, with its Adam mantel and pale damask covering protected by the overhanging section of roof that still remained. The bare walls stood like pale spectres, dimly perceived as they caught the uncertain light filtering through the darkness from the nearest street lamps before it disappeared in the black shadow of the overhanging roof, dark homeless ghosts whose footsteps were the slow intermittent drip of rain drops collected in the trees, falling on the sodden leaves below. The broken walls were wrapped in curious silence, compounded of a thousand small familiar sounds, above which his own footsteps seemed so loud that he stopped for a moment, stopped and went on and stopped again—abruptly, this time—listening, every nerve instantly alert.

He was not alone. He looked quickly over into the central garden, and turned sharply again as a sound of something like a pebble falling focussed his attention back on the ruined house.

There was someone at the top of the stairway. A black shadow of what he had thought was a jutting section of the broken roof had moved, and in moving dislodged a fragment of rubble. Why? he thought. Why should anyone be up on the stairway of a bombed-out house? He moved forward a step with the quick impulse to call out "Who's up there?" He changed his mind, walked briskly on past the house until he was halfway down the Square, crossed the road quietly, vaulted over the wattle fence into the garden, bent down and crept back until he could look up again at the shadowy stairway.

The deceptive interplay of sound and shadow could have fooled him, of course, he thought as he raised his head. But it hadn't. A dark figure was moving cautiously down the stairs—from nowhere. It was a man, almost at the bottom step; and as Dan watched he disappeared for an instant, and appeared again gripping the solid board fence put up to keep pedestrians from falling into the area. Dan heard the sudden shower of old rubble that fell as the man pulled himself up and climbed over the barrier. He hurried swiftly away into the night, moving noiselessly—too solid for a ghost, too silent for an honest man.

Dan McGrath straightened up and stepped out into the

73

path. The gate in the wattle fence was open a little. He started through it and stopped. There was no point in going over to Number 22 again. The man had gone, it was too dark to see anything. In the morning . . . He pulled the gate shut and turned back. The path he was on would cut through the garden; he could get out on his own side without going clear around the Square. He took half a dozen steps and froze to a dead stop.

A woman's voice spoke, distinctly and without warning, and very close to him. He jerked his head around, saw no one, and looked quickly the other way.

"I said, what interest have you got in my house, young man?"

He heard the words as well as the voice this time, and took a step toward the bench at the side of the overgrown path, in front of a large clump of black straggling bushes. He saw the pale surface of her face almost as if she were a face speaking, disembodied except for face and voice. She was staring steadily at him. As the face moved, he was aware that she had been sitting there and was now rising and coming slowly toward him. He took a step backwards involuntarily. There was something terrifying about the heavy-lidded eyes fixed on him.

7

WHEN the face coming toward him in the dark said, "I'm Caroline Winship," Dan McGrath was startled again by the quiet menace that he felt in those simple words. "This is my house. Why are you spying on it? What is it you want? What are you after?"

He was surprised to find his own voice steady. "Nothing whatever, Miss Winship. I was just coming by. I saw somebody on the stairs there. It seemed a funny place for anybody to—"

"I understand that you know my brother-in-law?"

"Miss Winship—" He stopped, trying to think how to make her believe him. She was close to him; he could smell the faint odor of some dry scent that reminded him of an aunt of his father's who thought once a year was enough to air her closets. Her head was trembling, almost with a palsied shake. Whether it was palsy, or anger, he couldn't tell. He had a strong belief it was not fear.

"Look," he said. "The answer is no. I do not know your brother-in-law."

The hooded eyes looked steadily at him.

"My brother-in-law is dead. I'm sure you've not come all the way to London to do his family, or any member of it, the great injustice of bringing him to life again. His wife is ill. She is a very susceptible woman. His daughter has been brought up to believe he was a—a kind and gentle person. I can't believe you would wilfully set out to hurt people whom you do not know and have no reason to hurt. Good night, young man."

He stood in the middle of the overgrown path watching her heavy figure move along it, her stick supporting her over the uneven ground, and then looked back, wondering, at the ruins of her house. She must have been out there waiting, not for him obviously, as she had no way of knowing he would come, but for her brother-in-law. It only made everything more puzzling. If her friend Mr. Sidney Copeland thought he was a confederate, and Mary thought he was a policeman, just what,

75

he wondered, did Miss Caroline Winship think he was, appealing to him simply as a decent human being? He looked over at Number 4. She was going inside. He saw her thick figure outlined in the door for a moment before it closed, and he looked up then through the plane trees at the top floor where his friend Mr. Pinkerton was. The light was on there. He could see a small oblong segment of it, beyond the stone coping. And the light shouldn't be on. A sudden cold hand gripped his heart as he went rapidly through the garden and across the street.

"Oh, he's doing very nicely." Mrs. Beckwith smiled at him as he cleared the top three steps. "You needn't have been worried. A little peculiar, perhaps. He *would* write a letter for me to put in the post tonight, and I thought it best to humor him." She fished in her pocket. "Would you like to see it?"

Dan shook his head. It was probably to the Lord Chamberlain, but that was someone else's problem. He opened the door quietly. Mr. Pinkerton was sleeping peacefully. He turned back.

"Thanks very much," he said. "How much—"

"Mr. Pinkerton paid me." She took off her cap and picked up her coat. "Two ladies and a gentleman came up to see him. A heavy-set lady and another who doesn't look very well. The young gentleman was quite anxious to talk to him. He just left a few moments ago. They didn't see him—or Miss Grimstead. She came up too."

"Thanks," Dan said.

Reflecting that he liked Mrs. Beckwith, he went back into his room. Eric, he thought, had got here first. That meant that Mary would no doubt be in for it. He put his hand in his raincoat pocket and took out her book. *"Masterpieces They've Never Found."* He looked at it for an instant, put it down on the table and hung up his raincoat. He looked at his bed and along the hall at Mr. Pinkerton's closed door, pulled the chair up to the table and sat down, knowing that once he got in bed no book ever written would keep him awake. He opened the book, and was next conscious of coming up from some bottomless abyss, cramped and cold, aware that he had fallen profoundly asleep and was struggling for breath. He jerked bolt upright and opened his eyes, and saw her.

The woman was there by his table, clutching at it with one hand, the other at her throat, gasping, struggling in a paroxysm of suffocation. Her face was swollen and suffused. He leaped to his feet and caught her by the shoulders, holding her steadily while she struggled and finally caught her breath. She sank exhausted into the chair that he pushed under her with one foot.

Cold perspiration stood out on his forehead, and his hands were shaking as he fumbled in his pocket for a cigarette. He remembered that she was struggling for air and put it back. Then, as he stood looking helplessly at her, he gave a sudden start of recognition. This must be Mary Winship's mother. She had the same thick dark eyebrows and long lashes lying like wet silk on her high cheekbones as the suffused swelling went down in the flesh covering them. There were streaks of grey in her hair, but it had been black, and was still curly, and she had the same pointed chin.

She was lying back in the chair, the pulse in her throat pounding, her breast rising and falling heavily under the silk padded robe she had wrapped around her. Then her eyelids, delicate, almost transparent, folds of violet, fluttered and opened. Her eyes were Mary's eyes, but faded and tired, as they met his in sudden mute and poignant appeal.

"I'm Louise Winship," she whispered. "Have you—a message for me? I'm Mrs. Scott Winship . . ."

She thinks you know him too. This isn't funny any longer.
This is getting grim.

He leaned forward and took her hands, clasped together in her lap, in both of his.

"Listen, Mrs. Winship," he said as earnestly as he could. "This is all a mistake. I don't know your husband. I don't know him at all. I've never seen him in my life. Please believe me."

Her eyes opened wider for an instant before she closed them and let her head sink back on the chair.

"Oh, I'm sorry," she murmured. "I thought . . ."

Her voice trailed off.

"I am too," Dan said gently. "If I could have helped you any way. You see, Mrs. Winship, this is the whole story about why I'm here . . . I met your daughter Mary during the war. I only saw her once, but I fell in love with her then. And I've come back now to find her. That's why I'm here now. I'm still in love with her. I want her to marry me if she will."

Her eyes had opened, wider than before. He smiled at her. "No mother ought to act this surprised when a guy says he wants to marry her daughter, Mrs. Winship."

"But it—it is surprising, Mr. McGrath. I wasn't aware she knew any Americans." She drew her hand across her forehead in a vague bewildered gesture. "I'm sorry. I expect perhaps there are lots of things I don't know."

He kept himself from saying "You and me both," and smiled down at her.

"You wouldn't want to tell me what all this is about, would you?" he asked soberly. "Maybe I could be of some use. Would it—do you *want* to find your husband? Your sister—"

He stopped, and went on. "Your sister said he was dead—"

78

Her hands, still in his, had become very quiet.

"I'm not just being curious, Mrs. Winship," he said. "Believe me. I've told you I want to marry Mary. I mean that seriously, Mrs. Winship. And it seems to me there's something going on around here that's got all of you six jumps ahead of the loony bin. Maybe there's something somebody could do."

"I—I don't understand you, Mr. McGrath."

It was just as well, he thought. She drew back, disengaging her hands.

"My sister Caroline prefers to think my husband is dead because she is a person of intense convictions. She thinks my husband treated me and Mary unfairly, a long time ago. She never forgets, or forgives."

He saw her pallid face quiver as she added hastily, "I'm not being disloyal to my sister. She's enormously kind and patient, and she's not a patient woman. She's taken care of me and Mary ever—ever since my husband went away. We had—no resources of our own, and I have asthma very badly."

"Lady, you don't have to tell me that," Dan thought. He felt the prickle of cold sweat on his brow again.

Mrs. Winship was silent for a moment. "You asked me if I want to find my husband," she said at last, speaking very slowly, almost as if she were speaking to herself rather than to Dan McGrath. "I do, desperately. I was terribly in love with him. It was all so—so difficult. I think I'm—"

She broke off abruptly, giving her head a quick bewildered shake.

"What am I—what am I saying?"

She made a sudden movement forward and pushed herself to her feet.

"I'm being absurd. Why should I wish to find him, Mr. Mc-Grath?"

She said it so breathlessly that he looked at her in quick apprehension.

"Why should—I simply misunderstood. I thought you'd seen him, and perhaps you could—tell me if he's well—and happy."

She went quickly to the door. "Good night. I'm sorry I wakened you."

He watched her move unsteadily along the hall. As she reached the head of the stairway beside Mr. Pinkerton's door and turned to go down he stood there still, looking quietly after her. He was suddenly, and only then, aware that he had seen her before. She was the woman he had seen coming out of the little Welshman's room—or going into it—before he knew who she was, and before he had gone into Mr. Pinkerton's room to find him lying on the balcony. He turned away slowly. From below he could hear a door open and close so softly that if he had not been intensely alert he would not have heard it at all through the creeping and oppressive silence of the sleeping house.

He looked at his watch and was surprised to find it was almost three o'clock. His sense of time, disrupted by the transatlantic change, was slow to readjust itself. He realized now that he must have been asleep much longer than he had thought, and remembered suddenly, thinking back, that he had sat down to read the book Mary Winship had left with him. He looked down at the table, then at the floor, and under the cushion in the chair. The book was nowhere in sight.

As he looked slowly around the small barren room he saw that something else was wrong. He went over to the dresser.

The slide fastener of his briefcase was halfway from the end, where it always stuck if it was pulled together in a hurry. He picked the case up and opened it. It had his toothbrush in one side, with a couple of handkerchiefs. In the other side was a letter from Richards & Case, Attorneys-at-Law, Baltimore, Maryland, wishing him bon voyage and success on his mission to London. It was the law office where a job was waiting for him when he got back home. He picked it up and looked down at the last paragraph again.

"This firm has a distinguished record in tracing unknown and missing persons. In view of the special nature and urgent demand of the situation in hand, we confidently expect you to uphold our reputation on the present project."

It was meant to be funny. They all knew he was coming to London to find a girl whose name he did not even know—on a wild goose chase he might as well get out of his system so he could settle down and go to work.

He closed the briefcase and put it down, wondering how long he had actually been asleep. How long had Mrs. Scott Winship been in his room with him dead to the world? If she had not had that sudden paroxysm of strangulation and waked him, would he ever have known she had been there—if the slide fastener had not stuck?

He picked up the briefcase, took the letter out and read the last paragraph again. He had not thought it was particularly funny when he had got it at the airport. Mrs. Scott Winship would have no way of knowing it was even meant to be. On the other hand—the book would have been on the table just in front of him, perfectly ordinary like any other red book. Not a book you would recognize and spot at once—unless you already knew and were looking for it.

And the only person who knew he had the book was Mary Winship. If she had come home . . . He shrugged his shoulders, glanced at his watch again, put the briefcase away and got out his pajamas. He seemed still to be getting more and more entangled in a web of circumstances, all pointing directly to Daniel McGrath as a heel of the foulest order. He was still trying unsuccessfully to figure it out when he turned off the light and went to bed.

"Breakfast is served, sir."

The white-coated waiter Dan had been sleepily watching for the last moment or two announced the fact with impeccable formality as he switched on the table light. It gave an enlarged effect of throwing open the doors of the master's chamber and summoning him forth to the luxurious comfort of his own morning room, to the manner born, with a fire burning cheerfully in the grate. As the bed was less than two feet from the table, and it was a minor miracle that the man had been able to see enough in the grey gloom seeping down from the single window in the mansard roof to lay the cloth and the gleaming array of silver-covered dishes on it without waking him sooner, Dan looked at him with admiration. He was at the door about to retire into the hall, and stopped there, looking back over his shoulder.

"Good morning, sir. I'm Pegott, your permanent valet, sir."

Dan said "Good morning," and reached for his bathrobe at the foot of the bed. Impeccable, he thought, really was the word for Pegott. He had understood the Pegotts of Old England were a vanished race, the gentlemen's gentlemen gone along with the barons of beef and Devonshire cream, as dead as Walking Stewart and the five-bottle men with gout and purple livers.

But the whole thing was a gross libel propagated by Opposition. The permanent valet proved it: his white coat and black bow tie, his adam's apple cradled in the starched angle of his wing-tip collar, above all his manners that enabled him to make a suite of one attic trunk room and overlook Dan's toothbrush and twisted tube of paste still on the towel lying on the dresser. Pegott was perfect of his kind, perhaps too perfect for his age, which could not have been more than thirtyish.

He was still at the door. Dan stuck his feet into his slippers, expecting him to say "Will there be anything else, sir? Thank you, sir?" Instead he said, "I beg your pardon, sir. Do I understand from the manageress that you are leaving us today?"

"I wouldn't be surprised."

"In that case would you permit me to have a few words with you when you have finished your breakfast, sir?"

"Sure," Dan said. Why not? he thought. He had had words with practically everybody else. More than a few with Miss Myrtle Grimstead, to say nothing of Mr. Sidney Copeland; with Miss Caroline Winship, with Mary herself—rather heated ones, on the whole, now he thought of them again—and possibly significant words with Mrs. Winship, and with little Mr. Pinkerton. He was curious about what they would be with Pegott. He looked at him with more interest.

Pegott bowed slightly. "Very good, sir. Thank you, sir." He started to open the door. "You understand, sir," he said, lowering his voice, "in my position one is bound to hear a great deal."

It seemed to Dan that the smooth facade of the perfect permanent valet had slipped for an instant as his voice sank, and that he had caught a glimpse of something other than complete impeccability. Hear, or overhear? he thought. He nodded coolly, looking at the man. It was the first time he had been aware of his face as a face. It was pasty, the eyes a little too close, and a little too bright. They met his in a sharpened scrutiny that might have had more point, he thought, if he had been staying on than it seemed to have, considering he was leaving that day. But the encounter was so brief that he wasn't sure. It could have been his own imagination entirely.

"I hope you will enjoy your breakfast, sir. I used to work for an American lady who was very particular about her coffee. Thank you, sir."

He was gone then with a slight bow, his facade intact again. Dan turned to his kippers and the morning paper, a little surprised to find the kippers excellent, the coffee drinkable and the paper almost solely concerned with the private lives of the movie stars. He was a little surprised again to look up and see Pegott at the exact moment he finished all three.

He pushed his chair back, started to reach down for his napkin, remembered the shortages and that he had not had one, and turned to the valet.

"What's on your mind, Pegott?"

A sharp tingle along his spinal column alerted him instantly as he saw that the man's facade had not only slipped but slid. Pegott was nervous. He glanced back at the door.

"You'll understand this is strictly confidential, I hope, sir."

There was a faint trembling in his voice that communicated itself to his hands. "It would be very awkward if—"

"All right," Dan said. "What is it?"

The whole train of the previous night's fantasies that six hours' sleep had robbed of its presentiments of fear and evil and of its poignancy and emotional tension was back with him.

Whether it was a communication of the man's nervousness or a sudden distaste he was unable to say; but he was acutely aware that nothing had changed overnight. He was precisely where he had been when he found his briefcase tampered with. That Pegott was under some extraordinary tension was clearer by the moment. His face had a kind of dough-like pallor and his occasional glances back into the hall and the narrowed lines at the corners of his eyes were furtive and cunning. The prickling sensation along Dan McGrath's spine sharpened.

This guy's no good. He's a louse or he's dangerous. Watch him, McGrath.

"What's on your mind, Pegott? Shoot."

He felt an instant subtle but very definite change in the atmosphere—or was it simply in the relationship of the two of them? The valet's nervousness disappeared. In its place came a suppressed excitement, as if he was confident now where he had not been before. As he leaned forward he made no attempt to conceal the backward glance he shot toward the hall. His breath came quickly, so close to Dan that there was no missing the sweet-sour smell of gin on it.

"I know where he is," he whispered. His voice broke with eagerness. "I know where *it* is. All I want is half what's coming. I could take it all but I want it in American dollars put by in New York."

He straightened up, his eyes, sharp and brightly acquisitive, fixed on Dan's as if he saw something in them he was not so sure of. He drew himself up, steadied one hand again on the table. "That's fair enough, I'd say, sir. Wouldn't you? There was no need to speak to you about it—except I understood you'd been making inquiries."

Dan nodded, looking at him.

"It depends," he said coolly, "on who you mean. And on what you mean by 'it.'"

The "who" he could guess. As the "it" was unknown to him he spoke with as casual unconcern as he could manage, not to betray that he did not know. As he said it, Miss Caroline Winship's words flashed into his mind for the first time since she had spoken them, out in the Square, in the dark overgrown path under the dripping plane trees. "I cannot believe you would wilfully set out to hurt people whom you do not know and have no reason to hurt . . ." Betray himself? It was the Winships he was betraying—Mary and her mother—listening to this man.

"The person you were making inquiries about, sir," Pegott said evenly. He had disappeared, with a kind of super-legerdemain, entirely behind the impeccable facade. "And the picture, sir."

His eyes gleamed and his lips tightened as he added quietly. "The picture I understand he sold—for ten thousand pounds—and neglected to deliver to the American gentleman who'd purchased it, sir."

With the overtones of the well-trained voice of the well-trained permanent valet there were undertones that Dan McGrath heard and understood, as he was meant to hear and understand. Pegott was not telling him a fact for his information. He was telling him so that he would know Pegott also knew, and knew the exact value involved. It was not information. It was a warning. Pegott had the word. McGrath needn't try anything on. It was being stated politely but without equivocation.

Dan thought rapidly. This was it. Mary Winship's father had sold a picture, collected £10,000 and absconded without the formality of turning the picture over to the rightful owner. The title of Mary Winship's book flashed into his mind. The picture, then, had disappeared with Scott Winship. It belonged, then, to whoever it was had bought it. Or to the insurance firm if it had been insured and the insurance collected and not repaid, depending on what deal the firm had had with the owner. They would have offered a reward, he thought; Pegott was after it.

"How much is the reward?" he asked.

He realized at once it was a blooper. Pegott drew half a step back. That was not what he had in mind. Or that was only a part of it. He was playing for higher stakes. What they were Dan had no idea. What he did have was an exceedingly clear idea that in this sort of business, conducted in this way, there were dangerous potentials. One of them was only too often the shadowy uncharted area where the quicksands of blackmail crept too close to the edge of the solid legal towpath it was safe to proceed along. The warning prickles crept back to his spine. Pegott was not a pretty fellow. Somehow, in spite of that, Dan had no doubt that he did know, or thought he knew, where Mary Winship's father was and where the picture was. And Mary's passionate avowal that her father was not a thief and her mother's poignant indecision and emotional uncertainty made them particularly vulnerable to the lure of the siren's song . . .

"Where is he?" he asked.

8

Mr. Evan Pinkerton finished shaving. His head was still a painful lump that throbbed unpleasantly whenever he turned it, but nevertheless he turned it once more to listen through the washroom door for Miss Myrtle Grimstead's managerial voice. He was in a state of acute nervous anxiety. She should have come up by this time, if the nurse had posted his letter, of which he was none too confident. Unless, of course, she had posted it and the estate agents refused to do anything about it. They might easily feel he had no right to insist on Mr. McGrath's being allowed to stay in the box room in the first place, and regard his request that he stay on as Mr. Pinkerton's personal guest as a brazen disregard of the prime function of rental property in the second. In any event, it was very important for him to see Mr. McGrath as quickly as possible, or he should not have got up at all. He really did feel seedy this morning, and looked it. Hardly anything he could think of, except fear that the American might actually take it into his head to go to the police and complain about his narrow brush with death, could have spurred him up and out.

Mr. Pinkerton put down his towel and shaving kit, and exclaimed with annoyance as he knocked off the washstand, and for perhaps the dozenth time, the old silver-backed military hair brush that belonged to the chef. His head swam dizzily as he got down on his haunches and recovered it from between the trash can and the scouring pot. Whenever anyone mentioned the chef, who shared the bath with him and Pegott, and now the young American in the box room—and everyone did mention him, the guests because he was a good cook and could disguise anything, from whale to offal, in a very edible fashion, and Betty the maid because he was what she called uppity and the only member of the staff Miss Grimstead stood in awe of— Mr. Pinkerton always saw a silver-backed military hairbrush on the floor by the scouring pot where he himself had just knocked it. He reflected now that although he had never seen the chef, in spite of the fact that his room was just three doors from his own, next to Pegott's, he must have picked up the wretched brush scores of times. This was the most painful of all, and the only time he had not been sure, for a moment, that he could get his hand down between the wall and the drainpipe without his head bursting. He got it down, however, and put the brush back on the side of the bowl, wishing very much the man would mind his belongings a bit better.

At his own door he listened again for some evidence of Miss Grimstead's approach, either in person or in writing, before he went along and put his towel and shaving kit away. Perhaps the nurse had thought his mind was wandering, and left the letter there in his room. He looked about for it as he put on his grey coat and tied his purple string tie. But it was nowhere in sight, and he went out into the hall again. His head still ached, and it jarred it to walk at all. He put his hand out against the wall to absorb some of the shock, and crept gingerly along like a cat on a muddy path until he reached the wall by Dan Mc-Grath's door. He put his hand out to knock.

"Oh, dear," he thought, "he's got someone with him."

He started to go back to his room when he heard Dan Mc-Grath speak.

"It depends on who you mean. And on what you mean by 'it.'"

Mr. Pinkerton stopped where he was, blinking. Dan

McGrath was annoyed at something. He could tell the tone of his voice from his own unfortunate adventure the night before.

"The person you were making inquiries about, sir."

Mr. Pinkerton stood there motionless. *Pegott*. Pegott was in there, talking to Dan McGrath, and up to no good. Mr. Pinkerton was sure of that. He felt a sudden warm flush of indignation. Pegott was carrying tales about somebody. That was why his voice had been a low murmur before Dan McGrath spoke. It might even be Mary Winship he was talking about. Mr. Pinkerton would put nothing beyond him. And then he gave an abrupt start that made a hot knife jab through his aching head as he listened, blinking his eyes in incredulous consternation.

It was Mary's father, not Mary. Mr. Pinkerton moistened his dry lips. Dan McGrath was asking where Scott Winship was, then the business about the picture. Why was he so anxious to know, that he was willing to listen to a person like Arthur Pegott . . . ? Mr. Pinkerton hastily put aside the fantastic idea that had slipped abruptly into his mind. It couldn't possibly be true.

He could hear the valet clearly.

"That I'm unable to say at this time, sir. All I can say is that I may be able to take you to him—sometime after I go off duty tonight, if you are interested, sir."

"He is not telling the truth," Mr. Pinkerton thought. He could tell that too, from the tone of Pegott's voice. He listened, fascinated, hoping very greatly, but increasingly against hope, that his friend McGrath would tell the man off properly for what seemed extraordinary impertinence indeed.

"I can meet you outside the house. Or most Americans are familiar with the American Express offices in Haymarket. At say ten-thirty or eleven, sir."

"Right. I'll meet you outside. But get this. The whole thing may be a washout. There may be nothing in it at all."

The idea that had come into Mr. Pinkerton's mind and that he had hastily dismissed darted back into it again. He felt a chill at his heart. Maybe that was what Dan McGrath had really come to London about. The romantic search for Mary Winship was a blind; it was her father, and the picture, that he was actually hunting for all the time. It was a trap, and he had fallen headlong into it.

"Oh, dear, dear me!" Mr. Pinkerton thought dismally.

"Very good, sir," Pegott said. Mr. Pinkerton could almost see him smile as he said it. Dan McGrath had sounded quite as false as Pegott had done when he said he did not know where Mr. Winship was at that time. They were a pair of outright falsifiers. He heard the sound of a cover being placed on a dish as Pegott added, "My father was quite sure there had been a mistake made. But as you say, sir . . ."

Mr. Pinkerton did not stop to hear any more. As he scurried silently back to his room, he heard Miss Grimstead's voice coming up the stairwell from the floor below. It was all sweetness and bright light, a shower of milk and liquid honey.

"Betty, Betty! Let's put the sofa from Colonel Mayhew's room into Mr. McGrath's. I'm afraid he's not really as comfy as he should be. And let's give dear Mr. Pinkerton Mrs. Jameson's eiderdown—"

Mr. Pinkerton got into his room and closed the door. The nurse had posted his letter, the estate agents had complied with his directions. He realized gratefully, his heart warming, that in whatever form the communication to Miss Grimstead had come, it must have been what his special friend in the estate agents' office invariably referred to as a stinker. The eiderdown was pure unearned increment. He'd not had one as long as he had lived there.

He was so pleased that he forgot his aching head and sat down on the side of the couch smiling happily to himself. Until he remembered. Dan McGrath was now his guest, at his expense. If he turned out to be a whited sepulchre, it was all Mr. Pinkerton's fault—and cost. He stopped smiling abruptly. A further idea came instantly into his mind. The Winships ought certainly to be told. The only question at all, as he thought of it, was which of the Winships he should tell. Miss Caroline as head of the family was the most obvious person, but he dismissed the thought as quickly as he would have done, if it had occurred to him to embrace a boa constrictor. Mrs. Winship was ill, he did not quite trust Eric Dalrymple-Hughes if at all. That left Mary Winship, and Mr. Sidney Copeland, the family friend. And, from what he now knew of Dan McGrath, he was forced reluctantly to the conclusion that Mary had got off to Paris. Mr. McGrath had most probably had no intention at any time of attempting to stop her from going. What had seemed to Mr. Pinkerton surprising apathy, and lack of a lover's heat, when he had first told him she was going, was now painfully clear to him. Mr. Sidney Copeland was therefore the only person he could really go to.

He stoically put his hard brown bowler on his sensitive head and left his room. Mr. McGrath's door at the end of the hall was open, and Mr. Pinkerton could hear him in the bath, the spray running. He was not singing, which Mr. Pinkerton thought was unhappily significant. He knew from the cinema that it was an invariable national custom. They even wrote popular songs about it.

It was almost noon when Mr. Pinkerton came dejectedly down the steps from Mr. Copeland's offices in Wimpole Street. He had waited two hours. In spite of the young lady in the luxurious reception room he knew very well Mr. Copeland had been in the next room, and that he was now in the blue motor car disappearing round the next corner into Portman Square. Mr. Sidney Copeland had refused to see him. Whether it really was because he wanted him to see his own surgeon—Mr. Pinkerton hadn't one and had never had—as the office assistant had tried to explain, or for some other reason, Mr. Pinkerton could only guess. The fact was still the same. He stood unhappily in the street. If he felt a bit more fit, he might gather sufficient courage to approach Miss Caroline. He suspected, however, he would never feel that fit again as long as he lived. He turned and started dejectedly along the street, when a taxi drew up in front of the house he had just left. He glanced back and stopped, blinking.

It was Mary Winship. She'd not gone to Paris. Dan Mc-Grath had really meant . . . Mr. Pinkerton blinked again and scurried back just as she was crossing the footpath.

"He's not there," he said hastily. "He's—he's left."

"Oh, Mr. Pinkerton!"

Mary Winship looked at him with quick surprise. Her cheeks flushed a little. She looked very pretty, except, he thought, that she was rather too pale, as if she's not slept very well. "What are you doing here?"

"I came to see Mr. Copeland about a—a matter. But he's not in."

He saw her hesitate and look up at the house.

"I saw him leave. In his blue car."

"Oh, really?"

Apparently she had not believed him before, but now did. He could see by the evident distress in her blue-black eyes that she had wanted so see Sidney Copeland even more than he had, and that now she wasn't sure just what to do.

He cleared his throat hesitatingly. "I—I wonder if you'd have lunch with me?" he asked timidly. "There was something I wanted to see him about too. Perhaps . . ."

She looked at him quickly. "Is it about my father, Mr. Pinkerton?"

He could see that she knew it was, even before he nodded his head, which was a mistake. It felt much better when it was still.

"Then I'd love to. I—I'm terribly worried. I know a place we can go to."

"You—you didn't go to Paris?"

They were in a taxi and almost to the Green Parrot in Regent Street before Mr. Pinkerton, dismayed by the sudden realization of what he was actually doing, or about to do, could find his voice to ask her that. He flushed a little as he heard himself putting the question that way.

Her eyes were fixed ahead of her. "I changed my mind. I spent the night with my uncle. Elliot Winship—you know, the architect. My father's brother. He's so vague I don't see how he ever makes up his mind to put one stone on top of another."

She twisted her hands together and bit her lower lip to stop its trembling.

"I still don't know whether he even heard what I was talking about. That's why I wanted to see Copey."

The taxi drew up in front of a small tea room with a large

green parrot sitting in the window. Mary opened her bag. "I'll pay him," she said, and had done so before Mr. Pinkerton could get his worn brown leather purse out of his trousers pocket. It had been one of the late Mrs. Pinkerton's methods of discouraging impulsive expenditure that he had never quite dared to abandon.

"It won't be so crowded upstairs this early." She led him up to a small table in a corner. "Now tell me."

But as Mr. Pinkerton looked at her she seemed so very young, and so unhappy, that his throat closed up. All he could do was blink at her like a bewildered owl. She put her hand out impulsively across the table and on his sleeve.

"I know it sounds dreadful, but it's not really. It can't be. There must have been some terrible misunderstanding. Because, don't you see, Mother's always told me wonderful things about him. She'd never have done if he'd been so awful—or if he'd even been capable of doing anything awful. There's something wrong, somewhere."

Her small pointed chin was high and her eyes bright and clear.

"Do you know what he's supposed to have done?"

In the face of her passionate conviction, Mr. Pinkerton was a little ashamed that his answer had to be on the basis of information that he had not come by in a really honest and legitimate fashion.

"Was it—something about a picture?"

"Yes. You do know."

Her attitude was so matter-of-fact that he found himself ashamed again, of thinking that a few tears, or a trace of them anyway, would have been rather more becoming in one so young. He saw too that she knew what he was thinking.

"You can't go on forever not facing up to things, can you?" she asked calmly. "That's always been the trouble. I think that's why Mother's always ill, and why Aunt Caroline gives the impression of being so—so hard and so bitter. She's not really. She's terribly sensitive, and terribly kind. If it hadn't always been such a mystery—I don't believe in having skeletons in the closet."

Mr. Pinkerton mentally shook his head. She had always been so sweet, whenever he'd seen her, and she was actually one of these modern young women.

"Well, perhaps," he said tentatively.

"You can't hide things," she said warmly. "They go on thinking I know nothing about it, but ever since I was a child . . . They should have *told* me. Then I'd have got used to the idea. You see, I knew Mother always had one of her attacks—she nearly dies with asthma when certain things happen. Like—when the flowers come. When they came yesterday, and she tried to hide them. And the time I found the copy of my grandfather's will on the desk, and read it—I didn't see why I shouldn't—and asked her where the picture he left her had got to. She wasn't really his child, her mother was his second wife, so he hadn't got to leave her anything, except that he adored her mother, and her too."

Mr. Pinkerton put down his fork and blinked at her, bewildered at the sudden flow of information all quite new to him.

"I mean, why should anyone be ill sometimes and not others? You see, for years now, she's always got three red roses, on October sixteenth, and in April on her birthday a little bunch of yellow primroses. I—I found out my father sent them. And she's always desperately ill. Last night, just before I left . . . I'd been so excited I hadn't noticed that either of them was upset. I went to her room and I saw she'd got her fur jacket out. I saw the flowers, and a note she'd got. I asked her what it was, and she wouldn't tell me and burned it up the minute I turned my back. The ashes were in a tray on her dressing table. She was already getting an attack."

Mr. Pinkerton ate his tinned fruit and watery custard without really noticing it very much. He remembered he had seen the flowers himself, last night, in the lift. What was it Mason had said about them? Bring on another one of her attacks, poor lady. Hay fever, he had said. So even the servants in the flats knew about them. But still . . . What Mary Winship said next startled him so much that he almost dropped his spoon.

"You won't believe this—but I—I got it into my head something *must* be happening to her. I decided she was being poisoned—deliberately, I mean."

Mr. Pinkerton swallowed hastily, adjusted his lozenge-shaped spectacles and looked at her in dismay. In his role of gadfly and leech on the stolid flank of Chief Inspector Bull of New Scotland Yard, he had had several rather unpleasant experiences with poisoners.

"Poisoning her?" he managed to stammer.

She nodded. "Deliberately poisoning her. It just shows you the state I'd got into. People quit acting like normal human beings when this sort of thing goes on. Last spring, when the primroses came, I took the rest of her food—she's always so ill she can hardly eat anything—I took the rest of her food to a chemist I know at the hospital. Of course all of us were eating the same food, but I didn't *know*. So that's what I did. He analyzed everything she ate for a whole week before I broke down and told Aunt Caroline what I was doing."

Mr. Pinkerton shuddered inwardly. "What—what did your aunt do?"

He was almost afraid for her to tell him.

"She was terrified, of course. First she thought I was out of my mind. Then she thought we ought to keep on with it another week. We did, but there was nothing at all. Just the primroses. And she was over it then, by that time."

"Is she—could she be allergic to—"

"But the roses too? And to three red roses. Not to a dozen red roses. And not primroses in the garden or anyone else's house? But I know what you mean. I thought of that. I've thought of everything. And then I—I asked a psychiatrist I know. He said it was all quite simple. She really doesn't *want* to see him. Not really, you see. So she gets sick so she can't. Instead of going out to see him she has to go to bed. He said there are millions of cases like it. And Mother is high strung and nervous, of course."

Mr. Pinkerton wondered. He knew nothing about psychiatry himself, but it did sometimes seem to him people were rather too confident about making judgments about other people's motives.

"And I'm afraid he's right," Mary Winship said. "You take the war, for instance. The blitz and all the rest of it. She was perfectly all right all during that. She took all that better actually than Aunt Caroline did. Of course the flowers stopped coming during the worst of it, but you didn't have time to think about escape mechanisms. That's part of the pattern, the psychiatrist said."

Of course that was true. Mr. Pinkerton knew it from his own experience. A neighbor of his in Golders Green who'd been a semi-invalid for years became an unmitigated nuisance as a fire watcher by night and a Nosey Parker into other people's dustbins by day, as indefatigable as a ferret. And his own rheumatism had entirely disappeared. Still—he rather liked what he'd seen of Mrs. Winship. It was better, of course, to *be* a psychiatric case than be poisoned, from her point of view anyway. On the other hand . . . He looked hesitantly at Mary.

"But I don't quite understand," he said timidly. "You say you know about—about your father and the picture, and you know there's some—some misunderstanding. And yet you seem to think your mother has some . . ."

Fortunately she seemed to understand what he meant, which at that point he himself actually did not. All he knew was that he was very much bewildered, and that there was obviously some really basic confusion in matters as they now stood. But as he bogged down Mary nodded her head.

"I know what you mean. And you're quite right, of course. Maybe Mother's just made him sound wonderful, and never told me so I'd never know he was—something else. Of course, she should *want* to see him. But I do know I've always thought I knew she expected him to come back to us some day. I'm sure of it. That's why I can't understand her always getting sick. And—you see, Mr. Pinkerton, I want to *do* something to stop all this, before it kills her. I don't believe she believes my father stole the picture. How could he? How could he take it and sell it and run away and leave the two of us before I was born even? And why should he go on tormenting us? I don't believe he'd do that. I don't believe my father could do it."

Her long black eyelashes were moist. Mr. Pinkerton was silent. It was a sturdy faith that he admired greatly—but she did not seem to realize that her father had not only taken the picture, and the money for the picture, but he had not turned the picture over to the man he had got the money from. If Pegott was right.

"And now that policeman's here, or whatever he is," she said. Two hot bright spots burned in her cheeks and her eyes were like molten sapphires. "He must have been following him, or he wouldn't come here just when my father comes here again, and turn up at Godolphin Square. And he's got my book—it's Aunt Caroline's really—about missing pictures. If he finds my father, they'll put him in prison. I'm not supposed to know that either, but I do. So I've *got* to find him first. I've got to find him and warn him that Mr. McGrath—"

Mr. Pinkerton's jaw dropped. He had entirely forgotten that he had himself had the same suspicion of Dan McGrath not three hours before, and that that was in fact his sole reason for being here now.

"Mr. McGrath?"

Mary Winship nodded. "He's—he's a beast." Her cheeks flushed hotly.

Mr. Pinkerton hesitated only an instant. "He's going to see your father. Pegott knows where he is. He's going to take Mr. McGrath to see him tonight. At eleven o'clock."

He blurted it out breathlessly. It was what he had intended to tell her until he had forgot all about it—an escape mechanism in itself, no doubt, as he'd been so tongue-tied in the taxi with her.

"*Pegott?*"

She was looking at him incredulously.

Mr. Pinkerton nodded. "That's what I went to see Mr. Copeland about. But he wouldn't see me."

"Oh, not Copey!" The flush died in her cheeks. "He'd—he'd do something awful. He hates my father."

"I—I thought of your aunt," Mr. Pinkerton said.

"She'd be worse." Mary gathered up her bag and gloves. "If

you think Mother's allergic to primroses, you ought to see Aunt Caroline if anyone happens to speak of my father. You'd best keep out of it, Mr. Pinkerton. It's a family row. A really serious one."

"I—I expect you're right," Mr. Pinkerton said apologetically. He put down sixpence for the waitress and took up the bill. "I—I wasn't meaning to interfere."

He followed her across the room to the stairway, feeling very old and seedy in the spring-like wake of her erect young figure and quick elastic step. She clearly had no need of him. He thought ruefully of his rather absurd efforts of the day before to bring her and Dan McGrath together.

"I think I'll go and see my Uncle Elliot again." She turned back to him at the top of the stairs. "He's vague but he can make sense when he wants to."

She started down, with Mr. Pinkerton at her heels, and on them, in fact, as she came to an abrupt halt where the stairs angled and she had a view of the dining room on the ground floor. She stepped backwards so quickly that he had to scramble aside to get out of her way.

"Quickly," she whispered. "Come back."

He scurried up the stairs after her, more than puzzled.

"Do you think we might have a pot of tea over by the window?"

The waitress gave her an unfriendly stare, about to say something about closing up, Mr. Pinkerton suspected, until she glanced at him. He was aware she was relenting in spite of the sixpenny tip. He must look as seedy as he felt. The scramble on the stairs had been acutely jarring to his head.

"My cousin's down there," Mary said coolly. "Eric. Who do you think he's with?"

"I don't know."

"Pegott."

She brushed a crumb off the tablecloth.

"Eric's up to something. He's a snob. He wouldn't lunch with Pegott unless . . ."

She was silent until the waitress put down their tea and left them. Then she smiled faintly. "I told Eric this was a quiet place where he wouldn't see any of his friends. You said Pegott was going to take Mr. McGrath to see my father tonight?"

"At eleven o'clock."

"But—how does Pegott know where he is? He never knew him."

She looked silently at Mr. Pinkerton for a moment.

"You know, I'd bet anything it's Eric that knows where he is. And he's using Pegott. Is Mr. McGrath ready to *pay* for information?"

The scorn in her voice was clear, though she spoke without any emphasis.

Mr. Pinkerton hesitated. "There's the picture, of course. And the ten thousand pounds—"

"The ten thousand pounds?" She looked at him blankly.

She didn't know about that, then, he thought miserably.

"Do you mean he—he's still got the picture *and* what it was sold— Just what are you saying, Mr. Pinkerton? You've started. Go on."

Mr. Pinkerton managed to tell her what he had heard outside Dan McGrath's door. "Of course, that's just what Pegott said to Mr. McGrath—"

Her lips were parted, the blood quite gone from her face.

"I—I'm so sorry," he said wretchedly. "I didn't—"

"It's all right. I'm glad you told me. I really see now why

Aunt Caroline had that book. I thought she was trying to trace the picture to—to get it back for Mother and me."

She sat quietly looking down into the tea cup for a moment, or seeming to do. He saw her eyes were really focussed sideways under the long curling lashes on the street below. She was waiting for her cousin and the valet to appear.

"Where is Mr. McGrath now, Mr. Pinkerton?"

"He was at the flat when I left."

She put her hand out quickly. "There goes Pegott."

The permanent valet had come out below. They watched him put his hat on and look along the road, a half-smile on his face as he swung onto a bus. Eric Dalrymple-Hughes came out then, his bored and unhurried air that of a man of the world who had got into bad company and was wondering how it had come about. He hailed a taxi and got in.

Mary Winship gave Mr. Pinkerton a quick smile, and picked up her gloves again. "You and I are going out to see Mr. McGrath. You *are* on my side of this, aren't you?"

Even if she had not rested her cool fingers lightly on the back of his shaking hand for an instant before she pushed her chair back, Mr. Pinkerton would still have been on her side. He nodded his head without even noticing the pain.

9

At ten minutes past four, Dan McGrath came back to Number 4 Godolphin Square, so far as he could see not a great deal wiser than he had been when he left it at eleven o'clock in the morning. He had at least learned, for one thing, that there were no copies of that other McGrath's book in any of the book-stores along Charing Cross Road, that the publisher had not regarded it as of particular importance and that in fact his was the only inquiry they had ever got about it. For another, he had learned, thanks to Betty the chambermaid, that Pegott was lunching with Mr. Eric Dalrymple-Hughes at a place in Regent Street called the Green Parrot.

"Mr. Eric's turned proper Socialist, sir. I expect he'll be standing for Parliament one of these days. I'd not have believed it if I'd heard it in church, sir, but I heard it with my own ears."

The information while interesting had not turned out to be of very much use to him. He had seen the two go in separately and come out separately. For a brief instant he had wondered, hardly believing his own eyes, if he was on the track of a wider conspiracy. There might be a hundred little grey men with brown bowler hats in London, but there was only one Mr. Pinkerton, he was sure, and certainly only one girl who did to his pulse rate what the girl who got out of the taxi with Mr. Pinkerton did. Too conspicuous himself, he did not dare follow them all in, but he had a third pint of weak beer in the pub across the street and saw Mary and Mr. Pinkerton in the up-stairs window, watching the street themselves until Pegott and Eric Dalrymple-Hughes took their separate departures. He had tried to follow the other two when they left, but Mary had disappeared into the Underground and Mr. Pinkerton had been absorbed into the protective drabness of the crowds in Oxford Street, as invisible as a jackrabbit in a snow-covered birch woods.

"Oh, Mr. McGrath!" He stopped at the door of the lift and looked down the hall. Miss Grimstead, smiling brightly, was leaning out of the office window. "Did you get your lunch properly, Mr. McGrath?" she inquired solicitously. "We're so short-handed, and poor Pegott's mother was taken to hospital just at lunch time."

"I was out, so it didn't matter," Dan said. "But thanks. I hope she'll be all right."

He got into the lift and pressed the button for the third floor. Either Pegott and Dalrymple-Hughes were in the business together, he was thinking, or Pegott was taking his wares to the open market. Which it was he would find out at eleven o'clock that night. He could let it ride until then.

The lift whirred to a stop. As he opened the door and got out he saw that Pegott was back. He was just coming out of his room, or going in—which, Dan could not have said. He then realized, as the man with his hand on the doorknob turned about, that it was not Pegott at all.

Nothing but the economy of the lighting arrangements on the top floor would have allowed him to make the mistake in the first place—that and the fact that the man was about the same height and was there at the permanent valet's door. Otherwise he was of quite a different cut. While Dan could not see him in any very illuminated detail, he got an impression of baggy tweeds, a slight build, an indefinable air of good breeding. The man was peering at him with quietly amused interest.

"Oh, I say," he said pleasantly. "I say, are you the American who writes books?"

"No," Dan said. "I can write my name, but that's about all."

"Oh, I see, you've got what you call a ghost writer, is that it?"

The man seemed more amused than before.

"But you *are* the American that my niece is in such a blow about, are you not? The chap that's hunting that wretched daub my sister-in-law thinks is Art?"

"Except that I'm not hunting it," Dan said. "I take it you're Miss Winship's uncle?"

"Right you are, I'm Elliot Winship," the man said. "I'm looking for the valet de chambre. What's his name?"

"Pegott?"

"That's it. You've not seen him about, have you?"

"He was here at breakfast."

Elliot Winship moved away from the valet's door and came closer to Dan. He appeared to have quiet greyish eyes, a lean sensitive face and sandy hair touched with grey.

"My niece spent the night with me," he said. "Seems to have got it into her head you're some sort of a *detective.*"

"No," Dan said patiently. "Just a gifted amateur."

Elliot Winship laughed. "Oh, I say, that does make it bad, doesn't it? Makes a pair of us mucking things up. And my niece. Seems to think this valet fellow's got something up his sleeve. Something to do with my brother."

In the uncertain light his face appeared to sober as he looked up at Dan.

"I say, you're not *really* here trying to kick up a row about something we'd all be most happy to forget, are you?"

"No, Mr. Winship," Dan said deliberately. "I'm really not."

Elliot Winship's face cleared instantly. "Relieved to hear it, old fellow. *Very.* Thought it was all nonsense. Perhaps we ought to consult with each other. Come round and lunch with me, will you? Tomorrow? Fifty-three Saint Giles's Terrace. Delighted to see you. One o'clock."

He stepped into the waiting lift. "Cheerioh," he said smiling. He pressed the button to close the door. Dan smiled back. He was relieved himself. With a brother who was obviously intelligent and pleasant, there was at least a strong likelihood that Scott Winship could not be a complete louse. Concluding that, he went back again in his mind to the misgivings that had been quietly developing there about the wisdom of meeting Scott Winship in the solid flesh. Maybe it would be wiser to let well enough alone. He had thought that a dozen times when he had been convinced that anything he was going to learn about Mary Winship's father was bound to be pretty discreditable.

At the pub opposite the Green Parrot he had had another and graver misgiving that was now deeply underlined by his meeting with Scott Winship's brother. In point of fact, whatever he said or believed, he actually was kicking up a row about something they all wanted to forget. He'd denied it to Caroline Winship out in the Square, and again to Elliot Winship, and to himself in pretending it was for Mary and her mother, to save them from Pegott's machinations. The truth was that he was playing along with Pegott, no matter what else he thought he was doing. And now that he knew Eric Dalrymple-Hughes was in it somewhere, there was no point in deceiving himself any longer.

He stood in the dimly lighted hall thinking it over, and decided suddenly to go out, take a walk, get a drink and think matters over a little further. He pressed the lift button and waited for the long slow ascent. To his surprise, the lift was there before he could get a cigarette out of the pack. Elliot Winship could not have gone down more than one floor. However, he reflected, there was nothing surprising about that. After all, he had relatives in the house. He got in the lift and went down and out into the Square and paced around the unkempt garden —being, consequently, not in his room when Mr. Evan Pinkerton knocked on his door to invite him to tea with Mary Winship.

What, he thought, striding around the damp paths, was he actually doing? There was only one thing he had any real concern with. In a few words, he should get on with his own business, which—also in a few words—was to marry Mary Winship. It was the best way to start protecting her. No fact, known or unknown, about her father and his past or his present, was going to affect his feeling about her. What he had accomplished so far was make the girl and her whole family sore at him. As a courting technique, he thought with a sardonic grin, it might be original, but it was hardly likely to be effective. It was quarter to six when he came back to Number 4. As he rode up to the third floor what he should do was clear in his mind. He should get hold of Pegott and do what he should have done in the morning, namely, scare the living daylights out of him.

Thinking he was even going to enjoy doing it, he closed the lift door and looked down the hall. The lights were on now. Mr. Pinkerton was in; he could see the faint glow through the old-fashioned keyhole under his doorknob. There was no light in Pegott's room. He went over to it and stopped at the door, listening. On the floor below he could hear the maid taking the tea trays away.

"I've got Mr. Pinkerton's—Mr. McGrath's not in," she was saying to someone. "Pegott can't say I'm late today, but I expect he'll find something else to grumble about."

"Not tonight he won't," Dan McGrath thought. He put his

hand on the doorknob and pushed gently. The door was not locked. He stepped inside, and closed the door behind him as he heard Mr. Pinkerton's door open.

"I'll just see," he heard Mr. Pinkerton say. "The lift's up. He must have come in."

He heard the little man trot along the hall and knock at the box-room door, wait a moment and knock again.

"I expect it was someone else," Mr. Pinkerton said.

"He's probably lurking somewhere in the dark."

It was Mary Winship. Dan winced. What she thought of him was more than evident in the tone of her voice, and the fact that what she said happened to be true made it no easier to take.

"Or he may have stopped to use his fatal charm on Grimstead. Eric's method. Perhaps he thinks he'll get some bacon for breakfast. Thanks for tea, Mr. Pinkerton. Oh dear, now I've got to go and really explain why I'm not in Paris!"

Dan heard her light footsteps on the stairs, and Mr. Pinkerton's door close again. He reached his hand out and switched on the light. He looked slowly around the room, instantly alert. It was much more comfortably furnished than Mr. Pinkerton's or his own, and at the same time extraordinarily bare. The reason could not have been more evident. Pegott was leaving. His luggage was packed and piled against the wall at the foot of the bed. One small composition-leather despatch case was lying open on the bed waiting for the last moment. He saw a hairbrush, a worn leather toilet kit, a pair of felt slippers, a pair of lavender-and-pink pyjamas in it—and something else, something red, only partly concealed under the neatly folded pyjamas.

His jaw hardened and there were tight narrow lines at the corners of his chilly blue eyes as he went over to the bed. He knew the name of the book under Pegott's pyjamas before he took it out. As he pulled it toward him a small can that had been lodged behind it rolled out. Champignons. He put it back, not interested in fancy loot filched from the kitchen larder. The loot he was interested in had come from himself. He opened the other McGrath's book on missing masterpieces. Written on the flyleaf in a delicate script he had not had light enough to see when he had opened it in front of the jeweller's window in the Strand was the owner's name. Caroline M. Winship.

He closed the book and slipped it into his pocket. That was the story, then. It was not Mrs. Winship who had walked off with the book and got the fastener of his briefcase caught after reading the letter in it. It was the impeccable Peggot in person. It was not only what he could hear but what he could see—and one Dan McGrath should have figured that one out. He thought of himself stupefied with sleep, the book on the table in front of him. It was no wonder that Pegott, having read that letter, should have been so confident he could sell McGrath his wares.

Dan looked at the luggage piled at the foot of the bed. Sell his wares, and skip. Pegott was all set. He looked slowly around the room again. Was he planning to get out before he served dinner at seven, waiting for Dan outside? Was he going to go through with dinner, pretending nothing was on his mind? He looked over at the wardrobe, the door of it closed, with the key in the lock, glanced around the room again looking for Pegott's white jacket, went over to the wardrobe, turned the key and opened the deal door.

He let the door loose so sharply that it swung open and banged against the table, and stood there silent and motionless, staring into the wardrobe. The impeccable Peggot had not got far. The permanent valet was not permanent. Pegott was there.

The noose around his neck was made of a green and orange tie. The other end was knotted firmly to a brass hook beneath the wardrobe shelf. Pegott lay in a cramped huddle on the wardrobe floor, his swollen tongue protruding from his purple cyanotic face, staring horribly at Dan's feet.

The telephone on the stand beside the bed jangled sharply three times. Dan hesitated, and picked it up.

"Yes?"

"Pegott!" It was Miss Myrtle Grimstead's disciplinary voice, not the charming one she reserved for favored guests. "Chef would like you to come down at once, *if* you don't mind."

"This is McGrath speaking," Dan said deliberately. "Pegott is dead, Miss Grimstead. This time you have got to call the police."

He put the phone down, crossed the room and opened the door.

"My fault," he was thinking soberly. It was doubly his fault. He should have called the cops last night. Mr. Pinkerton had not had a heart attack. Pegott had not hanged himself. The shelf in the wardrobe was made of flimsy wood not strong enough to hold the weight of a body that long. The wardrobe was locked on the outside. He had had to turn the key to open it. Attempted murder, and successful murder, within twenty-four hours.

He looked back at the key in the wardrobe door. If the same hand and the same mind was in both attacks, it was not the hand that had slipped the second time.

He stood in the doorway, waiting. It was becoming evident that someone did not want Scott Winship found—Scott Winship and his missing masterpiece—or the wretched daub his wife called Art. Or could it be that Scott Winship did not want to be found?

10

As Dan McGrath closed Pegott's door and stood by, waiting until Miss Myrtle Grimstead appeared, he became aware of the mouse-grey figure of Mr. Evan Pinkerton two steps down the stairway, his brown bowler in his hands, pausing there, looking at him across the stair rail. He seemed very unhappy in a dejected sort of way, as if Dan had let him down, or at least definitely not lived up to what he had clearly expected of him. As he blinked his watery grey eyes past him to the door of the valet's room, Dan thought that might be it. Mr. Pinkerton did not expect him to be on such visiting terms.

"We—thought we heard you come up," Mr. Pinkerton said, adjusting his spectacles. It was more in sorrow than in anger, as Dan recognized from his own home life in Baltimore, Maryland."

"Pegott is dead, Mr. Pinkerton," he said.

The little man blinked at him. "Pegott— Not *murdered?*"

As Dan nodded an expression of such aghast dismay came so suddenly over Mr. Pinkerton's face that it was comic. "Not you—*you* didn't—"

"No. Not me," Dan said. "But it was somebody."

He started to say "Somebody in this house," and stopped. He did not know that to be a fact, and he had become clearly aware of the necessity of assorting and segregating actual facts, as he actually knew them, from the whole welter of surmise and speculation he had been wading through ever since he had walked into Number 4 Godolphin Square. Fact it was his duty to tell the police when they came. Surmise and speculation it was his privilege to keep to himself.

"Miss Grimstead is sending for the police."

"Nine nine nine," Mr. Pinkerton said. He came up into the hall. "Nine nine nine," he repeated with sudden urgency.

"The little guy *is* crazy," Dan McGrath thought.

Mr. Pinkerton had his brown bowler clutched tightly in both hands. "I mean, you're to ring up Nine nine nine. That's Scotland Yard. The communication center. They send a man straight out from the Headquarters."

Dan nodded. He could hear the soft whir of the lift making its deliberate ascent. "I guess Miss Grimstead will take care of it. This is probably her now."

He heard her snap open the iron grille, and stood in front of the door.

"What's—"

Miss Grimstead started to speak and stopped, her eyes suddenly angry and bright in her pale face, as they glanced from Dan McGrath to the little Welshman.

"Oh, it's you two again. Bad luck pieces both of you."

She came quickly across the hall. "Where is Pegott? Open the door, Mr. McGrath."

Dan shook his head. "Nobody goes in there till the police come, Miss Grimstead. Sorry."

Her blue eyes blazed for an instant as she faced him. Mr. Pinkerton shrank a little, glad it was Dan McGrath's six feet three inches and not his substantially lesser figure there in her way.

"He may not be dead, Mr. McGrath," she said quickly and breathlessly.

"You can count on it," Dan said coolly. "He's very dead, Miss Grimstead. Did you send for the police?"

"Yes."

Both Dan McGrath and Mr. Pinkerton knew it was not true as her eyes shifted from one to the other of them.

"But I'd best ring again. If you'll let me in—"

"Not until the police come, Miss Grimstead. Nobody's going in there until they do. See? So why don't you run down and ring them. Nine nine nine."

She looked at him sharply.

"If you'd called them in last night when I asked you to, maybe this wouldn't have happened. They'll wonder why you didn't, Miss Grimstead. The way I wonder. The way I wonder why you're so damned anxious not to call them now."

Miss Grimstead took a step back, her breath coming quickly, two unhealthy purple splotches dark under the pink powder of her rouged cheeks.

"You're—making a mistake, Mr. McGrath." The muscles of her throat were so constricted that her voice came in a harsh labored whisper. "You don't understand. I don't want trouble here. Not for myself—for my people."

She put her hand out unsteadily and caught the bannister rail.

"I shouldn't have kept him on. I should have made him go."

She gripped the rail tightly. "I'll ring them. I'll go ring them now."

Mr. Pinkerton and Dan McGrath looked silently at one another. Her footsteps, slow at first, quickened until she was almost running before they heard her key fumbling at the lock of one of the flats on the floor below.

"I'm—afraid she's upset," Mr. Pinkerton whispered. He cleared his throat to get his voice in a more normal key. "Would you—would you say she's—rather frightened? Rather badly frightened?"

Dan nodded coolly. Mr. Pinkerton glanced tentatively at the doorknob. "I wonder what it is he's got that she wants to get before the police come? Do you—do you think we might—"

"No. Nobody goes in, Mr. Pinkerton. Nobody takes anything out. That's flat. And how's your head today?"

Mr. Pinkerton's hand began an automatic move upward, but he stopped it, blinking as he looked away from Dan. "I—I would really much prefer it if we made no mention of my head," he said earnestly. "I really wouldn't like to make trouble. I—I feel rather sorry for Miss Grimstead."

"Yes?" Dan McGrath said. "Me, I feel rather sorry for Pegott." He looked at the little man with a detached and sombre eye. "I'd feel sorrier if you were in his shoes right now, Mr. Pinkerton. You almost were, you know."

"Oh, I think that was a mistake," Mr. Pinkerton said hastily. "I think somebody thought I knew something I really didn't know at all."

"The whereabouts of Mr. Scott Winship namely."

"You are trying to find him, then?" Mr. Pinkerton glanced behind him. "Do you think it's quite safe?"

Dan smiled without amusement. "Mr. Pinkerton, I don't think it's safe at all. In fact, you can count me out from here on. Personally, I'd be a lot happier if I'd never even heard of the guy."

Mr. Pinkerton drew a relieved breath. "I'm glad to know that, Mr. McGrath," he said sincerely. "Because I—I rather think Mr. Scott Winship prefers to—to remain incognito, if I can put it that way."

Dan grinned at him. "I've sort of gathered that myself."

"And I think the family rather feel that."

"I'm slow, Mr. Pinkerton, but I figured that one too."

He reached in his pocket for a cigarette and caught his breath for an instant as his hand touched the book. He'd forgotten it. He glanced at Mr. Pinkerton. The little man was craning his scrawny neck looking over the stair rail and could not have seen the look of surprise on his face. Still, the book was hardly what Grimstead was after. Or was it?

Mr. Pinkerton had come unobtrusively a few steps closer to him, looking back as if the empty corridor were somehow full of invisible eyes, and lowered his voice as if invisible ears were listening.

"Do you think it's *just* because of the picture?" he whispered. "Because I stopped in at Somerset House. I looked at the will."

"His will? Scott Winship's will?"

"Sssh." Mr. Pinkerton put his finger to his lips, glancing behind him again. "No. I mean the elder Winship's will. Miss Caroline Winship's father. And I asked Mary. He was the one that left Mrs. Winship the picture. He died not long after they were married. He was an invalid a long time."

His face as he looked up at Dan McGrath seemed to brighten a little.

"I mean, if there was anything—well, odd, about his death—"

"Was there?"

"Oh, I don't know," Mr. Pinkerton said hastily. "I just meant if there was. I just thought—"

He stopped as Dan looked down at him with wry amusement. It was generally the nicest and mildest little people who dreamed up the wildest and most bloodthirsty solutions for simple problems.

"You mean, if he's murdered the old man as well as getting

away with the picture, he'd really have a reason for staying incognito, as you call it. That it?"

"Well, something rather like it," Mr. Pinkerton said modestly.

"It sounds screwball to me." He stopped abruptly, listening. "Here they are."

Mr. Pinkerton went a shade paler grey, and blinked like a small dismayed owl caught out at high noon.

"Well, I think I'll just go to my room," he said hastily. "I—I think I'd best lie down for a moment."

Dan watched him scurry back along the hall and into his door with much more haste than seemed reasonable in anyone with so obvious a talent for other people's business. He watched the door as he waited for the lift to go down and up again. Mr. Pinkerton was in his room, but he was not lying down. Dan could see the shadow of his feet at the crack under the door. The big keyhole under the brass knob no longer showed any light. There was funny business, he thought, all over Number 4 Godolphin Square. Maybe the war and the post war had done something odd to the British. Or to the British in Godolphin Square anyway. The only perfectly rational and reasonably ordinary person he had run into was Elliot Winship, the missing Scott Winship's brother. And he lived somewhere else. Maybe, he thought, it was the house. Nobody in it seemed to make normal everyday sense. Including McGrath. On second thought, McGrath certainly had to be included—and he had not yet been at Number 4 Godolphin Square a full twenty-four hours.

"You say this door was locked when you opened it, sir?"

The very large burly man from Scotland Yard standing by the wardrobe regarded Dan McGrath with troubled blue eyes.

He had cinnamon-brown hair, a cinnamon-brown mustache and wore a suit of cinnamon-brown tweed. He might have looked like a pleasantly domesticated, greatly oversize, cinnamon bear except that he looked more like a St. Bernard worried about a traveller in a snowy pass—mild as milk, deliberate, naively trusting, and not very bright actually. The plodding type.

"Right," Dan said. "I turned the key before I could open it."

He was sitting on Pegott's bed, the open despatch case beside him. Pegott's body was gone, and the photographers and fingerprint men, with all their assistants and paraphernalia. Chief Inspector Bull and Detective-Sergeant Smithson were there, and a uniformed constable was at the foot of the stairs on the second floor.

"Miss Grimstead tells me he's been looking very seedy lately," Inspector Bull said.

"I wouldn't know about that. I never saw him till this morning when he served my breakfast."

"That's right, sir. You arrived after tea yesterday and got your dinner out, I believe you said."

"That's right."

It was easier than Dan had thought it was going to be. He tried to focus his eye on the narrow rib of solid fact, to tread safely through the morass without deliberately lying in the first place and without being a heel in the second. He was thinking about Mary Winship and her mother. Maybe they'd have to be brought into this somewhere, but somebody else could bring them in, not McGrath.

Chief Inspector Bull was looking soberly about the room. "I don't want to keep you, sir. But perhaps you'd explain how you happened to open the wardrobe door in the first place? Were you looking for something in particular?"

"Yes. I was trying to find out if Pegott was going to be here to serve dinner. I saw his stuff was packed up."

He motioned to the luggage still on the floor at the foot of the bed. They had not opened it up, and Dan, waiting with some curiosity, decided it was his presence that was stopping them. "I thought I'd see if his white coat, or whatever he wears at night, was still there."

"I take it you'd rung for him and he'd not answered the bell, is that it, sir?"

"No. I'm in what you call the box room, temporarily converted. I don't have a bell."

"What was it you wanted of him, sir?"

"I have a suit that needs pressing."

It was not exactly an outright falsehood. He had two, the one he had on and the one hanging in the box room.

Inspector Bull was looking at the despatch case on the bed. The space under Pegott's folded pyjamas where the book had been yawned at Dan blankly, proportionately as big and empty as the space in his jaw would feel when his last wisdom tooth came out. But the Inspector did not notice it, and as it was in a sense Dan's own property—in the sense that Pegott had taken it from him while he was asleep—he saw no reason for calling it to his attention.

"Just one thing more, sir, before you go. You say you left the flat at eleven o'clock this morning and returned shortly after four? And went out again till round six?"

"That's right, Inspector."

"If you'd just tell us where you were—"

The suggestion was made with no apparent real concern, but McGrath had heard of alibis before.

"Sure," he said agreeably. "I went to Regent Street and had

a snack in a pub there. Don't know the name, but I could find it again, Inspector. After that I strolled around. I bought some stuff called Herbal Smoking Mixture. The sign in the shop window says it's cheaper and better than tobacco and good for catarrh. Try some, Inspector?"

"Thank you, no," Inspector Bull said.

"Then I walked through Covent Garden to look at the market, but I was too late, I guess. All I saw was some dead cabbage leaves and a few stray cats. Oh, except a sign, on the door into St. Paul's Covent Garden. It says 'In this Garden Sanctuary the Fouling of the Ground by Dogs is Deplored.' "

Bull nodded politely.

"Very good, sir. You'll be here in case we should want to see you again? You're not setting off anywhere immediately, I mean, sir?"

Dan shook his head and got up. He started for the door.

"Don't forget your hat, sir."

Dan looked around. He had forgotten he had automatically tossed his hat on the chair by the door before he had noticed the luggage at the foot of the bed.

"Oh, thanks. That is—"

The inspector was in sudden motion, across the room and in the doorway with the agility, ease and speed of an adagio dancer weighing nine stone instead of the eighteen he undoubtedly did weigh.

"*Pinkerton!*" It was a bellow only in the sense that it was the first time Inspector Bull had raised his voice above a sick-room monotone. Dan McGrath's heart sank a little. The man really was known to the police. And Inspector Bull must have ears in the back of his head; he had heard no noise of any opening door. He looked past Bull. Mr. Pinkerton was at the turn of the staircase, his hat clutched in his hands, and if ever guilt was written on a human face it was written there. He was backed against the wall, terrified.

"Come here, Pinkerton. Where are you going?"

Mr. Pinkerton came as one hypnotized, like a mouse summoned by a giant and inimical cinnamon-pied piper, blinking all the way.

"I—was just stepping out for a bite of supper, Chief Inspector."

Dan McGrath looked at him silently, with genuine misgivings as to what this aspect of things did to the entire situation. He had thought before that the little man was honest. Touched, no doubt, but really okay. But now, as Mr. Pinkerton went into Pegott's room at the Inspector's gesture, sidling in unhappily indeed without a glance at Dan, he seemed virtually on the point of collapse.

Dan stopped outside in the hall. He would have stayed there if the Detective-Sergeant had not come out of Pegott's room as Mr. Pinkerton went in—precisely, it occurred to Dan, so that he should not stay there.

"Do you know Mr. Pinkerton?" Dan ventured tentatively.

"Oh yes indeed, sir." The sergeant permitted himself a slight, and dour, smile. "Always in hot water, he is, one way or the other, sir."

Dan went along to his room. It was no wonder the little fellow was adamant about not calling in the police, the night before. That, however, was hardly the immediate point, which concerned one Dan McGrath and what he was going to do. He tried to take stock of the situation. It did not appear to be too good. One thing, however, was certain, he decided, thinking it over: no one got to be a Chief Inspector at New Scotland

Yard who was as guileless, unsuspecting and unperceptive as the large cinnamon-brown man appeared to be. There was obviously more than met the eye: a kind of sign language, for one thing, he thought, remembering how Bull had occasionally nodded at one or the other of the men making their examination of the room and Pegott—his pockets, the necktie, the knot in it that had strangled him, and his shoes. They had all seemed to have some special interest in his shoes, carefully taking them off before his last grim descent in the service lift. A dumb show, he thought with a grin, but probably not so dumb as it had seemed to McGrath. There was obviously more than met the eye, and they were not through with him. McGrath ought to make up his mind where he stood and what he was doing there, and he ought to be quick about it.

He went over to the table and turned on the light. An envelope was lying on top of his briefcase. He picked it up and tore it open.

> *Sir. Our friend will meet us at 12:30 tonight at Number 22 opposite. £250 in American currency or by draught on an American bank will be acceptable if proper discretion in the transaction is guaranteed.*

He read it twice, crumpled it up and put it in his pocket. Pegott would have written it, obviously, after he came in from lunch with Dalrymple-Hughes and some time before he was unable ever to write again. Had he been in contact of some kind with Scott Winship? Or was this a part of some put-up job . . . Pegott and Dalrymple-Hughes at one end, himself at the other? One thing seemed certain: Pegott was skipping out in any case and he wanted American currency. The packed luggage was no deception. On the other hand, the murder of Pegott was evidence of something else again. Thinking of that, Dan came back to the one fact that he appeared to have—and that he wished he did not have.

He did not know the exact moment at which the impermanent valet had been killed, but it was some time between his return from lunch at the Green Parrot in Regent Street and ten minutes to six o'clock when he had found him on the floor of the wardrobe; and at fifteen minutes past four or thereabouts he had seen Mr. Elliot Winship with his hand actually on Pegott's doorknob—whether going in or coming out he could not tell. And the lift had been only one floor down when Elliot Winship had somehow given the impression, at least, of being on his way to the ground floor and out into the Square. And one other fact flashed into his mind that he wished also he did not have. It was actually in his own pocket. He took the red book out and looked at it without pleasure. He had been a fool to take it and a fool to keep it without telling the Inspector about it. He opened it up, looked at Caroline Winship's name on the flyleaf, closed it again and looked at his watch. It was twenty-five minutes past six. He looked down at the other McGrath's book steadily for an instant, slipped it back into his pocket and went out into the hall. All this had been serious enough before the murder of Pegott. It was more serious now. The only sensible thing to do under all the circumstances, and for more reasons than one, was what he should have done before: namely give the book back to its owner and make a serious effort to explain that he was genuinely and exclusively concerned with one thing, to marry Mary Winship.

11

O<small>N THE</small> first floor he concluded that the door at the end of the corridor on his right must be the one he was looking for, if Miss Caroline Winship's sitting room overlooked the Square as Mr. Pinkerton had told him it did. The low murmur of voices inside broke off sharply as he knocked on the white painted panel. The silence seemed ominously intense as he waited. He was about to knock again when the door opened abruptly. It was Eric Dalrymple-Hughes.

He stared silently for an instant, said "Oh," and relaxed into a bored nonchalance that was patently too studied.

"I'm Daniel McGrath. I'd like to speak to Miss Caroline Winship."

"My aunt is—"

"Ask him to come in, Eric."

Miss Winship's heavy voice cut him off curtly. He shrugged and stepped aside. "Come in, will you?"

As Dan went into the small foyer he was aware of sharp misgivings now that he was about to confront the woman he had met out in the dark in the Square the night before. He had not thought of Dalrymple-Hughes being there. As he put his hat and raincoat on the chair and went on into the room the misgivings ceased to have any doubt about them, and if he could have turned back he would have done it. Mary Winship was standing in front of the fireplace, her hand gripping the wing of her mother's chair. The surgeon Mr. Sidney Copeland sat rigidly in a chair turned sideways from the desk. Miss Caroline Winship was in a large faded yellow satin chair across the fireplace, and the empty chair that completed the half-circle was evidently the one Dalrymple-Hughes had left. Five pairs of eyes were fixed on him, each concealing, or making no attempt to conceal, the same livid resentment he had seen last in Miss Violet Grimstead's. They were motionless, ringed round him in the shabby-luxurious room, watching him, waiting silently.

He came on in as coolly as he could. There was nothing here he hadn't asked for. He was an alien, barging into their private lives, uninvited and unknown. He could see his own family in a situation of the sort. Except that the alien wouldn't be in the living room; he would be out in the front street brushing off the seat of his pants.

"What is it, Mr. McGrath?"

Miss Winship moved her ponderous body in the yellow chair, her fingers tapping the frayed satin of the arms, twitching a little like a cat's tail. Her brilliant brown eyes smoldered under their heavy lids as she looked steadily at him. "Will you sit down?"

"Thank you."

He took the empty chair in the semicircle.

"Close the door, Eric, and sit down."

Seeing Caroline Winship in the light for the first time, Dan had the impression of a gnarled oak on a storm-swept plain. He felt a sudden inexplicable twinge of sympathy for her that astonished him as he returned her steady unblinking gaze. Masterful women are the most easily deceived, he thought as her nephew drew up a chair and sat down, examining the tip of his cigarette with his brows raised. Miss Winship's eyes rested obliquely on him for an instant before she looked back at Dan McGrath. A brief flicker that might almost have been amusement lighted the sombre brilliance of her eyes.

"You find it difficult to begin, Mr. McGrath?"

There was no doubt about that, though trying to think about it he could not say which of them made it most so: Mrs. Winship pale and intent and withdrawn, Sidney Copeland openly hostile, restraining himself with apparent effort, Mary Winship with her chin proudly up and her eyes burning.

"I thought maybe I could be of some help, Miss Winship," he said as calmly as he could manage. "I guess I'm wrong. The police are coming back. They'll question me about Pegott's murder. I—"

"Why should you think it has anything to do with us, Mr. McGrath? I take it you do think so?"

"It seems to have some connection."

"Which you feel you have got to tell the police?"

"I'll have to tell them Pegott was planning to take me tonight to see Mr. Scott Winship."

He kept his eyes steadily on Caroline Winship's, not wishing to see any other person in the room. After Mrs. Winship's startled gasp, the silence in the room grew, intense and electric.

"You are brutally tactless, Mr. McGrath." Miss Winship's sombre voice was rigidly controlled.

"Sorry. So are the police. There's not much time. I thought you ought to know about it. It may be a coincidence that he was killed before he got the chance. I don't know. I wanted particularly—"

She motioned Sidney Copeland, who had half risen from his chair, back with an imperious gesture. "You have been deceived. My sister's former husband is not alive, Mr. McGrath. If he were, he would not confide in a valet. The Winships are not in the habit of associating with servants."

"I'm merely telling you what I've got to tell the police, Miss

Winship. If you don't mind I'll go on.—That Pegott some way got the quite erroneous idea I was prepared to pay him to get in touch with Mr. Winship, presumably about a picture Pegott said was in his possession. That he offered—for a price—to take me to him tonight. Also, that your nephew lunched with Pegott today."

Miss Winship stared silently at him.

"That is false, Aunt Caroline." Dalrymple-Hughes leaned back in his chair and brushed an invisible speck from his trouser leg. "If Pegott said that he lied."

"He didn't lie, Eric." Mary Winship spoke quietly. "You did lunch with him. I saw you. At the Green Parrot."

Miss Winship, still silent, turned to him. "Tell me the truth, Eric."

"Well, as a matter of fact, I did." He smiled easily at her. "On your behalf."

"On *my* behalf?"

"As head of the family. I was going to tell you tonight. Pegott thought we might like to overbid his American client here." He waved his cigarette toward Dan. "I said I'd got to take it up with you. Don't ask me how Pegott comes into it, because I don't know. But he—seems to have got it into his head that Aunt Louise here knows perfectly well where Uncle Scott is. I rather gathered he'd done a bit of detective work following her about when we've had the idea she was too ill to leave the flat."

Louise Winship shrank deeper into her chair, her face ghastly pale.

Eric Dalrymple-Hughes got up coolly. "You haven't got to believe me if you like. I had no intention of mentioning it at all. It's no pleasure to me to know I've got a thief for an uncle. I'd much rather they'd not find him, frankly. But I've no intention of being accused of murdering Pegott just because he decided to tell me a lot I'd not known before. Fortunately, I've got an alibi, if it interests Mr. McGrath. I hope he's got one—because I've got several things to tell the police myself."

He moved away from the motionless semicircle in front of the fireplace.

"Eric—sit down."

Miss Winship's voice was like a lash catching him in the face, his angry flush the welts it left as it struck.

"I'll not sit down, Aunt Caroline. Frankly, I'm through with the lot of you."

He looked around the circle. "I'll tell you this too. I don't believe Scott Winship ever stole the picture. I think Aunt Louise sold it herself and kept the money and kept the picture. I don't know Scott Winship. He may be the half-saint half-devil he's made out to be, but I'll bet he's got some jolly good reason for hiding out. I'll bet he's been living right here in London all the time. I'll bet he's never left it at all. More than that, I'd bet that every one of you except Mary—old Copey and Elliot Winship and all of you—knows damned well where he is. And I'd not blame him for fighting clear of this hole where every penny farthing you get you've got to get down on your knees and beg for like a poodle for a biscuit. I'm fed up, I tell you. I'm clearing out."

He did not slam the door as he went, but the effect was not different.

"Insolent puppy—" Sidney Copeland had again half-risen from his chair. He sat down abruptly again as Caroline Winship shook her head.

Dan was watching Mary and her mother. Louise Winship

had closed her eyes. She sat with her head bowed a little, pale but not seemingly either shocked or surprised by the tirade that swept over her. Mary Winship had stiffened, shocked and angry.

Dan got to his feet.

"Thank you, Mr. McGrath." Caroline Winship's voice had an extraordinary quality of sombre deliberateness as she drew her breath in deeply. "I think you'd best go now. We don't know what your business here is. I can only hope it no longer concerns any of us."

"It concerns one of you," Dan said. His eyes were fixed on Mary. He took three steps across the space in front of the fireplace and stopped in front of her. He put his hand out, tilted her chin up, bent his head and kissed her abruptly on the mouth. "That's my business here. It's the only one I have, Mary. The only one I have ever had. Good night."

He was halfway up the third flight of stairs to his own room when he realized what he had done.

"Good God," he thought. "They'll think I'm a—"

He could not offhand think just what. Insolent puppy would be a milder term for him than it had been for Dalrymple-Hughes. Nobody knew better than McGrath that getting sore had never helped him. But sore he had been. He could not get her white shocked face out of his mind. Or the feel of her cold hostile lips on his own. "You've torn it, McGrath," he told himself. "Wrecked the works. You're in England, you creep. You're not in Hollywood. Apologize and get the hell out—that's all that's left for you, McGrath."

And moreover, he thought suddenly, he still had the book in his pocket. Although how, or at just what point, he could have brought it out and handed it over, he could not imagine—

not, certainly, without making himself more unpopular than he already was—even, he reflected further, if he had thought of it, which he had not.

He went on up, trusting the book was something that it might be a very good idea to skip altogether.

12

S IR CHARLES DEBENHAM, Assistant Commissioner of the Metropolitan Police, regarded Chief Inspector J. Humphrey Bull with a mild twinkle in his eyes. Not that there was anything amusing about the murder of Arthur Pegott, valet at Number 4 Godolphin Square. Or indeed anything basically amusing about Bull himself. It was the slow, ponderous incredulity with which, after eighteen years of dealing with people who murdered other people in the Metropolitan Area of London, as well as occasionally farther afield, Bull still approached each new example of man's inhumanity to man. He reminded Debenham of Wells's description of that American writer chap's prose style—a hippopotamus trying to pick up a pea out of the corner of his cage. Although he knew no hippopotamus ever got the pea with one falcon swoop as quickly, if still inexplicably, as did the large stolid man standing there looking down onto the Embankment, once he had made up his mind. It was the laborious, minute grubbing for facts, the painstaking reluctance to accept them as such, the patience of a water buffalo, and an occasional intuitive brilliance that Sir Charles Debenham still found it difficult to remember at the beginning of a case.

"I don't like the looks of this thing, sir," Bull said. His face was even more concerned than usual. "Pinkerton's not telling me the truth. But that's on account of this American out there. Pinkerton's what he calls a—a pushover for the Americans."

"Ah, yes. That's that Bird Watcher's game the Americans play. The rosy-breasted push—"

"I doubt if it's the same, sir." Bull looked even more troubled. "I believe he means he's extremely fond of them. But the American—his name's McGrath—isn't telling the truth either. He found the body. He says he came into Pegott's room to see about getting his trousers pressed—coming in directly from the street without first going to his own room two doors off. He'd got his hat with him and forgot it when he started to leave. That's ridiculous. Then there was a book in his pocket. I'd say it had come out of the valet's case on the bed. There was a hollow space still under his pyjamas the same size. It's clear he came into Pegott's room to see him about something important, saw his luggage packed up, and was concerned enough about something to look in the wardrobe."

"What's his story?"

"I've not asked him yet. I thought we'd wait to see what he did next. He went down to the Winships' flat."

Debenham's eyes lighted slowly. "The *Winships?*"

Bull nodded. He opened his despatch case on the corner of the Assistant Commissioner's desk and took out a yellowed sheaf of papers.

"You remember the name, sir. And we've heard of Arthur Pegott before too." He unfolded the sheaf. "Pegott was in trouble when he was seventeen. Pilfering, money and cigarettes. He was remanded to his father's custody—respectable stonemason, lived in Battersea. He seems to have gone straight enough for a time. McFarlane thinks he was mixed up in the sale of clothing coupons here last year—not enough evidence for an arrest. Some little trouble in the Army and discharged after ten months. He's been at Godolphin Square three and a half months. Miss Grimstead the manageress says she was worried about taking him on. He'd always been at fancier establishments—bigger pay and tips. She taxed him with it, and says he was uppity about it—said if he wished to come there she'd jolly well ought to be glad to get him. He was excellent at his job when he chose to be."

"And the Winships? The name—"

"You remember Inspector Pulham, sir? Reggie Pulham?"

The Assistant Commissioner nodded, smiling. "Reggie Pulham and his *idée fixe*. Very well. Some picture. He nearly drove us out of our minds."

"It's the same Winships, sir. You remember he used to go and see every amnesia case reported?"

Debenham nodded. "I remember the *idée fixe* without remembering what it was about."

"It was about a Scott Winship," Inspector Bull said. "He was crocked up in the last war—shrapnel head wounds. He was in hospital in Sussex. Used to disappear and turn up at the place he'd lived at as a child. The fourth time they decided to let him stay there. He got well finally and married his cousin. That's the Mrs. Scott Winship at Number Four Godolphin Square, sir, where the valet Pegott was killed. They'd been living at Number Twenty-two on the opposite side until they were bombed out in '44."

Bull took up one of the yellowed papers.

"Let me give you some of the facts, sir. I wasn't on this case but they were talking about it down in the canteen this morning. Carson knew it best. This is a statement by Andrew J. Myers, American art dealer, reporting a picture presumably painted by Vermeer of Delft, purchased by him second October 1925. On fourteenth October he went to Number Twenty-two Godolphin Square to collect the picture and was refused it. He called in the police, ringing from the house. When P. C. Baker got there he'd sent for the receipt and cancelled cheque. Miss Caroline Winship, who owned the house, was there—Mrs. Scott Winship was ill, with a doctor in attendance—and Miss Caroline Winship, Myers, and P. C. Baker went to the second floor, unlocked a bedroom that had been occupied by Miss Winship's father, an invalid who'd died in August, and found the picture missing from the wall where it had hung and where Myers had seen it and bought it on second October.

"Miss Caroline Winship said the picture belonged to her sister Mrs. Scott Winship, and that her brother-in-law Scott Winship, from whom Myers had bought the picture, was abroad. Myers and P. C. Baker left the house. That afternoon Sergeant Pulham, he was then, went back with Myers. Miss Winship's solicitor was there. It was agreed Myers would be forced to take action against Scott Winship for recovery of his property. The next afternoon, fifteenth October, Myers came to Pulham and said they'd settled. He'd got his money back and was withdrawing charges. That's what we have officially here."

Debenham picked the file up as Bull laid it in front of him and glanced through it.

"Which is when Reggie Pulham started hunting through secondhand shops and barrows?"

"Yes, sir. But it was really Winship he was hunting, not the picture. He found out that Winship had been living down in Kent at the lodge of Mrs. Winship's sister's place near Sevenoaks. Scott Winship had left to come up to town on business early the morning of the second October, when Miss Caroline Winship was to be in Richmond for the week. He took Myers the American dealer to the empty house at eleven-thirty and sold the picture: five thousand pounds paid then and another five thousand pounds to be paid on delivery. The two of them went to the bank and Winship cashed the five thousand pound cheque in Myers's presence. When Pulham got to this point, he decided Winship's mind had blanked out again or he was the victim of foul play. He learned then Winship had told his wife he was going to Paris for a week. She'd not expected him home that night —of the second October. He's not been seen by any of them since. She didn't worry about him till the second week. She came up to town on the twelfth, afraid to tell her sister, who'd assumed Winship was down in Kent supervising her farm. And the next day, which was the day before Myers turned up to collect his picture and pay the balance of the price, she got a letter from him from Monte Carlo—or she and her sister too said it was from Monte Carlo. Pulham didn't see it. Miss Caroline Winship was furious with him, her sister being as ill as she was in addition to everything, and flung it in the fire. The letter said he'd done his wife a great injustice and would come back when he could to make it up to her. She was in a state of collapse already. That was when her sister called in the doctor. At this point, neither the wife nor the sister knew the picture had been sold—and had disappeared before delivery. It's a big house, the picture was hanging in the bedroom they'd closed after the father's death and wasn't likely to be immediately missed. And then, on fourteenth October, sir, when the dealer came round to collect, it turns out the man, the five thousand pounds *and* the picture have all vanished."

"It was Caroline Winship who paid the American back?"

"It must have been, sir. She's the only one of them that's got any money. Carson says she talked to Pulham just once. He went to see her with his amnesia theory. She's supposed to have said she expected the shock of having five thousand pounds might have brought the amnesia back, but the picture didn't belong to him in any case, she never wanted to hear his name again, and if he turned up at Twenty-two Godolphin Square, which was Pulham's idea, she'd call the police and have him thrown in gaol. She's a bitter woman."

"Well, five thousand pounds is something to be bitter about, Bull. Never having had that much, I can still imagine how I'd feel having to pay it out for somebody."

"Right, sir." Inspector Bull agreed soberly. "And if you'd got to take care of the sick wife and the child—it was born the following March—I dare say it's not surprising."

He got to his feet. "That gets us a far cry from Arthur Pegott, sir. But I've always believed in coincidences. Pegott could have got a much better post in a dozen places in the West End. It looks to me—"

He chewed at his tawny mustache.

"You think Winship's come back to Godolphin Square?" The Assistant Commissioner smiled faintly. "Just don't take over Pulham's monomania. Or have you done already?"

Inspector Bull shook his head. "I don't believe so, sir. But I would like to find a picture of him—without asking his wife or sister-in-law for one. It could be, of course."

A smile flickered through his mild blue eyes.

"I know he's not Pinkerton. Or the American. Though an interesting thing happened last night. The American got his supper out and came back to his room at twenty minutes to ten. Smithson was in the serving pantry behind the lift. At eighteen minutes past twelve, McGrath came out of his room and went downstairs. Constable Mathers reported that a man came out of the flats at twenty-three minutes past twelve and walked round the Square, smoking his pipe, until thirteen minutes to one. First Mathers thought he was just taking a stroll, but it started to rain about half-past twelve, so Mathers kept an eye on him till he went back into the building. Smithson says he was back in his room at ten minutes to one. It looks as if he expected to meet someone who didn't show up. Nobody else left the house except the servants and Mr. Sidney Copeland. He's a surgeon in Wimpole Street, an old friend of the family.

"Then there's a nephew of the Winship ladies, Eric Dalrymple-Hughes, actually the son of a first cousin of Caroline Winship who died out in India. His father married again and was evidently glad enough to turn the boy over to his wealthy relative to bring up and educate. Dalrymple-Hughes came downstairs with his suitcases at a quarter past ten. I was in the office talking to the manageress and I suggested he wait until today. He said if the police wanted him to stay there they'd got to be prepared to pay the rent for his flat. When I went up to talk to him ten minutes later, he'd cooled off considerably. He said he'd lunched with Pegott yesterday. The man had had something to tell him. They'd seen his cousin Miss Mary Winship and Pinkerton lunching there, so they'd put it off. Pegott was supposed to see him yesterday evening, then, but he states he's got an alibi for the time of Pegott's murder."

"What time was that?"

"I asked him, sir. He said he didn't know, of course, but he'd left Pegott after lunch and hadn't got back to the flat until six o'clock when the place was overrun with policemen. I thought it was best to let him think about it a bit. I'll see him today. He's got the wind up about something. He's a proper spiv, I'm afraid, sir. I'd not say he's the sort of person to lunch with one of the lower orders, if I may say so, any more than McGrath's the sort to worry about his trousers not being pressed. Now if it was the other way round, sir . . ."

13

WHICH was in a sense unjust to Dan McGrath. If he was not worried, he was at least slightly concerned about the rumpled state of his lower as well as upper garments. Twenty minutes strolling in the midnight rain dripping from the trees in Godolphin Square had not done much for either one, and his packing technique had done nothing to improve the decent blues he was wearing now. Laundry and pressing seemed to be a problem Miss Myrtle Grimstead left solely to the personal discretion of her tenants. On the other hand, Elliot Winship was hardly likely to be critical, Dan thought, remembering the rather weary-looking oatmeal tweeds he had had on himself there in the hall the day before. And if he had to go to lunch in a blanket he would not have hesitated long. Elliot Winship he had got to see. It was very clear that the leisurely and unobtrusive methods of New Scotland Yard were not as undeceptive as one might think. If it had not been for the rain, and the frail glow of the street light glancing off the policeman's cape out in the Square the night before, he might easily not have spotted the fact that he was there, nor would he have known that Detective-Sergeant Smithson was in the serving pantry behind the lift shaft, if Mason had not brought him a nice hot cup of tea along about one-fifteen. The ivory tower he was to all outward appearances abiding in, so far as the police were concerned, was a snare and a delusion. Even his old friend Mr. Pinkerton had deserted him. Coming out of the washroom the little man had seen him and run for his room, any resemblance to a frightened rabbit being too marked to miss. Pariah McGrath. Even Betty had looked at him reproachfully when he suggested maybe she could get his trousers pressed. Still, it was a good try.

As he rang the bell at 53 St. Giles's Terrace, the green door of Elliot Winship's neat compact little Georgian residence overlooking Kensington Gardens was opened by a solid and respectable person whom he took to be Mr. Winship's daily woman. The door opened exactly the number of inches she required to look out of.

"I'm Mr. McGrath. Mr. Winship expects me for lunch, I believe."

Her face fell into far more reproachful lines than Betty's as she reluctantly opened the door full and stood aside.

"Put your hat there, sir. And wait in here." She nodded to the room at the right of the narrow hall. "I'll tell him you're here. Mr. McGrath, is it, sir?"

The reproachful look was transforming itself into something more tight-lipped as she turned and plodded up the stairs.

"He forgot to tell her," Dan thought. He stepped into the small drawing room.

"It's an American gentleman, sir. He says you asked him to lunch. And you *promised,* sir. If you'd have told me, I could have brought in a bit of fish or—"

The door upstairs closed before Dan heard the rest of it or Mr. Elliot Winship's unhappy reply. He felt a sharp twinge in his own conscience. He'd forgot he was in a rationed world, that here people did not have food to throw around. He glanced at his hat on the hall table. It was too late. The door upstairs had opened again, and someone with feet less heavily plodding than the woman's was coming down. Dan turned from the fireplace to meet him, and stood for an instant, not openmouthed but very near it, as Elliot Winship came briskly into the room.

He was barely recognizable as the same man. He was as neat and glistening as the brass firedogs on his own hearth. His hair was meticulously brushed, his chalk-stripe grey flannel suit had not a wrinkle in it, his black shoes gleamed, his blue striped shirt, starched collar and maroon tie were immaculate. Only his eyes were recognizably the same, and his voice as he spoke.

"Oh, I say. Frightfully glad to see you, Mr.—I'm so stupid about names—"

"McGrath," Dan said.

He felt a slight twinge of half-amused annoyance. It was utterly apparent that Elliot Winship had not only forgotten his name, but had no memory of ever having seen him before in all his life. The mild but desperate scratching around in his mind could not have been clearer.

"I say, do sit down, won't you? What about a bit of sherry? Or gin and orange. You Americans aren't sherry drinkers, are you, really? Do sit down, I'll get it. Mrs. O'Neill is temperance and won't touch the stuff. I say, I'm sorry I've no cigarettes."

He opened a box on the table. "I'm afraid I'm out. I seldom smoke myself. It's so much trouble to find the things."

He started out the door and stopped. "I say, why don't you come along up to my diggings? It's so blasted precise down here. Do come along."

Dan followed him up the stairs. Through the closed doors of the domestic reaches of the house he could hear a vehement rattle of pots and pans. They went along to the front of the house. Elliot Winship's diggings were not precise, but the diagrams and drawings the room was full of were orderly and well-dusted.

"I do hope you're not in any frightful rush. Lunch is always late on—"

Mr. Winship stopped, pondering. "On Wednesday. I say, it is Wednesday, isn't it? As a matter of fact, lunch is late every day in the week."

He smiled at Dan. "The whole business of food is so stupid in England. It's all anyone talks about. It's a great bore."

He was at the cellarette at the end of the room against a temporary partition of composition board where a wall had been blown out, rattling along, still trying hard, Dan saw, to remember him.

He turned suddenly with a happy smile. "Oh, now I place you," he said. He laughed heartily at his own stupidity. "I'd got the name McDermott in my head. And I thought it was *next* week. You're from Frazier-Heath, of course, about the plans for—"

"No," Dan said. He took the glass of lukewarm gin and orange squash his host held out to him. "I'm afraid you don't remember me, Mr. Winship. I'm from Number Four Godolphin Square. I talked to you yesterday afternoon. You were hunting Arthur Pegott. The *valet de chambre* . . ."

He stopped slowly. The expression on Elliot Winship's face as he put his glass of gin and orange down on the corner of the desk could not have been more ludicrously blank.

"Arthur Pegott?" It sounded like "Pigett" as he pronounced it. He looked anxiously at Dan. "Whatever was I looking for anyone named Pegott for? I—I've no idea whatsoever. But I'm sure you're right," he added hastily. "I have the most appalling memory."

"Perhaps it's just as well, as he was dead at the time."

Elliot Winship had picked up his glass. He put it down abruptly again and looked still more blankly at Dan. "Dead?"

"Murdered."

Mr. Winship stared.

"Look, my dear fellow," he said. "What *are* you talking about? I am so sorry, but—you *are* in the right house, aren't you? This is Fifty-three Saint Giles's Terrace. My name's Elliot Winship. I'm an architect. You're sure you've not made some—some sort of error, of some sort? I mean, well, *really,* you know!"

The expression on his face was so compounded of anxiety, solicitude and profound disturbance that the fantastically bizarre doubt that had been creeping negatively round in the background of Dan McGrath's own mind sharpened into positive action.

He hesitated for an instant. "I think you invited me here for lunch today, Mr. Winship, didn't you?"

"Well, my dear fellow—I'm delighted to have you. And, of course, I may have done. But, frankly, I have no memory of it. Frankly, the only place I could possibly have met you yesterday —unless I stopped you in the street—was at my club. But do wait a moment."

He went to the door in the composition wall and opened it. "Oh, I say, Mrs. O'Neill. Did I say where I was going yesterday after lunch?"

Through the doorway Dan could see the solid figure, her face flushed, coming out of the kitchen door.

"You did not, sir. Because you never went out. You worked all afternoon on them drawings I took to the post office for you at six o'clock, sir. The ones for the Dorrington Town Council. You'll remember, sir, if you'll stop to think of all the fuss and bother they've been to you, sir."

"Thank you, Mrs. O'Neill."

Winship closed the door and came back. "Remarkable woman. Memory of an elephant. Have some sherry, won't you? Now let me see. What were we saying? I remember. Well, I'm delighted you've come anyway. An American friend sends me food parcels, and Mrs. O'Neill hides them until someone unexpected drops in. Mrs. O'Neill has an acute mania for emergencies, I'm afraid."

He looked vaguely out of the window, off over Kensington Gardens.

"Pegott," he said. "Pegott. I'll ask Mrs. O'Neill if she—"

"It's not important, sir," Dan said. "He was the valet—permanent valet, I believe they called him—at Number Four Godolphin Square. You *are* the brother of Scott Winship, aren't—"

"Oh dear God," said Elliot Winship. He put his glass abruptly down. "You know, I do get so irritated at all this nonsense about my brother. I thought Number Four Godolphin Square sounded curiously familiar. That's where his unfortunate widow lives. Assuming she is his widow, not his wife. Of course, the thing's so utterly fantastic. My niece was here yester-day—the day before. I don't know, I'll ask Mrs O'Neill. Some time recently. She thinks he's back again. I must say it sounds perfectly ridiculous to me. Good Lord, Scott's not a ghoul—why should they think he's about haunting them every seven years? It's nonsense. If he were back, he'd come see me. We were great friends. He was four years older than I. A charming fellow. I mean, really charming."

Mr. Winship shook his head slowly. "You know, I've never been able, my dear fellow, to believe Scott was really such a swine. I was up at Oxford when it happened. I suppose Louise has always kept thinking he'd come back. He'd always got some kind of curious wanderlust. Marriage was not his dish, really, and managing Caroline's farm in Kent must have been an ap-palling chore, with an ill wife. I thought then that just the pros-pect of having a baby to look after too was too much for him—in his condition—so he skipped out. I could understand that. Reprehensible, of course. But I can't understand his selling a valuable painting that belonged to his wife—it was a lost Ver-meer, or so the American dealer believed—selling it and pocket-ing the money. That is hard for me to believe."

He gave Dan a quizzical deprecatory smile.

"Of course, I don't want to believe it. I'll admit that. None of us likes to think he comes of tainted stock. But, if Scott took that money, I know he was mentally ill. He couldn't have done it, otherwise. And he had got a lot of nasty stuff sticking in his brain from the war. Shrapnel, and that sort of muck. I was aw-fully fond of him, you know. But I say, you're not interested in my family history, are you? I—I really mustn't keep you. Per-haps you *will* lunch with me, one day soon."

143

He looked around as Mrs. O'Neill appeared at the door.

"There's a man downstairs, sir," she said severely. "From the police. I do pray you've not gone and got yourself in trouble with *them,* sir."

"I sold my motor car, Mrs. O'Neill," Mr. Winship said with some dignity. "Show the gentleman up, will you please? Dear me," he added anxiously as she went down the stairs again. "I *did* sell it, didn't I? Some time ago. They were always picking it up and hauling it off some place. Blasted nuisance, you know. Mrs. O'Neill will be very annoyed."

The heavy tread of solid boots on the staircase seemed suddenly to depress him. He was trying anxiously to recall what it was he could have done, as he rose and went toward the door. Dan saw the startled surprise on his face as it was not a blue uniform there but a tawny cinnamon-brown creation, and knew it was only a pallid reflection of the surprise that must have been on his own face as Chief Inspector Bull nodded soberly at him. He put down his glass and got to his feet.

"That's all right, sir," Bull said. "Sit down." He introduced himself to Elliot Winship. "I'm here about a man named Arthur Pegott."

Winship's face was blank for an instant, and brightened. "Ah yes, of course. I was going to ask Mrs. O'Neill about him." He went to the door, called her and waited, smiling at them. When she appeared he said, "Mrs. O'Neill—do we know anyone named Pegott? Arthur Pegott?"

"We don't *know* him, sir." Mrs. O'Neill spoke with strong disapprobation. "We knew his father. A respectable, God-fearing man. He did work for you before the war. We never knew his son. He came here to see you—a month ago, I think it was, sir. I never liked the look of him, sir—a proper bad one he is and always has been, to my mind. I'd have none of him. Never comes near his own mother. He pretended he wanted to sell some of his father's moulds. What's his father to him? More likely bringing tales about the other Winships, sir. I told him we wanted none of him in this house."

"Oh dear me," Elliot Winship said nervously. Dan McGrath saw that Inspector Bull was listening with quiet attentiveness.

"I told him so far as we were concerned Mr. Scott Winship was in his grave, and decent people should let him rest in peace. And I never heard hide nor hair of him again, sir, till I saw in the paper this morning he'd been found dead in his own cupboard. Good riddance, if you ask me, sir, and your lunch is getting cold on the table."

"Dear me," Winship said again as she went out. He looked at Bull. "I'm afraid we don't know Arthur Pegott, Inspector."

"It was really about your brother I came anyway," Bull said. He seemed to Dan to be as imperturbable as a friendly yak. "Have you got a picture of him? A photograph or a snapshot?"

Elliot Winship shook his head. "I've got a sketch of him that I did when he was ill. Mrs. O'Neill saved it when we got an incendiary." He motioned toward the temporary wallboard. "All my pictures and papers were destroyed. It's in the dining room."

He went out and returned in a moment with a small framed pencil sketch of a thin-faced man, his head bandaged, a crutch under one arm.

"It's not very like. But he wasn't himself of course. I wanted to photograph him—this was for a competition for a war memorial—but he couldn't bear the click of a camera then."

He propped it up on the mantel and looked at it. "It's not Scott, really," he said, shaking his head.

"May I take it, sir?"

Elliot Winship hesitated a moment, looking oddly at Bull.

"Do you think he's come back?" he asked quietly. He was silent for a moment. "It's been twenty-four years. He'd be fifty or so, now. I'd like to see him. Could a man forget, and remember, after that long? We were very happy as children, in Godolphin Square—especially when Caroline and Louise were away at school. Grandfather loved his pictures. He made us love them too—little barbarians, we both were. High tea with him was a sort of beautiful mystery. I suppose now some of the pictures were pretty bad—Edwardian taste, you know. That's why I didn't feel too strongly about it when the house was destroyed. I like to think they were all Titians and Correggios, and I'd have hated to see that young boor Dalrymple-Hughes get them, and bring in some supercilious bounder from the Tate and have him say a hundred quid for the lot. I dare say the frames are honest pear wood, or perhaps the Americans will buy them. One's dreams are frightfully valuable, these days."

He stopped, suddenly remembering, apparently, that an American and a policeman were there in the room with him.

"Oh, I say," he exclaimed. "I do babble on. I'm so sorry."

He took the sketch from the mantel, looked at it a moment and handed it to Bull. "You may take it, but do tell Mrs. O'Neill so she won't miss it. And if you find him, I'd like to see him. I have room here, and I'm sure Mrs. O'Neill could do for both of us."

"Thank you, sir." Bull took the framed drawing. "You've not seen him, I take it, sir?"

Elliot Winship shook his head. "Not since I made that

sketch. I've not seen his wife but a few times. I was *persona non grata* in the house. Caroline felt he was an ingrate of the lowest order, as I think she easily might, and it extended to me. His daughter Mary started coming to see me during the war. We've become very fond of each other."

Elliot Winship brightened. "In fact, I gave her the only picture I had of her father—in uniform in the last war. I'm sure she'll have it. Have you asked her?"

"I'd rather say nothing about it to the Winship ladies, just now, sir." Inspector Bull turned to Dan. "I was on my way out to see you. But if you've not had your lunch—"

"I think Mr. Winship would excuse me, Inspector."

Mrs. O'Neill was the only doubt he had, and he tried to avoid her offended gaze as she let them out the front door. He followed Bull down the steps.

At the bottom Bull turned and looked at him.

"You've got something on your mind, Mr. McGrath?"

Dan nodded. "If you're asking me, I'd say you could take that sketch back and leave it with Mrs. O'Neill."

"Why do you say that, sir?"

"Because," Dan said slowly, "Mr. Scott Winship is—back. I've seen him. Seen him and talked to him—outside Pegott's door at quarter past four yesterday afternoon."

He felt something chillier in the atmosphere as he thought about it, though it was not a particularly cold day.

"He's the spitting image of his brother Elliot, Inspector—a little older, lighter sandier hair, a lot seedier. A lot happier, too, some way. More of a sense of humor than his brother. He told me he was Elliot Winship and invited me to lunch here today."

He hesitated for a moment as the two stood there on the

sidewalk by the police car, Chief Inspector Bull looking at him silently.

"Mr. Scott Winship knows everything that's going on, Inspector. And if he could come out of that room after he killed Pegott—or even if he didn't kill him, if he just *saw* him—and be as casual and charming and amused as that guy was, then that shrapnel must have wrecked any moral sense the guy ever had. Scott Winship has a sense of humor, all right, Inspector, but it's a damned queer one—and I think he's playing some kind of a joke on everybody."

14

AT TWENTY minutes to three o'clock the postman going indifferently about his business in Godolphin Square came to more active life and set off toward the top of the road a short distance ahead of the small man in the shoddy grey suit and faded brown bowler who had come out of Number 4. Mr. Pinkerton, his furled umbrella clutched in one hand, nervously adjusted his steel-rimmed spectacles with the other as he glanced behind him to see if anyone was following him out of the house.

It was seldom Mr. Pinkerton told a deliberate falsehood, and almost never to his friend and former lodger Chief Inspector Bull. But desperate times demand desperate remedies. Having denied any and all complicity with Daniel McGrath, the Winships en masse and Arthur Pegott in particular, in any degree whatsoever, and having kept his mouth miraculously shut in spite of the siren song that Scotland Yard *per se* whispered in his inner ear, he had now come to a number of distressingly regrettable and even grim conclusions.

He had come to them quite on his own, behind the locked door of his bed-sitting room on the third floor. The first was that Mary Winship's father was not dead, as Miss Caroline Winship averred, but very much alive, and definitely somewhere in or about Number 4 Godolphin Square. He had even been emboldened to subject Miss Myrtle Grimstead to extraordinary scrutiny on the strength of it. The second was that Mr. Scott Winship could now only be thought of as having turned, in some way, into a cold-blooded, cruel and ruthless person. The third was that unless he was laid by the heels, they could all of them be victims. There was no doubt in Mr. Pinkerton's mind, among other things, that Mary Winship was right in believing her mother was being slowly poisoned to death, though he had not figured out how it was being managed. But in general, piecing together the bits and fragments of information he had got from Mary, and from searching his own mind for discarded memories of his own observations since he had lived in the house with the Winships, he had gathered himself what he regarded as a formidable body of evidence supporting those conclusions.

Why, Mr. Pinkerton thought, had he himself been murderously attacked, immediately after he had, in a way, pretended knowledge of Scott Winship's continued existence? Why had Pegott, who had been listening at the keyhole, and who had or claimed to have definite knowledge of Winship and his original crime, been brutally murdered just as he was apparently on the point of divulging it? And why did Scott Winship send the flowers twice yearly, effectively keeping his wife from believing herself a widow so she could marry Sidney Copeland, when he quite determinedly had no desire to return to her himself?

He had been spurred on to his third conclusion by the incident of the chambermaid Betty when she came to make up his bed that morning. The girl was badly frightened.

"I don't know what to do, I'm that worried, sir," she had whispered, looking anxiously at the closed door. "It's my key. The one that opens all the flats. I couldn't have lost it off by itself, sir, but it's gone." She held up the wide metal ring she carried hanging by a ribbon tied to her apron belt. "It was missing last night. Sarah didn't let on to Grimstead when she was giving her what for for not turning down old Miss Winship's bed. She would be the one to make the complaint, sir, but Sarah told me because we're not supposed to let it go off the ring. I'd not let it go. And it was on yesterday morning. Somebody must have pinched it when I was making up the rooms."

Mr. Pinkerton remembered how he had involuntarily reached up and touched his bruised scalp, and glanced nervously at the door he'd been at such pains to lock before he'd gone to bed the night before. If Pegott's murderer had taken the key, he would still have got it. There was no flat in the house he could not creep into any time he had a mind. A cold shiver had gone rippling through the grey fluid of his meagre spine.

"What must I do, sir?"

"You must tell Chief Inspector Bull when he comes," Mr. Pinkerton had said. "He'll be here today. You must tell him at once. It's—not safe for—for anybody. But don't tell anyone else. Not Sarah or the porters or the chef—"

"No fear, sir."

He had tried to wipe the dismay off his face as he saw it reflected on hers.

"The chef's that balmy he'd not hear me if I did. But it's a —a wicked thought, sir, isn't it?"

It was indeed, and Mr. Pinkerton was faced with a certain reluctant sense of his own responsibility. He wondered if he ought not to find Bull and tell him himself, immediately, before anything else could happen at Number 4 Godolphin Square. He had the uneasy feeling that he had been a quixotic fool not to have told Bull about his own incident, and about Scott Winship and the picture. But the grim satisfaction, if he might think of it as such, that a least part of his conclusions were damningly corroborated by the disappearance of the girl's key gave him heart. It was conclusive proof that the murderer of Pegott was undoubtedly familiar with the interior workings of Number 4 Godolphin Square—probably even personally known to Arthur Pegott—or to them all.

As he passed the postman on his way to the top of the Square, Mr. Pinkerton, his small grey ego supported and prodded on, had given up his role of sedentary theorist. He had a slight tendency to shiver at his temerity, and what he might possibly be doing, but he kept stoutly along until he came to Tottenham Court Road, and hesitated only a moment before he opened the door of Guillaume, Florist. Inside he stopped short, blinking with dismay as he recognized the girl at the end of the counter. He sidled back hastily, reaching for the door, but he was too late; Mary Winship turned her head. As she saw him, her face became as waxy white as the tin pot of gardenias on the counter beside her.

"Mr. Pinkerton!"

He could see the words framed on her lips, and there was a startled look in her eyes that she suppressed quickly, trying to smile at him.

He swallowed, moistened his lips and managed to speak. "Oh, hello, Mary. I just dropped in to get a few . . ."

He went up to the counter, looking around the small shop desperately. Chrysanthemums, he noticed, were six shillings each, and roses half a crown. It was absurd for him to be buying flowers anyway. Tomatoes were three-and-six a pound. ". . . a few figs," he said, spotting the box next to the tomatoes, and before he realized that the two-shilling sign meant they were two shillings each. He had an awful vision of Mrs. Pinkerton rending her shroud in horror. "I mean, a fig," he said hastily.

"No—that's not true, is it." She shook her head at him. "You're here for the same reason I am. To find out about the—the flowers."

Mr. Pinkerton nodded unhappily. "It—it was just an idea I'd got, thinking it over."

"Something, miss?" The woman behind the counter turned from the cash register as her other customer moved away. "Sophie!" she called over her shoulder, through the door into the rear of the shop. "The gentleman wants some figs."

"One fig," said Mr. Pinkerton nervously. "One will be quite sufficient."

He looked at the girl in the faded blue smock. Her eyes were red and so was her nose, and her sullen mouth twitched at the corners as she took one fig out of the box and put it in a small paper bag. The woman waited impatiently for Mary to make up her mind.

"I wanted to ask you about some flowers that were sent my

mother the night before last. Three red roses. Mrs. Scott Winship, Four Godolphin Square."

The girl taking Mr. Pinkerton's reluctant four sixpences dropped one of them. She got down on her knees to get it from under the wooden counter, and scrambled to her feet.

"Get on with your work, Sophie."

The girl edged past Mary and vanished into the back room.

"Winship?" The manageress opened her dog-eared order book. "Delivered at a quarter past six, miss. I hope there were no complaints. We can't accept responsibility for flowers after they're received and signed for."

"I want to know who sent them."

"That's no business of ours, miss." The woman closed the book sharply.

"I know," Mary said quietly. "I thought you might help me. My mother's been getting flowers from you for years. Primroses in April, roses in October—"

"I'm sorry, miss." There was a truculent finality in the way the woman pushed the order book closer to the cash desk and shut her lips together. She was defensively stony-eyed as she said, "We've got many standing orders. No one's ever made a complaint before."

"I'm not complaining. I'm just asking. My mother gets the flowers, not during the war—"

"Our records are mostly gone, miss. We were in Oxford Street before we were bombed out. My father was killed, and his two assistants. I was working in Plymouth. I've just opened here again last year. It's not been easy, miss. And we don't give out information about our orders anyway."

The woman included Mr. Pinkerton in a glance of stony

resentment, and turned as the bell over the shop door rang. "Something for you, madam?"

Mr. Pinkerton plucked at Mary's sleeve. "I think we'd best go," he whispered nervously. "Let's go have a cup of tea."

The woman was still watching them out of a corner of her eye. It was an abortive venture.

"She—she seems to think I'm blaming her," Mary said. They stood in the street outside the shop, defeated and dejected. Then they both turned quickly at the low call behind them.

"Miss! Oh, miss!"

The shop assistant, in the doorway of the hall leading to the upper floors of the building, motioned them to come to one side of the shop front, out of sight of the woman inside.

"It's all my fault, miss," she whispered. "I sent the roses. Arthur Pegott rang me up and told me to and he'd give me money, but he never did, miss. I paid for them myself. That's why she's so cross about it. He came all around me, miss. Two months it was, he came to the shop and pretended he was going to open up at one of the posh hotels and wanted a girl like me to manage for him. He took me to the pictures and the dog races. I told him everything I could think of. She has got some old order books, and I let him look at them when she was at market. When I rang him up yesterday morning, he said I could whistle for my six shillings. He was going to Canada where the girls were smarter and not such silly fools. And now he's dead. And I *was* a silly fool."

"Oh, thank you!" Mary said. "And I'm sorry about Pegott."

She took a ten-shilling note out of her bag and put it in the girl's pocket.

"Oh, no, miss. That's not what I want." She thrust the note back into Mary's hand. "I'd not be happy if I was to take it,

154

miss. It's just that I meant nobody any harm. I've got to run, miss—she'll have a proper fit if she sees me here."

She ducked back into the doorway and disappeared. Mr. Pinkerton and Mary Winship stood looking silently at each other.

"Why on earth should Pegott have sent my mother the roses, Mr. Pinkerton?" she asked at last.

The little grey man shook his head. He was as bewildered as she was. They walked along for some time in silence.

"I've no idea at all," Mr. Pinkerton said then. "Unless—"

He stopped. The only idea that he had in fact got was too preposterous.

"Unless he's seen my father send them? But—he's only been at the flat this summer. Do you think he knew my father before he came?"

They had come to a small tea shop in Charing Cross Road. Mary stopped abruptly just inside the door, delaying the weary-looking postman about to come in behind them.

"Do you think that's *why* he came to the flat, Mr. Pinkerton?"

"Two, sir?" An efficient woman in a red dress motioned them to a table in the center of the room. "One, sir?" She seated the postman beside Mr. Pinkerton at the same table.

"You know, there was something odd about Pegott," Mary Winship said. "He listened at doors. Eric caught him at ours once."

Mr. Pinkerton nodded. He was as oblivious to the postman sitting by him as Mary Winship was, and glanced at him at all only because he could not recall, thinking fleetingly about it, ever having seen a postman sitting down.

"So did I," Mr. Pinkerton said. "The afternoon Mr. Mc-

Grath spoke to me. Or rather the afternoon I spoke to Mr. McGrath."

Two bright spots grew in Mary Winship's cheeks. "I'd rather not talk about Mr. McGrath." The waitress put the pots of tea and hot water down in front of her. "Milk?"

Mr. Pinkerton nodded again. He was distressed at the abrupt dismissal of his friend the American. He must have done something regrettably offensive, from the blue-black sparks shooting out of her eyes before she picked up the teapot and changed the subject.

"Another thing," she said. "Eric's spent more time than yesterday's lunch with Pegott. Several times when I've gone in his flat Pegott's been there, smoking a cigarette. He'd sneak it behind him and say 'Will there be anything else, sir?' I thought it was racing and Pegott was placing his bets for him. But I'm not so sure now."

She looked across at Mr. Pinkerton.

"You could do something for me if you would."

"I'd be very happy to."

"I'd like to know where Eric goes and what he does all day. I know it sounds underhanded and all that. But I'd—I'd really like to know. He's still at the flat. He made a brave show last night, about leaving us all, but this morning he's there—the charming repentant—and Mother and Aunt Caroline accusing me of being hard and unfeeling."

Mr. Pinkerton looked at her anxiously. She lowered her eyes, a faint flush growing in her cheeks.

"I really want to find my father, Mr. Pinkerton," she said, her apparent irrelevance bridging the gap Mr. Pinkerton's devious mind had already leaped over.

"Are you sure, Mary? I mean—"

"I know what you mean." She spoke quietly without raising her eyes. "They told me a lot of things last night I hadn't known before."

She opened her bag, took out a picture and handed it across the table to him. "My uncle gave me that. It's my father when he was a young man."

Mr. Pinkerton looked at a smiling and debonair youngster in the uniform of a major in the last war.

"I know he'll have changed, but you can keep it. He was about my uncle's height, five feet nine or so, and sort of sandy-haired, my uncle says. It may help. I've got my own picture of him—in my mind. I'm sure I'd know him any place. If he walked in here now, I know I'd know him."

Curiously, Mr. Pinkerton thought, a man was walking in just then. Mr. Pinkerton glanced past Mary's dark head at him. He was grey-haired, mild and unassuming in appearance, as he hung his hat on the wooden tree by the cashier's desk and turned to look for an empty place to sit. There was a seat at their table, beside Mary. He glanced at it, then at the postman, solemnly drinking his tea, at Mr. Pinkerton, and at Mary, or at her back which was all he could see. And then, and it seemed extremely odd to Mr. Pinkerton, he turned quietly round again and took his hat off the tree.

"Here's a place, sir." The efficient woman in red held up her hand. The man shook his head silently and went out. The woman looked at the cashier and shrugged.

"I'm sure I'd recognize him," Mary was saying. "So you keep that, and give it back to me some time."

Mr. Pinkerton looked at the photograph, removed from its original folder, and put it carefully in his coat pocket. He sat there blinking. Something strange and very puzzling seemed to have happened to him. He knew Mary Winship was talking still, about her father, but he seemed to hear her only in the most vague and far-off way. He was held fast in some extraordinary sphere of the most complete unreality. It was as if he had stumbled on some magic phrase, or picked up some magic stone. Something totally inexplicable had materialized, and as inexplicably vanished, as if he had forgot the phrase or dropped the stone.

"It—it must be the blow on my head," he thought. "I must have gone a bit balmy. I really must."

He could not for the life of him have described his sensation, or anything about it. And it could not have had anything to do with the man who had come into the tea shop and gone out. He did not know the man; he had never seen him before. A hundred Londoners come into tea shops every day, change their mind and go out to go somewhere else. Mr. Pinkerton told himself that very firmly. But an odd feeling of dismay persisted there in the pit of his stomach. It was disturbing in the extreme.

15

HE WAS still disturbed, and still unable to rid himself of the persistent feeling of dismay, when he put Mary on her bus in Oxford Street.

"I promised Copey I'd come and help him this afternoon," she said. "He's got to make a speech and his secretary's got a cold. Poor old Copey. I'm beginning really to feel sorry for him. I used to resent him frightfully. I didn't know till last night he was my father's surgeon. His first private patient after he got out of the army. That's how he met my mother. It's hard to imagine any man being that faithful for that many years, isn't it?"

She smiled for the first time that afternoon. "It's hard to think of Copey as a romantic heart at all, isn't it?"

Mr. Pinkerton nodded. Considering what Mr. Sidney Copeland had said to McGrath, he must never have had a very high opinion of his first private patient. And not unreasonably, perhaps, considering the opinion Mr. Pinkerton had formed of Scott Winship with far less personal knowledge than his surgeon must have had. The thought quickened the latent anxiety troubling his own conscience. He looked at Mary Winship, the quick smile she gave him as she glanced back from inside the bus before she sat down touching the taut strings of his small grey heart with a poignant and unfamiliar music. In his heightened state it seemed to him that some shadow of despair, malign, almost evil, hung over her dark young head, and that the shining armor of faith she wore was only a delusion bringing her closer to the pit.

He turned away, blinking his watery grey eyes. "Oh, dear!" he thought. "I'm really daft."

He felt gingerly at the bruise on the side of his head, and adjusted his lozenge-shaped spectacles as he glanced hastily about to see if anyone was particularly noticing him. People had been committed for seeing shadows hovering about. But none of the hurrying people jostling each other in the accepted postwar manner seemed concerned with him, and he crossed the road, not because he wanted to cross it but because it was the path of least resistance. The traffic signal had changed, and the crowd surged across, taking him along, stumbling not to be overturned in the middle of the road.

On the opposite side he disentangled himself and scurried to a protecting shelter at the side of the door into the Corner House. He stopped to catch his breath, and gave suddenly such a start that his head pounded and his brown bowler hat contracted to an iron band gripping it. The man he had seen leave the other tea shop was coming out of the Corner House. The mild faraway look in his eyes changed in an instant as they met Mr. Pinkerton's directly. He dodged out through the crowd at the entrance to Mr. Pinkerton's side, and took two steps straight toward him. Mr. Pinkerton's heart stopped beating for an instant before it started to beat like a woodpecker on a wormy limb. The man's eyes brightened. He leaned forward, close to Mr. Pinkerton's dumfounded ear.

"The wicked *shall* be repaid—*and* the good!"

He intoned the words in a hoarse singsong whisper, and before Mr. Pinkerton could even sort them out in his bewildered auditory channels, he leaned forward again and prodded the little man's shoulder sharply with his forefinger.

"The wicked *shall* be repaid—*and* the good!"

Then Mr. Pinkerton, blinking his eyes desperately, suddently stared about him. The man was gone. He had been absorbed by some fantastic legerdemain into the streams and crosscurrents of the tea-hour mass movement. Mr. Pinkerton licked his dry lips and tried to swallow. The man was gone—gone, that is, if he had ever been there at all. Mr. Pinkerton adjusted his spectacles with a shaking hand, his knees very uncertain. A taxicab drawing up to the kerb let out its passenger, and Mr. Pinkerton made a dash for it. There were few times in his life that he had taken a taxicab when there was a bus, or a bus when he was able to walk, but for once parsimony was a dull jade.

"Four Godolphin Square, please."

He sank back into the seat and closed his eyes.

"The wicked *shall* be repaid—*and* the good!"

Suddenly he opened his eyes and sat up straighter in the seat. He might have imagined the words. He might even have imagined the prodding forefinger on his shoulder. But he could not have imagined the odor of fresh onions on the man's breath. They were too scarce. Mr. Pinkerton could not remember when he had smelled, much less tasted, a fresh crisp green onion.

He leaned forward and spoke to the driver. "You may let me out here, please." Fortunately the meter still registered ninepence. He was quite willing to expend eleven-pence to be assured of his own continued sanity.

"The wicked *shall* be repaid—*and* the good!"

"Wot's that, sir?" The cabbie looked at him in alarm, and then at the tuppeny tip there in his hand. "I tyke you, mister," he said with a grin. "It's in 'eaven I gets my reward." He chuckled cavernously at his joke and pulled off, leaving Mr. Pinkerton, appalled at himself, on the street corner. He had not meant at all to repeat what the man had said.

"I really must be more careful," he thought, nervously glancing about him. It did not occur to him then, or when he got on a bus at the next corner, that for the first time since he had left Godolphin Square there was not a postman anywhere in sight.

At the moment Mr. Pinkerton was getting off his bus to walk through from Oxford Street to Godolphin Square, however, a postman was in communication with Chief Inspector Bull in Battersea. Bull was in his car in front of the house in

Pilkington Crescent where Arthur Pegott's mother, her lined face stained with tears, sat with two friends drinking tea behind the drawn faded blinds, still stunned and unable to believe.

"My Arthur was always such a good lad, sir." It was a cry from the womb that Bull had heard many times—of men who murdered as well as men who had been murdered, of thieves and worse than thieves—and it was always a sobering thing, moving him to a compassion his job had taught him to resist or be blinded when it was most necessary to see. He listened now to Detective-Constable Weedham's report. At the Corner House a man had come up to Mr. Pinkerton and whispered something to him. Mr. Pinkerton, apparently terrified, had jumped into a taxicab. Weedham had lost him, there being no other cab in sight. He had got the cab number.

"Forget it, man," Bull said patiently. "He'll not take it far."

He spoke through long acquaintance with the habits of his deceased landlady's relict. The fact, for instance, that he had been impelled to take a taxi at all was important.

"Who was the man who spoke to him?"

Weedham had had his eyes on Mr. Pinkerton, the street was crowded, and the man had disappeared at once. Bull scowled. He was genuinely fond of the little grey Welshman, and genuinely worried. The pseudo-postman had been an attempt to protect him, assigned the instant the American, after his curious luncheon at Mr. Elliot Winship's, had told Bull about the lozenge-shaped spectacles caught in the inside folds of the afghan that Mrs. Bull had herself knitted for Mr. Pinkerton. Bull hesitated. There was no doubt of the little man's instinct for nosing out the salient figures in a spot of trouble—or their nosing him out, Bull had never been quite sure which.

"Did you see the man at all who spoke to him?"

From his position, Weedham could not see him sufficiently to make any identification, and the man had disappeared at once. Bull sighed patiently. The idea that he had more than once was in his mind again: arrest and detention—for withholding vital information—until they had got whoever it was who had apparently tried to get Mr. Pinkerton out of the way and had got Pegott out of the way. He started to tell Weedham to go to Godolphin Square and take the little man into custody the minute he appeared. He changed his mind as an idea occurred to him.

"Carry on where you are," he said. "See if you can pick up the man who spoke to him. I'll take care of Mr. Pinkerton myself."

As he said "Godolphin Square" to his driver, his placid blue eyes had what might almost have been called a twinkle in them.

But Mr. Pinkerton had already left Godolphin Square. He had, in fact, not quite reached the top of it when he saw Eric Dalrymple-Hughes coming toward him, not from the flats but from the garden through the gate in the wattle fence. Mr. Pinkerton hesitated only a moment. The memory of his abortive visit to the florist, which he was aware would probably have turned out even worse had he asked the questions instead of Mary, had dampened his confidence in himself as a private investigator. But he had promised Mary. At least, he had in a way promised her.

"The wicked *shall* be repaid—*and* the good," he said to himself. "I must stop saying that," he added hastily. Still, there was no doubt in his mind as to which category included Eric Dalrymple-Hughes. He scurried across to the opposite side of the road, went a short way along a side street and waited until the young man appeared in the road headed toward Oxford Street. Mr. Pinkerton hurried back and set out on his own side, keeping fairly abreast of Dalrymple-Hughes across the road. The black Homburg hat and the square elegant shoulders were simple to follow. The young man never looked back, and Mr. Pinkerton, dodging in and out in the crowds, had only one real anxiety. That was lest Eric Dalrymple-Hughes's destination should turn out to be some gilded den of iniquity. He would then have had no idea of what to do, his experience in that field being greatly limited.

Not that Old Bond Street was likely to be the center of such activities, but Old Bond Street led into New Bond Street. Mr. Pinkerton more than a little anxious, came to an abrupt stop on the heels of an irritated lady in front of him and to the equal irritation of the man behind him. Dalrymple-Hughes had turned into a shop three doors ahead. Mr. Pinkerton edged along and stopped, blinking, acutely disappointed. The most fevered and puritanical imagination could hardly convert the shop he had entered into a den of any sort. The worn sign over the door was its own sufficient accolade of solid respectability.

"Jno. L. Turnipseed & Sons Ltd.," Mr. Pinkerton read. "Iron-Mongers. By Appointment. Founded 1796."

Mr. Pinkerton peered in through the murky window. Dalrymple-Hughes had put his stick and lemon-colored gloves on the counter and was looking about him. Mr. Pinkerton, seeing the man who came to wait on him, realized that any inquiries he might make after Eric had left would get short shrift. The sons of Jno. L. Turnipseed did not look as if they would encourage inquiries about their customers or their purchases. He peered deeper into the gloom into which Dalrymple-Hughes had gone to the rear of the shop. Insignificant as he was, he could not hope to barge boldly in without the young man's noticing him eventually, so he stayed where he was. When Dalrymple-Hughes came out carrying a small parcel, Mr. Pinkerton was waiting for him, faithful to his task if slightly depressed by it.

Two hours later, in his own room on the third floor of Number 4 Godolphin Square, he was even more depressed. His feet hurt also. He took off his solid black boots and put on his slippers. He would have liked very much to put his feet up on something, but Mrs. Pinkerton had never allowed it, and it was folly to give too many hostages to a fickle jade. Dalrymple-Hughes had worn him completely out. Following him to Turnipseed's had been one thing. Following him from there to Camden Town to a second ironmonger's had been too much, even if they had gone by bus part of the way. Mr. Pinkerton sat down on his sofa, leaned his head back against the crocheted antimacassar and closed his eyes. He then opened them quickly as someone knocked on his door.

"Oh, dear!" he thought as he said "Come in" wearily. It was the first time in his life that he had not sprung eagerly up to admit his so infrequent callers.

"Hi, there, oldtimer."

Dan McGrath opened the door and came cheerfully in. He stopped short. "Hello—you're pooped."

"I expect I am," Mr. Pinkerton agreed tentatively. "I've— I've had a rather difficult day."

He blinked his eyes. There was something suspiciously like tears in them as he thought Dan McGrath was going to burst into laughter. But he did not.

"You sure look it," he said. He sat down as if he belonged there, or at least had come to stay. "What happened? Come on, Mr. P. Tell old McGrath all about it."

Mr. Pinkerton blinked again. There really were tears in his eyes this time. It was the first occasion in all his life that anybody had ever called him Mr. P. It was a friendly thing, and Mr. Pinkerton badly wanted a friend.

"Come on," Dan said. "Put your dogs up here and tell your old chum all about it."

He pushed up the only other chair in the room, lifted Mr. Pinkerton's surprised feet into it, and sank back into his own chair. "What's the dope?"

Mr. Pinkerton sat rigid for a moment, his feet barely touching the worn tapestry seat. But nothing happened. There was no blowing of trumpets, no mouldier than usual smell in the place, no vinegary-cheeked apparition materialized in the cupboard door. He took a deep breath.

"The wicked *shall* be repaid—*and* the good," he said happily.

Mr. McGrath uncrossed one leg and crossed the other. "Okay," he said, staring a little. "Okay." He groaned inwardly. "If this guy isn't nuts," he thought, "I am. And this is the character that that damn Chief Inspector says I'm to ride herd on from here out."

"I mean, that's what the man said," Mr. Pinkerton explained hastily.

"I hope he's right," Dan said amiably. "Now suppose you tell me what *you've* been doing."

16

INSPECTOR BULL knocked on the door of Miss Caroline Winship's flat on the first floor of Number 4 Godolphin Square, and waited with a feeling of comfortable complacency that he would ordinarily have been the first to suspect. He had, to the best of his belief, knocked up a century. Two of his problems, worrisome nuisances at any time but especially so when he had got a murder on his hands, were, if not solved, at least merged into one which he expected would thereby take care of itself. Instead of two gifted amateurs (the Assistant Commissioner's expression) diligently mucking up the tracks he was laboriously and painstakingly trying to sort out and follow, he had managed to set them to minding and circumventing each other. With the American looking after him, Mr. Pinkerton could be counted on to keep out of dangerous trouble, and with Mr. Pinkerton to occupy McGrath's waking hours, Bull confidently hoped the same for him. Which only proved him to be a human and not a Papal Bull, hence lacking the virtue of infallibility.

There was only one thing about the arrangement that disturbed Bull, not as a law-enforcement officer but as a man who had once collected Dresden and Chelsea shepherdesses until he found one more exquisite not made of porcelain and married her. It was the American's sardonic rejoinder when he made his appeal to him to look after the little Welshman.

"Why not?" McGrath had said. "Whoever said three's a crowd?"

It had taken Bull a few moments to understand what he meant, even though he knew about the girl. McGrath had explained why he was in London when he had given his summary of what had happened since he had been there. On the other hand, Mr. Pinkerton had been underfoot, and rather a help, in fact, when Inspector Bull was courting Margaret. Still, Americans, he understood, had thrown off chaperones, with other Old World impediments, and he had not seen the girl herself.

He saw her now as she opened the door of her aunt's apartments.

"I'm Inspector Bull of New Scotland Yard," he said.

Knowing something about the Americans, he was a little surprised that this was the girl one of them had crossed the Atlantic to find again. There was nothing startling or flamboyant about her. She had a delicate pointed face and a soft crown of dark curly hair, very little lip rouge, and no bright red lacquer on her fingernails. Her eyes were beautiful, he could see that. And she was alive, intensely alive, just then, poised like a dark flame in the doorway, taut with some inner emotion, controlled but very evident. Fear, or anxiety—he could not tell which.

"I'd like to speak to your mother, Miss Winship."

"I'm sorry. My mother's ill. She has asthma. She's had a terrible attack this afternoon."

He looked at her closely. That was it, then. It hadn't seemed to him the stark, smiting sort of fear his appearance or the sound of his name sometimes produced in a house of trouble.

"Can you come back later?" she asked.

He started to nod and move away. Some instinct deterred him. Some quality in the atmosphere, or in the girl herself, as tangible as the acrid odor of a fire smoldering in the cellar, seeping up through the cracks and rat holes of a dilapidated house.

"Your aunt, then, Miss Winship. I'm sorry to disturb you, but my business is urgent."

"She's got spirit," he thought as she tightened her grip on

the door, blocking his way, indignant sparks shooting out of her blue-black eyes. Then as abruptly she released the door and drew it open.

"Come in," she said curtly. She stepped aside. "My aunt's with my mother. Mr. Copeland, of Wimpole Street, is with her too. We've sent for her own doctor. I'll tell my aunt you're here."

Bull looked about him in the sitting room. Luxurious but shabby, their own furniture and objects, not the management's, the room but not its contents refurbished since the war. Four windows overlooking the garden in the Square. A door on either side of the one he'd come through from the foyer. It was through the door on the right that Mary Winship had gone, and in the brief opening of it before she had closed it again he could hear the hideous gasping struggle the asthmatic woman was making to get her breath, and the murmuring voices of people with her. Then as Miss Caroline Winship appeared, Bull suppressed an involuntary step backwards at the speechlessly silent but deadly rebuke on the woman's face. Her heavy-lidded eyes were burning brilliantly. She closed the door quietly and motioned her cane toward a chair.

"You wished to see me, Inspector?"

"I'm sorry to—"

"Get on with it, please. What do you want?"

She sat rigidly upright in the faded yellow satin chair.

"I want to know what you knew about Arthur Pegott, Miss Winship."

"Nothing whatever, Inspector. Except that he was an unpleasant and obsequious servant who was remarkably efficient at his job, and remarkably well-trained compared with the rest of the staff we put up with here. About his private life I know nothing at all."

"I want to know in particular, Miss Winship, if he had any connection with your brother-in-law?"

"My—"

"Mr. Scott Winship," Bull said evenly. He was a mild but also a stubborn man.

As she settled back in the yellow chair, releasing her grip on her stick, she reminded him of a heroic figure by Epstein if one could be thought of as becoming animate and settling into a chair.

"I see," Miss Winship said. Her voice mirrored a faint light that moved in her eyes. Was it some kind of ever so polite contempt? Bull wondered. He was not sure. "Aren't you belaboring a dead horse, Inspector?" she inquired slowly.

"That's for you to say, Miss Winship. I'm told you were out in the Square the other night. A man was at your house opposite here. My informant got the impression you were there to see him."

"You're holding me responsible for the impressions Mr. McGrath picks up, Inspector?" Her heavy brows lifted ironically. "He's a very impetuous young man."

"I dare say, ma'am. But the valet Pegott offered to take him to see your brother-in-law, Miss Winship. And the picture. I expect you know what I'm referring to."

"I should, Inspector, since it cost me six thousand pounds— to prevent the dealer from prosecuting. I sold two farms in Kent to find the cash."

Bull nodded. "You can't be expected to have any very friendly feelings for Scott Winship, ma'am?"

Miss Caroline Winship drew a deep breath and expelled it slowly. "You may say that, Inspector." She pronounced each word distinctly. "You might say a great deal more. I'm a violent and vengeful woman. I have an antediluvian reverence for the sanctity of private property and the inviolability of contracts. Scott Winship respected neither."

Bull hesitated an instant. "Do you remember Sergeant Pulham of the Yard, Miss Winship?"

She thought a moment, and nodded. "Yes, I do. He was very helpful with the American dealer. It was he who suggested the extra thousand pounds—as a heart balm, I presume. Twelve hundred was agreed on, but he returned me two hundred the dealer had given him—what he called Sergeant Pulham's 'cut,' I believe. I was surprised then that there were honest men."

"Sergeant Pulham always expected Scott Winship to come back to that house—as he'd done when he was ill before."

Bull watched her intently beneath the surface of his placid gaze.

She put her hand out, gripped her stick, drew herself forward and to her feet. Her brown eyes were brilliant burning coals, her mouth shut for an instant like a vise. When she spoke her voice was tense with subdued passion.

"I don't know what Sergeant Pulham expected, sir. But I will tell you this. *I* am not afraid of my brother-in-law—if, as I do not believe, he is alive. I who have the most reason to be am the only person who is not afraid. Look at my sister—is it *love* that brings on these horrible attacks that nearly kill her whenever she thinks he is near? What happens to men whose brains are injured, Inspector? Do they become admirable creatures, or do they become tigers feeding on the human heart?"

Miss Caroline Winship struck the carpet with the ferrule of her stick.

"You ask me if Pegott had any connection with Scott Winship, Inspector Bull. I do not know what company he keeps. It may be ghouls and monsters and evil things. It may be thieves and valets. But *I* have no fear of him, Inspector—dead or alive."

"Why do you keep your house on the opposite side of the Square, Miss Winship? You have had large offers for the ground it's on. You've tried to get a license to rebuild it just as it was before it was bombed out. I'm told—by people in this house, Miss Winship—that you sit here watching it day after day."

Her burning eyes were fixed on his for a moment. Then she said, with extraordinary calm, "You may say it's my reverence for the sanctity of private property, Inspector." The ironic overtone struck him with the violence of another unspoken rebuke as she turned back toward her sister's door. "You will excuse me now. I've told you I am a vengeful and determined woman. Good afternoon, Inspector. Let yourself out when you wish to go."

Bull stood for a moment where he was. Then he turned and looked across the Square to the naked ruins of the house, softened in the early evening dusk. It was a trap baited to the death. An impressionable man in spite of his stolid tawny bulk, Bull felt a faint shudder course along his spine.

He went out into the hall and up two flights to Mr. Pinkerton's room, knocked on the door and opened it, and stood staring.

"Pinkerton!" he said.

His former landlord, clad in his bright pink-and-purple dressing gown, was stretched full length on the sofa, lolling like a sybaritic rabbit against the pillows propped under his head, his stocking feet sticking out from under the green and red afghan Margaret Bull had knitted for him. As if that were not sufficiently incredible, he was smoking an American cigarette, and on the chair pulled up beside him was a glass of beer. It was a scene of debauchery such as Inspector Bull had never hoped to see, having known the late Mrs. Pinkerton's high and rigid standards of propriety and total abstinence. Tobacco was an evil in any form, but a cigarette was a coffin nail straight from the foundries of the archfiend himself.

Bull looked at Dan McGrath, coming in through the long windows from the balcony, with a twinkle in his eye. He had asked him to look after Mr. Pinkerton, not start sapping his moral fibre, as they said.

"No, no, stay where you are." Mr. Pinkerton was attempting to scramble out of the sofa and the dilemma he was in. "I won't disturb you."

He turned to Dan. "I just dropped up to say there'll be an inquest tomorrow at nine o'clock, sir. We'll have to ask you to appear."

He turned back to Mr. Pinkerton. "What did you find out at the florist's in Tottenham Court Road this afternoon?"

Mr. Pinkerton inwardly shook his head. There was something very frustrating in the omnipresence and omniscience of New Scotland Yard. "Just that it was Pegott sent the flowers to Mrs. Winship the other day," he said meekly.

Bull nodded. "And who was the man who spoke to you outside the Corner House?"

"I don't know. I—I never saw him before. 'The wicked *shall* be repaid—*and* the good.' That's what he said to me, Chief Inspector—just that. He—he was quite mad, I expect."

Bull looked at him intently.

"Mrs. Winship has had another of her attacks today," he said after an instant. "I've been talking to the staff. Pegott came in from lunch a bit before three o'clock yesterday. There was no one in the kitchen except the three maids getting ready for tea. The porter, James Belcher, had gone to the chemist's to get some medicine for Mrs. Winship. Miss Grimstead was minding the telephone and filling out forms with a representative from the estate agents."

He turned to Dan. "No one saw the man you say you saw, Mr. McGrath, at Pegott's door there. Either come in or go out. You're quite sure you did see such a man?"

"Quite, Inspector," Dan said.

"Mary and I heard him talking to somebody," Mr. Pinkerton put in, nodding at Dan. "We'd been listening for him. We were going to ask him in for tea."

"I'd like you both to come to the inquest," Bull said. "He may show up there. And your man too, Pinkerton. Both of you take a look round."

He nodded and started out. Dan McGrath took a step toward him.

"Say, before you go, Inspector," he said, "Mr. Pinkerton and I've been trying to figure things out. We've got a couple of ideas—"

"I expect you have, sir," Bull said patiently. He took out his watch and looked at it. "I'd be very glad to hear them, but not now. I've got to be at Headquarters in fifteen minutes. Pegott's young lady Sophie Barnes is being brought in to question. I expect she'll be able to tell us something more about him."

He looked down at Mr. Pinkerton. He had led them to Sophie Barnes, but there was no use telling him so. He was already a bit above himself, lolling there like an Indian potentate in his coat of many colors.

"I'll see you both in the morning. Good night."

Mr. Pinkerton adjusted his spectacles and looked at Dan.

"I expect I should have told him about Eric and the ironmongers." He shook his head regretfully. "But I expect he knows about it anyway. I'm afraid I'm very stupid. I—I should have known that postmen don't take time out for tea."

He was a little hurt that his friend should have had him trailed like a common felon. "I—I'm afraid I'm a bit of a cat's-paw," he said, taking another sip of his beer. It was a source of constant inferiority to him that he really abominated the bitter stuff. He would much rather have had a cup of strong hot tea, but he did not want Dan McGrath to know he couldn't take it, as the Americans said.

Dan did not at the moment appear to be concerned with his likes or dislikes. He had turned back to the window and was looking out across the Square, his brows drawn together.

"I'd swear she was out there, watching for him," he said with sudden vehemence. "My busting in is what put the kibosh on it. The whole thing's screwy, Mr. P., but it's got to be that way to make any sense at all. Scott Winship must come back there—for some reason or another."

Mr. Pinkerton sat up among his pillows, which were Dan's, brought from the box room at the end of the hall. He blinked his eyes and swallowed in sudden excitement.

"Mr. Mc—I mean, Dan," he said. His voice shook a little. "Why don't we go and see? He might come tonight. If he had had to kill Pegott, it's perhaps—well, the way you lawyers put it. Time is of the essence. Maybe Scott Winship goes there and watches this house—and that's why he can slip in here when the porter's out on errands. Maybe he even stays there. There are plenty of walls he can hide behind, if he goes upstairs—the way you saw him come down. Maybe—maybe he's over there now —just waiting—"

Mr. Pinkerton disengaged his feet from the afghan and put on his slippers, looking excitedly up at Dan McGrath. His face fell then.

"Well, it's not impossible, you know," he said timidly. "And I know I'd not be much use to anybody. But I could—I could stop out in the street, and—and whistle if anybody came."

He put two fingers in his mouth and gave a loud clear whistle.

"Of course, if it were Miss Caroline, I'd probably be too nervous to make much noise," he said sheepishly. "But if it were anybody else . . . Shouldn't we try it, Dan? It'd not do any harm if it turned out to be a—a washup—would it, really?"

Dan McGrath was shaking his head. Not at the idea, because it was one he had had for some moments entirely on his own. But letting the little Welshman go with him was a horse of a different color. He'd promised Bull to keep Mr. Pinkerton out of trouble. As the stark gaunt angles of the ruined house across the Square loomed vividly in his mind he was seeing again the dark slinking figure creeping down the staircase, and hearing again the hollow echo of the dislodged rubble as it dropped into the area under the street.

"No, Mr. P.," he said calmly. "Get that idea out of your head, and but quick, my friend. There's no use sticking your neck out. Remember what happened to Pegott?"

Mr. Pinkerton sat back on the sofa, crestfallen. He felt he had imposed on Dan's friendship, but he was rather disappointed, nevertheless, at his friend's lack of daring and initiative.

"Of course, if you'd rather just go to bed—" he could not help saying.

"Right," McGrath said cheerfully. "That's what we're both going to do."

"I do wish I'd found out what Eric bought at the ironmongers'," Mr. Pinkerton said.

"Probably a bolt for his door, if he's found out Betty's key is missing," Dan replied, and was more right than he knew at the moment.

17

IT WAS two hours later when he slipped quietly out of his own room and down the stairs. He stopped in the middle of the hall. Mary Winship was coming slowly up from the first floor. She looked tired and exhausted, very pale and very lovely.

"Mary!" He went quickly toward her.

She stopped, her hand on the newel post, and looked at him. She was too worn out to remember that he had offended her the night before.

"How is your mother, Mary?"

"She's better now. She's asleep at last."

"Mary—I'm sorry about last night. I didn't mean—"

"Oh, it's all right. It doesn't matter. Aunt Caroline says you've been to the police."

"Did you want me not to go?"

She shook her head. "No," she whispered. "No. But I don't believe it. I won't believe it till I've got to—that my father—"

She turned her head away.

"Gosh, I'm sorry, Mary." He wanted to put his arms around

her and comfort her if he could. But she seemed too remote and her despair too private and personal for him to intrude upon.

"I was over at Copey's when Miss Grimstead rang for him to come to Mother," she said. "He told me you could never tell what brain injuries might do. Oh, if I only had some money of my own and could get somebody not connected with the police to find him, and put him somewhere where he could be taken care of, if he's ill—I talked to my Uncle Elliot tonight. I'm going to see him again tomorrow."

She shook her head like somebody shaking off a bad dream.

"I'm so confused, between what I've wanted to believe and what I've got to believe. All my—my fairy castles seem to be collapsing at my feet."

"If I'm one, I haven't collapsed."

Dan grinned at her suddenly, grinning at his own effrontery as well. McGrath, the castle in Old Spain. She looked up at him quickly and laughed herself, half laughing and half crying too from sheer exhaustion.

"Oh, Mary!" She was in his arms then, not at all remote, the weight of her despair lifted with the enchantment of another heart to share it. "I'm going to take you away from here, Mary."

"Not yet. Not now." She drew away from him and turned her head, listening down the stairs. "Aunt Caroline *will* be shocked," she said. "I've got to go to bed."

"Not up here," Dan said sharply. "I thought you were downstairs—"

The fact that she was down with her aunt and mother, close to the street and the porters' room and offices, had been the reassurance he'd given himself ever since Mr. Pinkerton had told him about the missing key.

"I am, but Aunt Caroline's taken my room to be next to

Mother. Copey and Eric are in hers. So I'm in Eric's. But it's quite all right. Come look."

She moved over to the door of Eric's flat. It was at the rear of the house, a small sitting room with a bedroom opening off to the right. "There. You see?" She pointed to the door frame. A shining new brass bolt was fastened to the white painted wood, the other half fastened to the solid door. "I don't know what Grimstead's going to say when she finds out about it. Or why Eric thinks he's in any particular danger. He was working at it when I came up to call him to dinner. He'd not answered the phone."

It really was what Dalrymple-Hughes had gone to the iron-mongers' for, after all. Dan examined it critically. It was a solid if amateurish and not very neat job.

"I suppose it's on account of Pegott," Mary said. "I don't know who told him about Betty's key. Aunt Caroline heard about it from Sarah at tea. I suppose it's his conscience. He's being frightfully mysterious about something or other—I mean, seriously."

Dan tried the bolt, and the door with the bolt closed. He went into the bedroom and the bath and looked around. It was the only door to the flat, and the bedroom window opened on an enclosed air shaft down to the kitchen area. There was a second bolt on the bedroom door.

Dan went back into the sitting room. "I don't want you to stay here tonight," he said soberly. "I don't like it."

"I'm not afraid," Mary said calmly.

"I am."

"I'm not at all. Eric's always dramatizing himself for his own ends. I'm not nearly as worried about him as I am about—"

"About?"

She looked away for an instant. "Aunt Caroline, and my Mother. Aunt Caroline's frightened. I know she is. She says she's not, but I know. The way she breathes and sits there. She's frightened for herself, and for Mother too. That's why Copey's there tonight."

A soft tap at the door startled them both. Dan unbolted the door and opened it.

"Oh. Locked in, are you?"

Miss Myrtle Grimstead's shock at seeing him and seeing Mary there behind him in Eric's sitting room went through a kaleidoscopic series of gulps and grimaces to final articulation and a waggish shake of her red-tipped forefinger.

"You *are* naughty, aren't you? And poor old Grimstead, she didn't mean to intrude. She just came up to see if you were all snug and comfy. But she'll never breathe a word to anybody."

Miss Grimstead's tongue was moving on syrup-smooth, but she had spotted the bolt and lock fixed to the newly painted door and doorframe.

"Dear me!" Her managerial eyes sharpened and her lips tightened. "Dear me, it does look as if someone didn't wish to be disturbed. It does indeed."

Miss Grimstead backed out of the doorway with a waggish flutter of her pencilled eyebrows. "Don't let me disturb you. I should never think of disturbing either of you. But it *is* naughty of you, isn't it?"

She pulled the door shut behind her. There were two bright spots burning in Mary Winship's pale cheeks. Dan looked at her.

"Did she know you were here? Or did she come to see Eric?"

"Eric, I expect. He's—quite a pet of hers. I doubt if she much cares if I'm snug and comfy."

Dan McGrath's face was still sober as he let himself out the front door into the deserted Square. There was something very curious about the manageress checking on the comfort of her guests twenty minutes before midnight when the rest of the house was in silence, the lights in the halls reduced to a minimum. Mason was nowhere to be seen. Dan had looked for him on his way down to tell him to keep his eye on Mary's door. The office window was closed. Miss Grimstead had apparently vanished into her own apartments. There was no light under her door that Dan could see as he came down the last flight of heavily carpeted stairs.

In the street he glanced up at the Winships' flat. The curtains were drawn, but he could see a narrow ribbon of subdued light down the center of the middle window. Aunt Caroline would hardly be standing watch out in the garden with Mrs. Winship ill enough to need both her and Copeland on hand, and Eric there too.

Dan stopped and fished in his pocket for a cigarette. He was uneasy. He glanced across the garden at Number 22. It stood out like a single tooth in some disease-blackened gum, the luminous, almost frosty clearness of the night giving it strange dimensions, and a brooding emptiness that he had not felt in it before. Some trick of the light or of his own heightened imagination made it seem to have some quality of movement, as if it were stretching out strange inimical hands through the shadowy strip of trees and dark low-lying shrubs to the house he had just left. He knew it was absurd, and that the animate qualities he was endowing it with were ones it could not possess—the product of the hours he and the little Welshman had discussed it, as well as of the profound uneasiness he felt at leaving Mary back there, no matter how securely bolted behind her door.

He glanced back at the front door and started. A man was coming out, so quietly Dan had not heard the door open. Nor could he hear it being closed; he was only able to see that it was, and that the man was coming down the steps.

"Oh." Sidney Copeland recognized him first. "What are you doing out here?"

It was an abrupt and irritating demand.

"Just taking the air," Dan said. "What are you doing? I thought you were staying to look after Mrs. Winship. Let's both be rude, shall we?"

"Mrs. Winship has considerably improved. I have a full day tomorrow. I prefer to sleep in my own bed."

"It's always a good idea," Dan said. He was sorry as he said it. Copeland wasn't a bad sort. He was a friend and mainstay to the desolate woman who was Mary's mother. But somehow he managed to rub McGrath the wrong way. He was too damned British, Dan thought—aware that Copeland undoubtedly thought the same thing about him as an American. Manners might not make man, but they certainly could keep a couple of them from ever getting together.

"Good night, Mr. McGrath."

"Good night, Mr. Copeland."

It was ridiculous of both of them—the formal jerk that was the modern counterpart of the bow of another era before two men called in the seconds and arranged to meet at Richmond Deer Park at dawn.

"And I said he was probably Scott Winship in disguise." Dan grinned sardonically to himself in the dimly-lit street, and started walking in the opposite direction from that Mr. Sidney Copeland was taking. He heard the staccato echo of his footsteps in the empty Square, and heard his own, a longer and slower beat punctuating Copeland's precise rapid tread.

At the bottom of the Square, Dan slowed down and moved across the road to the wattle fence round the center garden. If Copeland had gone and Mrs. Winship was resting quietly, Aunt Caroline might come out . . . He came to a sagging place in the fence, put one long leg over it into the garden and pulled himself over. He went cautiously and quietly in among the straggling overgrown maze of unclipped shrubbery until he was through it and to the fence at the other side. He dropped his cigarette and crushed it out with his foot on the ground, looking up at the open stairway disappearing into the black imponderable shadows of the projecting portion of the roof. As Mr. Pinkerton had said, anybody could hide up there, waiting, watching—or, if a wanderer, could return with only a frail vestigial memory of a happy childhood to guide him, bewildered, struggling to reconstruct his destroyed life in its destroyed walls.

The stairway winding gracefully to the hall that had been, and was an open balcony, was empty. Dan followed it with his eyes, up to the second storey from the drawing room floor, trying in his own mind to reconstruct the house as he had seen it when he waited there in the Square during the war, hoping Mary would come out the street door, or that he'd see her look down out of the drawing room window upstairs, or a bedroom window on what he'd call the third floor but the English would call the second. All that was gone now, dissolved and powdered rubble.

His senses sharpened, suddenly alert. He had heard the same sound before—when the bit of rubble was dislodged and fell down into the dark cavernous hole that had been the cellars below the street; when the man had climbed over the wall before Miss Winship's voice had come out of the dark, freezing him into a solid stationary lump.

He went forward as noiselessly as he could, looking for a gate or a low place in the wattle fence. Then exactly what happened Dan McGrath never fully knew. It happened instantaneously. There were dark running figures on the stairway, a subdued shout from out of the black shadows, pounding feet on the hollow stairs, and as McGrath sprang forward to clear the fence, a hand gripped his arm in a vise of steel.

"Sorry, sir—you're Mr. McGrath? Sergeant Dick. Stay where you are, sir." The man released Dan's arm and sprang across the fence. Dan swallowed, staring across the darkness.

"Got him, sir!" He heard a voice, solid but triumphant. "Easy. Take it easy there. Get him to the car."

He could hear sounds of a struggle.

"Wasn't there another one, sir?"

It seemed to Dan there had been half a dozen, the garden suddenly alive with moving figures converging on the wall in front of Number 22. And as suddenly and silently melting away, or into the solid group around the man they'd taken, who was now quietly being led to the car parked toward the top of the Square. Dan watched in silence from his side of the wattle fence. He felt much like a small boy being rebuked for playing cops and robbers. He stood there with his arms hanging down at his sides, looking at the quiet street and at the car, backing to turn in the narrow strip of road.

It was a hollow sort of anti-climax, all so neatly and efficiently and quietly managed that he felt rather like a fool. "I guess Scotland Yard can manage without you, McGrath," he thought with a wry grin. He stood there. In a moment a man came along the road from where the car had been. Another car was coming into the Square. The two stopped as they passed, and the second one came on.

The man in the road called out. "Mr. McGrath? Sergeant Dick again, sir. I'm sorry I had to startle you. We've been waiting all evening—we didn't want things to go wrong."

"My fault," said McGrath the magnanimous.

"We're taking him to Divisional Headquarters, sir. Inspector Bull expected you might be about. He's meeting us there; he wants you to come along, if you don't mind, and see if you can identify him. He's bringing Constable Weedham from the Yard, too, sir."

Dan McGrath thought quickly. Weedham was the man Bull had told him Mr. Pinkerton had given the slip when Bull appointed him, McGrath, to take over unofficially. If he was bringing him along, and bringing McGrath in, it must mean he thought his catch was one of two people—either the man he had himself seen coming out of Pegott's room, or at his door, who'd said he was Elliot Winship, or the man who'd stopped Mr. Pinkerton outside the Corner House and said, "The wicked *shall* be repaid—*and* the good."

The officer in charge at the Divisional Headquarters in Solomon Street looked at the clock on the wall. "Inspector Bull will be here in a very few minutes, sir." He went back to his writing. It was twenty-five minutes to one o'clock. Dan read for the fourth or fifth time the notices of men and women wanted by the police and the list of personal and private property that had been stolen or otherwise illegally removed from the premises of their legitimate owners. He was thinking anxiously of Mary Winship, and how simply a quiet knock on her door would make her forget and open it . . .

"Here he is now, sir."

Bull nodded to him. He looked like what he was, a man who'd been routed out of his bed and a sound slumber to dress hastily and take up the chase again.

"He's along here, Inspector." A constable on duty opened the door and led the way through an antiseptic-smelling corridor to the block of cells on the floor below. "Given us a good deal of trouble, he has too, sir. Quite mad, in a quiet way, sir."

"I think I might recognize him, sir," Detective-Constable Weedham said. He and Dan followed the large figure of the Inspector.

"Here he is, sir."

Dan looked in through the barred door. Sitting on the edge of the narrow iron bed was the man the officers from Divisional Headquarters in Solomon Street had booked for trespassing on bombed-out property at Number 22 Godolphin Square. He did not look mad, nor did he look like a vicious type. In fact, Dan thought, he looked very near to tears.

He did not quite know what to do when Inspector Bull looked round at him.

"I asked you to take care of him for me, sir—"

Bull spoke with pained deliberateness. He turned to the constable. "Open up," he said. "Come out here," he said to Mr. Pinkerton.

Mr. Pinkerton came, slowly, trying hard to look as if he'd not really much rather be dead.

"I—I didn't mean any harm," he said wretchedly. "And he *was* there, Chief Inspector. I thought somebody ought to go, and Mr. McGrath wouldn't go with me. And he *was* there. I kept telling them there was another man, but they'd not listen to me. But there was another. He got off down the back stairs. Truly, Chief Inspector. He tripped me and threw me over."

Mr. Pinkerton straightened up a little. "And I can prove it."

He put a shaking hand in his grey coat pocket and pulled it out again. In it was a square of light brownish Harris tweed, more oatmeal-color, actually, than brown.

"It's—it's his coat pocket," Mr. Pinkerton said shakily. "I had got hold of him, and it tore loose when he jerked away and ran."

Dan McGrath took the square of tweed out of Bull's hand. He nodded slowly. "That's right, Inspector," he said. "That's the stuff my man's suit was made of—the man I saw at Pegott's door. I could see it when he got in the lift."

Inspector Bull took the small piece of cloth silently. His broad back was a solid wall of disapprobation as Dan, with Mr. Pinkerton scurrying miserably along beside him, followed the three police officers back along the antiseptic corridor. The officer at the desk was waiting, the telephone in his hand.

"It's the C. O. for you, sir."

"Bull here."

Dan and Mr. Pinkerton stopped as the Inspector spoke into the phone. He sounded still not unlike his namesake, put out and annoyed at some small beast of the field hidden among the buttercups. Then his big face sobered abruptly.

"Right," Bull said at last. "I'll be out there in five minutes."

He put down the phone and turned to Dan McGrath and the little man at his side. "There's more trouble at Godolphin Square. Mr. Eric Dalrymple-Hughes has been found murdered in his bed. His skull smashed with a sledge hammer."

18

M<small>R.</small> P<small>INKERTON</small> and Dan McGrath went back to Number 4 Godolphin Square from the Divisional Headquarters in Solomon Street, silent in the back seat of the police car, Inspector Bull silent in front with the driver, lost in a grim lethargy of thought that made his sudden physical and mental activity once they had got to Godolphin Square all the more surprising. They did not see Eric Dalrymple-Hughes, but following the Inspector, half automatically, into the Winship flat they saw Miss Caroline Winship. She was in the sitting room in the worn yellow satin chair, backed up against the fireplace, beleaguered and alone, her stick gripped in one hand, her heavy face working, livid and suffused, her brilliant eyes under their folded lids dull-glazed, with the paralyzed horror of one who had looked on Medusa's head, unable to turn away.

She seemed as if she had had some profound physical shock, a cerebral hemorrhage even, Dan thought, except that her hands opened and closed in sharp spasms, working as her heavy face worked. If she recognized either of them they had no way of knowing it. Her eyes moved over them to the closed door of her sister's room, and back, slowly and painfully, through them again to the other door, leading to her own room, where Bull and the police were, and all that remained of Darymple-Hughes lay in its final conflict with violence and death.

She shuddered horribly again, closed her eyes and bent her head down on her hand just as Bull opened the bedroom door and came out. The robust ruddiness of his own face had taken on the color of jaundiced putty.

"I'm sorry to disturb you, Miss Winship, but you must tell

us what happened here. The night porter tells me you called to him?"

She nodded painfully. "I'd gone to sleep, in my niece's room to be near my sister if she woke. Mason was cleaning the stair carpet. The vacuum woke me. I looked in on my sister. She was asleep, but I couldn't get back to sleep myself. I went in my room to get my medicine I'd left in here. I didn't turn on the light. I knew where it was on the table. I started back this way."

She motioned to the door he had come through.

"But he seemed so quiet. I stopped and listened. I thought he'd slipped out. I was annoyed, because I thought one night he could stay in if my sister and I wanted him. I switched on the light. I saw him."

A shudder racked her heavy body. She shut her eyes again, her mouth working in spasms of remembered horror.

"I must have fainted. I was on the floor when I tried to shout. I could hear the vacuum going, but I couldn't make him hear me. I crawled out and called to him. And he came. I should never have allowed him to sleep there. I never really believed—"

She broke off, strange dry sounds coming from her throat as she rocked her body back and forth. "He thought it was me," she managed to say then. "The blow was meant for me."

"What time did your nephew go to bed?"

"Early. Before the rest of us. He was cross and impatient, about eleven o'clock. Mary stayed down, and Copeland stayed until Louise seemed quiet for the night. Copeland decided to go home. I'd gone to bed when Mary went upstairs. Copeland was in here. He left a note."

She nodded toward the desk. "We were all exhausted. The vacuum outside the door was what woke me."

"Who does this belong to, Miss Winship?" Bull put his hand out to the officer behind him and took the thing he had been holding, the handle wrapped in a red-stained wash cloth. It was a small sledge hammer, the head smeared, dark and ghastly.

She looked away. "It was Eric's. He brought it downstairs with him. He said it was for—protection. I thought it was a joke, in very bad taste. Until—until I saw it lying on the counterpane when I switched on—"

An abrupt thin ringing sound from the bedroom cut her off. She turned her head sharply. "That's my alarm. Who set it for—"

She glanced quickly up at the Dresden clock on the mantel above her chair. It struck two soft lovely notes.

"Who set it for two o'clock? I keep it set at half-past seven. Why should anyone—why should Eric—?" She stared blankly at the bedroom door.

They went out into the hall. The police had persuaded the other tenants to go back to their rooms. Mason the night porter was there, and Miss Grimstead, clutching her old woolen bathrobe about her uncorseted hips, half managerial and half hysterical, at one moment ordering Mr. Pinkerton not to step on the cord of the vacuum cleaner, the next wringing her hands in the despair of the helpless.

"Mr. McGrath went out a few minutes before twelve," Bull said curtly. "Mr. Copeland a bit later. Where were you, Mason?"

"I was below in the kitchen, sir. Everyone was in by 'arf past eleven and I'd made tea for them that takes tea. It was my understanding Mr. Copeland was spending the night 'ere. I was down putting out powder for the cockroaches, sir. The chef's that touchy 'e don't believe in killing God's creatures." He jerked his head toward Miss Grimstead. "But as I told 'er, the guests are touchy too. They don't like God's creatures crawlin' all over the victuals they've got to eat."

"We have very few roaches, Inspector," Miss Grimstead came partially to herself. "And if the chef is a bit peculiar," she added tartly, "so are all good male cooks—all of them I've ever had to do with. And these days you can't pick and choose. You've got to make do with what you can get, and Mason knows it."

Bull intervened between the glowering porter and the tight-lipped manageress. "What time did you come back upstairs?"

"It was ten minutes to one, sir. I was late getting on with the stairs and 'alls. I started at the top and came down. I was through 'ere and down at the bottom." He motioned to the ground floor. "I'd never 'ave 'eard 'er, poor lady, but I kicked the cord, and when I tried to pull it down it got caught, and I 'ad to come up and unloose it. I'd never 'ave 'eard 'er in there groaning with the machine going. Pitiful it was, sir. 'Er in a 'eap on the floor by the door trying to make somebody 'ear. And 'im there on the bed—worse'n I ever see in the bombing, sir. That was at five-and-twenty to two o'clock, sir."

Bull pieced it together. From twelve, when Sidney Copeland left the house, no member of the staff was in the halls until Mason came up fifty minutes later. From then until approximately one-twenty, he was upstairs with the vacuum cleaner going. It was an old model, and Mason, cleaning up there with it, could hardly have heard anyone slipping down the heavily carpeted stairway. No phantom tread was needed at Number 4 Godolphin Square, at least not on the lower floors where the carpets were new and the pads not worn as they were on the third floor where Mr. Pinkerton and Dan McGrath lived.

Dan McGrath was trying to piece things together too. It

was half-past twelve when he got to the police station. It must have been at about quarter past when the melee broke out on the open staircase across the Square, leaving Mr. Pinkerton to hold the bag—and, Dan thought, the torn square of oatmeal-colored tweed. Why Eric Dalrymple-Hughes . . . Dan glanced along the hall to the door behind which Caroline Winship sat, alone with horror—and with terror, perhaps—in spite of the stolid figure in blue stationed there in the hall to protect her. She had refused to allow them to wake her sister or her niece or to call Sidney Copeland to come back.

"Of course, if he'd still got the key . . ." Mr. Pinkerton said in his small timid voice. He spoke in a hush that had fallen for a moment on the weary group in the hall as Inspector Bull chewed at the corner of his tawny mustache, his brow wrinkled and his mild blue eyes darkly troubled.

Bull turned slowly to him. "Key? What key?"

Mr. Pinkerton remembered, and caught his breath. "That Betty, the chambermaid, lost," he said weakly. "Or—or had stolen." He moistened his grey lips and tried to move a little closer to his friend McGrath.

Inspector Bull came as close to glaring as he had ever done —at Mr. Pinkerton, at Mason and at Miss Myrtle Grimstead.

"I have no idea what he's talking about," Miss Grimstead said tartly. "Mr. Pinkerton must be mistaken."

Bull looked at him, like a man counting not ten, or fifty, but a hundred, before he spoke.

"Where is the maid?" he asked patiently. "Does she live in?"

"She's not with us any longer," Miss Grimstead said. "She left without notice just before lunch. She'd got some wild tale that she'd rung up her young man and that he was afraid for her to stay on here and wanted to marry her at once. She certainly made no mention of a missing key to me, and Sarah said nothing about it this evening when it was time to turn down the beds."

"They—they were not turned down," said Mr. Pinkerton stoutly. "The girls were afraid to tell you the key was gone."

Inspector Bull was still looking at his unfortunate friend. He turned to the manageress and the night porter. "Leave the vacuum cleaner here," he said. "I'll see you in the morning, ma'am. Go on with your duties, Mason." He turned to the two officers with him. "Carry on," he said. "I'll be back down in a few moments."

Only Mr. Pinkerton and Dan McGrath were left there with him. He ignored McGrath.

"Pinkerton," he said. "Come up to your room. I should have known . . ." Dan had the impression of a man never overly articulate now utterly bereft of words. "You'll tell me all you know about this affair. If you don't, I'll—I'll put you behind bars and keep you there."

He did not add "till you rot," but there was no doubt in Dan's mind that it was what he meant. Or in Mr. Pinkerton's. He edged along the bannister to the stairs, and if he had been as seedy as Miss Grimstead would have said he could never have made it up as fast without really having a heart attack. Bull and Dan followed with a heavier and slower tread.

Outside the door of Eric Dalrymple-Hughes's flat Dan stopped. "I think it would be a good plan to look in on Miss Mary Winship, Inspector Bull," he said gravely. "She's got to know. She'd probably like to be with her aunt. And there's something here I think you ought to see."

Bull hesitated, and nodded. Dan rapped at the door, remembered there was a whole room for her to hear through, and knocked more loudly. He knocked again.

"Try the door, sir."

"It's bolted. That's what I wanted you to see. He bought two bolts at the ironmongers' this afternoon."

He put his hand on the knob as he spoke, turned it and pushed. The door opened. The light was on at the desk in front of the window. Dan went across the room.

"Mary!" The cold sweat stood on his forehead, pricking it sharply, and his voice was hoarse as he called her again. *"Mary!"* He went quickly to the bedroom door and opened it. The light was on there too and the room empty.

"Easy, sir. Take it easy."

Bull's quiet voice and solid bulk behind him were like brakes applied to a car careening madly down a road. Dan drew up sharply, his heart an icy lump. The bed had not been slept in. He looked around, and froze for an instant into rigid intensity. There was a wardrobe—like Pegott's wardrobe—against the wall between the fireplace and the window looking down into the air shaft to the kitchen area. He went across the room white-faced and put his hand out.

"Steady, sir. You'd best let me do that."

Bull was at his side, but he had already jerked the wardrobe door open. There was nothing in there but Eric's suits and over-coat and a neat row of shoes propped up by their heels on a rack at the bottom. Dan took out his handkerchief and wiped the icy sweat off his forehead. His hands were shaking.

"Where do you suppose she's gone?"

The Inspector was looking at the shoes, calmly removing one pair after another, looking at them attentively and deliber-ately.

"She was going to bed when I left her. She promised to bolt both doors and not let anybody in."

Bull put down the last pair of shoes. He looked at the bolt on the bedroom door, and round the room.

"She's left all the lights on," he said soberly. "There's no sign of anything wrong. She must have gone out purposely. I'd not worry, sir. It looks as if she's safer outside this house than in it."

He went back into the sitting room. "If you knew where she'd be likely to go . . ."

"I don't." Then Dan remembered that he did know. There were two places: her uncle's in St. Giles's Terrace, and the place in the Adelphi she'd gone to from the train in Watterloo the first night he was in London—the night he'd found her again after six years of waiting. And Bull could stand there, stolid and imperturbable. McGrath was made of hastier metal. He took one look at the Inspector, said "I'm going after her," and went out. Bull got to the door in time to see him going down the stairs three at a time. He stopped, halfway to the stairs himself, shook his head, went back into the murdered man's bedroom and opened the wardrobe again, thinking about the bad moment he had himself had until McGrath had jerked the door out. He had felt the cold sweat on his own brow, and he had seen Eric Dalrymple-Hughes, as McGrath had not done.

He started methodically to work on the pockets of the suits hanging on the brass rod at the top of the cupboard. In less than a half hour he closed the door of the flat and went on up to Mr. Pinkerton's third floor bed-sitting room. Somewhere in that half hour a faint ray of light had begun to glimmer, though he had found only two things of interest in the small flat. Like Pegott, Dalrymple-Hughes had planned a voyage. Unlike Pegott, he had apparently been content to travel in a sterling area, where he could spend pounds and not be restricted by travel and currency regulations. It was interesting to Bull because the cheque book locked in his desk drawer showed a balance of three pounds, eight shillings and sevenpence—adequately explained, he thought, by the second item of interest, which was the counterfoil of the last cheque drawn. It was in the amount of one hundred pounds, and the entry on the counterfoil was "Self for A. Peg."

Bull opened the door of Mr. Pinkerton's room.

"Well, Pinkerton," he said.

"Well, Inspector." Mr. Pinkerton adjusted his spectacles and glanced apprehensively past Bull's great cinnamon-brown bulk. "Where—what have you done with my friend Mr. McGrath?"

"Your friend Mr. McGrath has gone out to find his friend Miss Winship," Bull said placidly.

"Oh, dear," Mr. Pinkerton said. He shook his head dismally. "I—I'm afraid this is all a very dangerous business," he said timidly. He glanced hesitantly up at the Inspector, and took courage. "Dan McGrath can say it's because I'm so—so repressed that I have to escape into what he calls bizarre whimsy all he likes—but I still think, Chief Inspector, that . . . Well, if you'd sit down a moment, I could tell you what I think."

He went on, even though it really was fantastic, the Inspector listening silently and gravely, and to Mr. Pinkerton's surprise even nodding his head, almost, from time to time.

19

THE impelling need, as national and characteristic in Dan McGrath as Bull's stolid patience was in him, to translate his anxiety into some form of action however irrational, succumbed abruptly to an equally native common sense and pragmatic realism as he pounded along toward the bottom of the Square. This was London. The chances of his finding a taxi in these parts at three o'clock in the morning were nil. If Mary was at her Uncle Elliot's, charmingly vague though Uncle Elliot was he could easily be expected to be pretty sore also, routed out of bed a second time, first by his niece and second by McGrath. The occupants of Adam Street, Adelphi, would no doubt be the same, especially as he did not know the particular flat or the particular house even that Mary had planned to go to the night he'd stopped her there, under the street light, in front of a whole block of houses and flats.

Stopping to figure it out, he could see no reason to think she would go to either place anyway. She would have had to stop in her own room and get her bag and coat, at the risk of waking her aunt. He stood at the end of the Square, frowning, his anxiety, that had been so acute when he saw her empty bed and had relaxed somehow at the idea she was at her uncle's or Adam Street—away from Godolphin Square, actually—seeping back into his mind, sharpening again. He looked at the dark rectangle of the garden down the center of the Square, at the clumps of black rhododendron, remembering Caroline Winship out there in the night. He also remembered the invisible hand of Detective-Sergeant Dick that had reached out and held him in his tracks. He looked over at the gaunt remains of Number 22, silent and deserted now after the abortive flurry of the attempt to catch the phantom of the dark.

He went round the end of the wattle fence, toward the bombed house, staying on the soft ground so as not to attract the attention of Bull's driver, dozing behind the wheel of the car in front of Number 4. Across the road from Number 22 he stopped, hidden in the shadow of the fence and the over-grown shrubs, his eyes intent on the open staircase and the pale expanse of plastered wall rising up to the dense black shadow cast by the broken projecting roof. There was no sound except the shivering claque in the plane trees overhead. It was like some child's game that had taken on a real and frightening signifi-cance, as if he had asked "Am I warm?" with none to answer but the dry dead lips of the ghosts whispering in the sear and yellow leaves.

Then he knew suddenly he was not alone. There was some-one in the garden across the fence.

He took two steps in that direction. "Who's there?" He meant to keep his voice down, but it was sharpened as he thought he heard behind him something that sounded like a low moan. It could have been only the breeze in the plane trees, or a swinging damper somewhere among the chimneypots.

A quiet voice answered him. "It's me, sir—Dick again."

The detective from Divisional Headquarters eased himself over the wattle fence. "I came back after our little fiasco, sir. Did you hear something over there? I've been here half an hour. It's seemed all quiet, but I thought I heard something just now. There it is again."

He went across the narrow strip of road to the barrier in front of the ruined house, Dan beside him. They stopped there, listening. A soft moan that was not the breeze in the treetops or a whirling damper in a chimneypot came again from somewhere on the other side of the barrier. It was followed by a slow scraping sound, as if a foot moved painfully, grating over the rubble and fallen plaster. Sergeant Dick jerked his electric torch forward. A sharp beam of yellow light pierced the black emptiness of the cellars, its bright arc describing the broken masonry before it leapt up to the balcony and reached the graceful hanging stairs, flying down it then until it reached the bottom, and stopped with an abrupt jerk on the dark slight figure huddled in an unconscious heap on the stone floor at the foot of the stairs.

Dan was across the barrier, clearing the open space that dropped down into the area with a leap that had only fool's luck to commend it. "Mary!" He knelt down, gripping her cold hands, and bent to listen to her heart. "She's alive." His voice sounded not like his. "Let's get her out of here."

Sergeant Dick threw the torch beam on the solid strip of masonry that had been the wall between this and the house next door and that went to the street. "Steady, sir. I'll give you a hand." He stopped for an instant, listening intently, and swept the torch around, up the stairs, into the black hollows on either side of them, before he helped Dan pick the girl up. "Careful, sir. Watch your footing here."

Dan carried her across the Square, running, the Sergeant ahead of him opening the wattle gates. When they came to Number 4 the porter on the ground floor turned, staring.

"Call Mr. Sidney Copeland," Dan said. "Get hold of him right away."

The lift was too narrow and too slow. He carried her up the stairs, Mason with him fumbling for his key.

"Here's 'er flat, sir."

"I'm taking her upstairs where we can bolt her in," Dan said curtly. "Where's Inspector Bull?"

He was coming down from the third floor, took the last three steps in one and was at Eric's door before Mason.

"Get a doctor," Dan said urgently. "Call Sidney Copeland, won't you?"

"We'll get a doctor." Bull looked at the girl, put his hand on her pulse, lifted her eyelid with his thumb and forefinger. "She's coming round, sir. I'll not get Copeland, I think. One of our own men. Mason, you get Miss Grimstead."

He went across the room and picked up the telephone. "Put me on to Scotland Yard." He turned back. "Dick, you go over to that house—go through it from cellar to garret. Get two men on it with you. Keep a watch there till I tell you to take it off."

Dan put the girl gently down on the bed. "You're taking Mr. Scott Winship seriously at last?" .

It was an offensive thing to say and he knew it, but he was in an offensive mood.

"I've taken him seriously from the beginning, sir," Bull said.

Mr. Pinkerton crept quietly back into his room and closed the door. From his crow's nest at the top of the stairs, peering over the bannister rail, he had seen Miss Grimstead come running up to the flat that had been Dalrymple-Hughes's. He had seen the doctor come, and a young woman in the uniform of a nursing sister but who looked very much like a young woman he had once seen at New Scotland Yard in a uniform of a different sort. Bull had not left, nor had Dan McGrath, but Miss Grimstead had gone, stopping outside the door and leaning against the wall a moment in such patent relief that he had not needed Mason to tell him Miss Mary had come round, with no bones broken, and was now asleep under a sedative.

"And you'd best go to bed, sir," Mason had said very sensibly, as Mr. Pinkerton's teeth were chattering as effectively as if they had all been his own. "I've got to get on with my work."

So Mr. Pinkerton was back in his own room. He felt worn out and exhausted, like an orange that Inspector Bull's patient interrogation had squeezed the last drop of juice, even pulp, out of and thrown into the gutter for the dustmen to pick up and carry away in their burgundy-colored sacks and bags. Except that he did not smell quite like an orange. He still smelled unpleasantly of antiseptic from his brief stay in the Solomon Street gaol. In stir, like an old lag, he thought wretchedly. He glanced at himself in the mildewed mirror, not able to tell, quite, whether it was mildew or prison pallor, or whether his face merely wanted washing. He took off his clothes and put on his patched nightshirt, too tired, really, to make the trip to the washroom until he decided the washing might remove the antiseptic memory as well as dirt.

He put on his slippers and got his soap and towel from the rack inside the wardrobe. He did not put on his dressing gown. The stripes were a little too gay, as tired as he was, and McGrath was belowstairs and Pegott was dead, so no one would see him. Nevertheless, he peered cautiously out into the hall before he slipped out of his room and scurried along the darkened corridor to the bathroom door. He opened it, and stopped petrified in his tracks, sure finally and with no possible room for let or doubt that he had completely and irretrievably lost the last vestiges of his mind and the last tattered remnant of any sanity he had ever possessed. He was staring directly at himself. He was there in the doorway, but he was also there inside the bathroom, himself in his long white nightshirt, wanting only his slippers and his steel-rimmed lozenge-shaped spectacles.

He had left his spectacles on the bureau under the mildewed mirror, so that the image of himself staring back at him had blurred and confused lines. He could still see, however, what he was doing. He was brushing his hair with the chef's silver-backed hairbrush.

"Oh, dear, dear, I *am* balmy," he muttered to himself, and tried to edge back out of the doorway. Then he blinked violently, moistened his particularly dry lips and tried to swallow when suddenly the other figure of himself put down the hairbrush and padded with horny toes and calloused feet scraping on the waxed floor covering directly toward him, one finger raised, pointing at his palpitating chest.

"The wicked *shall* be repaid—*and* the good!"

Mr. Pinkerton, gulping, edged back into the hall. The other man, barefooted in the long nightshirt, padded along with him. Mr. Pinkerton's heart felt as if it was in his mouth choking him. He edged round surreptitiously so he could back down the hall to his own door. But the man stopped. He raised his bony finger and spoke again.

"Stone walls do not a prison make, nor iron bars a cage!" With that he turned and strode like a prophet, barefooted, his nightshirt flapping about his bony ankles, along the hall to the door of the room next to Pegott's. He opened it and looked back at Mr. Pinkerton. Then he bowed.

"A very good night to you, sir. Vengeance is mine, saith the Lord."

Mr. Pinkerton was alone in the hall. "Oh, mercy me!" he said, and ran the rest of the way to his room. He would have pushed the bureau across to block his door, but it was heavy and he did not want to make any noise. As Miss Grimstead had said, however, you had to make do with what you could get, these days. That could apply to a chair as well as a chef. He could get the chair in front of the door, and did, quietly but with considerable relief before he sank down on the side of his bed and wiped the cold sweat off his brow with the sleeves of his patched and worn nightshirt.

"Peculiar" seemed to him a very mild word for Miss Grimstead to have used. He thought for a moment of going downstairs and telling the Inspector, but he gravely doubted if he had strength enough to go out of his door again in the close future. "And I must get myself some pyjamas," he thought as he laid his head on the pillow and closed his weary eyes.

20

INSPECTOR BULL left the Bulls' semi-detached villa in Hampstead at half-past seven o'clock that morning. He had got in three hours' sleep, a bath, a shave and a clean shirt. He had also got a report of the young woman on duty with Mary Winship, who was still asleep. Mr. McGrath had been persuaded to go to his own room and go to bed shortly before five. The rest of Number 4 Godolphin Square was apparently quiet and apparently secure.

Bull's first call was in Wimpole Street. He found Sidney Copeland at breakfast.

"I want to talk to you about Mrs. Winship's illness, sir."

"I'm not the physician, you understand? I'm a surgeon. But I did discuss it with him at length. It's a psychotic disturbance, Inspector. In effect, an allergy upsetting her vasco-motor system. Apparently connected with the memory of her husband, and his reappearance in several forms."

"The flowers, for example, sir?"

"Right," Copeland said. He put down his coffee cup. "The flowers. You understand, Inspector, this is difficult for me. I've been very fond of Louise Winship for a great many years. I've waited to marry her for a long time. There have been times when she's agreed to take legal action to free herself from this man, but each time she's had a serious attack of her asthma."

"You really want to marry her, sir?" Inspector Bull asked deliberately.

Sidney Copeland's ascetic face reddened. "I've said so, Inspector." He pushed his chair back. "If you will come with me, I'll give you as much of the history of Mrs. Winship's illness as I can, as briefly as I can. We're both busy men. I'm sorry I was not called in when Mary was found last night."

"This morning, it was," Bull said. "We preferred to have—another opinion."

"Unbiassed?" Copeland looked at him, raised his brows and opened the door into his surgery. "Sit down, Inspector."

Bull stopped forty-five minutes later at Guillaume's, Florist, Tottenham Court Road.

"My father and his assistants were killed when the shop was bombed out in Oxford Street," the manageress said resentfully. "Most of our records were destroyed. These are what are left. I came down early to get them out for you. Sophie talks about things she doesn't know about. I'd sack her if I could get anybody else. I can't tell you much—this is all I know."

His third stop was in the Strand at the offices of the building concern where Nancy Pulham was secretary to the manager.

"Here they are, Inspector Bull." She handed him a bundle of papers tied with a brown shoe lace. "Father would love to know he'd helped you any way. He'd always been going to write a book, so give them all back to me—some day I'd like to write it for him or get somebody who can. I've taken out all the references to the Winship case for you. It was always his favorite case, you know. Mother called it 'Pulham's Folly.' He called it 'The Doctor's Dilemma.' He'd be surprised to know Mr. Copeland's got ahead the way he has done."

His fourth stop was his own small office overlooking the Embankment. He hung up his hat and stood at the window a moment, looking through the plane trees, watching a coal barge move slowly up the Thames until it disappeared under the bridge. Big Ben's solemn deep-tongued voice boomed out nine of the clock. He turned to his desk and picked up the telephone.

"Send him along," he said patiently. Then he took out his horn-rimmed spectacles and polished them thoughtfully for several minutes before he perched them on the end of his nose.

"Well, Pinkerton," he said. "What is it now?"

Mr. Evan Pinkerton sidled into the office. He always sidled nervously in there, as if he were in some kind of invisible custody, yet with the concerted forces of Law and Order hot on his heels.

"It—it was the chef, Chief Inspector," he stammered. "He's the one that thinks the wicked shall be repaid . . . He wasn't away last night, he was there. I saw him. And—if he doesn't believe in poisoning roaches, he'd be hardly likely to be poisoning Mrs. Winship. So my theory's gone. Although I expect that doesn't necessarily follow," he added hopefully.

Bull waived the point. "The chef was preaching in Hyde Park the afternoon Pegott was killed," he said patiently. "A constable reported about him. He was standing by because a couple of young ruffians were heckling the man in a threatening manner. He was also quite safe last night." Bull smiled faintly. "He was like you. In gaol. He was trying a competition with a Communist street meeting in Lambeth and was taken into protective custody. They sent him home shortly after one o'clock. There was a report here when I looked in on my way home this morning."

He eased himself back into his chair. "He's quite harmless, they say, except out on the street when he sees a—a brand to pluck from the burning."

His sober face lighted again, slightly, for an instant. "I expect your sins have found you out, Pinkerton. Anything else?"

Mr. Pinkerton shook his head. He was nevertheless a little relieved that the chef had been talking about his own stone walls and iron bars, not about Mr. Pinkerton's. He hesitated for an instant. "You told me to tell you everything I could think of, Chief Inspector. I've not been able to think of anything else except one thing that is very trivial. Miss Winship called me 'Mr. Pilkington' once. I expect she was put out, at the moment, because she thought Dan was an American antique dealer trying to buy her mantelpiece."

Mr. Pinkerton was really only trying to gain time, hoping that perhaps Bull would break down and tell him something. But the Inspector gave no sign of breaking down anything except possibly the chair that he was leaning his enormous bulk backward in.

"Well, good-bye, Chief Inspector. I expect you'll be out later?"

"I expect so," Bull said. "Cheerioh."

He watched Mr. Pinkerton close the door and listened to his scurrying footsteps along the narrow corridor. He pushed up his horn-rimmed glasses then and started going through Inspector Pulham's notes one by one, reading them soberly and carefully while another part of his mind wandered up and down, in and out, round the intricate maze of fact and surmise, impression and doubt, that he was immediately concerned with, picking a path here and abandoning it at a dead end there, assorting and reassorting, trying to reach out and grasp the frail thread that would lead through the dark labyrinth.

Suddenly he took off his glasses and put them sharply down on the desk, in effect discarding them—saying, in effect, "How blind I have been." If he had not been blind, he would have seen it all clearly without the aid of written words. He sat there for a moment, reached down and pulled open the drawer that had the neatly labelled exhibits the Prosecutor would take to Court. A small sledge hammer, not the one that Eric Dalrymple-Hughes had been killed with but another, taken from the room Sophie Barnes had led them to the night before, where she had met Pegott in his pied-à-terre in Bayswater. He looked at it a moment, and the cold chisel that had been with it, wrapped in a towel marked "4 Godolphin Square" in Pegott's bureau drawer. He put them back, took up the book that had been in Pegott's despatch case, taken out by Dan McGrath and finally given to Bull when McGrath had decided to tell everything he knew. He turned to the page he had marked with a slip of paper.

"Of special interest to me," wrote the Boston McGrath, "has been a small picture reputedly a Dutch Master, sold by an Englishman, reputedly a gentleman, for what in these days of less enthusiastic purchases of old canvas seems a fairly large sum.

The opinion of the dealer who bought the picture but never received it—and which he freely admits was second-sight in view of the circumstances surrounding the transaction—was that the owner was aware it would not stand up to present-day microscopic and X-ray tests, which were agreed upon at the time of sale. Dealers are human, and loathe to admit their errors. In this particular instance, however, error was the easier to admit as the dealer suffered no loss, either in his pocket or his prestige, as his mistake has never come to light for his fellows to see and point their fingers at.

"The picture quietly disappeared, the family quietly made restitution. It would not be the first time that a reputed old master has vanished, or been taken off the market, before its authenticity could be determined. Nor the first time that an heir has found his heirloom Chippendale to have been made in Grand Rapids, Michigan. If the family has money enough, they are frequently glad to draw in their horns and continue to point out Great-great-grandfather's Chippendale to undiscerning friends, not to dealers. *Caveat Emptor!*"

Bull closed the book and let his eyes rest for a moment on Inspector Pulham's dog-eared notes.

"Caveat Emptor," he thought. Let the buyer beware. He shook his head silently. He had come very close to being a buyer himself; he had just next to bought Inspector Pulham's *idée fixe.*

He pushed the notes back and got to his feet. Pegott's luggage was stacked neatly in one corner of the small room. He went over to it, opened the despatch case that had been lying on the murdered man's bed, and stood looking down at it. He went back to his desk and picked up the telephone.

"Put me on to Inspector Carson. I'm not going to the inquest on Arthur Pegott," he said when the inspector was on. "Adjourn it as soon as possible, for further information." He made two other calls, thought a moment, and took up the phone a fourth time. "Put me on to Mr. Sidney Copeland in Wimpole Street."

"Inspector Bull here," he said when he heard the surgeon's dry precise voice. "I have to ask you to go to 4 Godolphin Square, Mr. Copeland. I've put a nurse with Mrs. Winship. I'll be there to talk with her in a few minutes. I think it would be wise for you to be present. I know you've a full day ahead, sir. I think it would be better if you come of your own accord."

He put the phone down and got up. Big Ben was striking ten slow sonorous notes from the tower above the Houses of Parliament on the river embankment. He listened until the last note died above the hoot and clamor of motor traffic across Westminster Bridge and the scurry of the taxis and trams in the street below. He looked at his watch, got his hat ond put it on, ignoring the telephone ringing on his desk. It rang again as he opened the door, a short and somehow urgent demand that made him stop, close the door and go back.

"Bull here." He listened, intently after the first few words. "Repeat that."

The voice in his ear came from the sergeant on duty downstairs.

"A man here says his name is Winship, sir, and you're looking for him. He's come to give himself up. He says to tell you his coat is torn—the pocket has been pulled off, sir."

Inspector Bull took his hat off mechanically, and dropped it on his desk. He stared blankly out of the window, for an instant, at nothing.

"Send him up," he said.

He put the phone down. His mild blue eyes, sober and not a little perplexed, moved from Inspector Pulham's notes to the book written by the Boston McGrath, and from there to the drawer of exhibits, and across the room to Pegott's despatch case on top of the pile his luggage made in the corner. He stood there for several moments, moved around then to his chair and sat down, leaning forward, his eyes fixed on the door.

21

D<small>AN</small> M<small>C</small>G<small>RATH</small> tapped lightly on the door of Dalrymple-Hughes's second-floor flat and waited. He was back from the inquest on Arthur Pegott, an hour and a half lost getting there and back, with the coroner's proceedings taking seven and one-quarter minutes before they were adjourned until another day. Mr. Pinkerton had not showed, nor the man he was supposed to look for, nor anyone he could conceivably imagine to be the little Welshman's friend calling down anathemas on unrepentant sinners. There was no one he had ever seen before, and not even Inspector Bull. He rapped impatiently on the door again. It was eleven o'clock and he still had not seen Mary.

"Oh sir, she's gone downstairs." Sarah, the maid who had taken Betty's place, put her head out of the door of the flat across the hall. "The nurse helped her down. She *is* a sight, sir. It's a blessing she wasn't killed too, I expect, if you want to look at it that way. A detective was here talking to her too, sir."

"Thanks." Dan started down the stairs. He had a certain

not unnatural reluctance about barging in on the Winships again; but it was no place for Mary, and he was going to get her out. Scotland Yard might well be tops, taken over a hundred years, but they were too blasted casual to suit McGrath—too casual and too damned deliberate. It was good the British were law-abiding people, or the whole population could get its throat cut while Inspector Bull sat on his derriere. He knocked at Miss Winship's door.

"Oh," he said. "You're here."

Mr. Sidney Copeland equally repressed any enthusiasm he may have felt at seeing Dan McGrath on the other side of the door.

"Is there something you wish, sir?" His hand stayed on the door.

"Yes. I wish to see Mary. If it's all the same to you."

Come on, McGrath. Stop being a bloody fool. Be nice to the gentleman.

"I'd like very much to see her, sir. Sorry to have to bother you."

"Come in."

He went in as Copeland stood aside.

"Hi, there." It was all he could say, seeing her, and she was all he did see, for a blurred profoundly grateful moment, sitting up in a big chair, in her dressing gown, one taped ankle resting on an ottoman, one wrist taped and a square patch of white bandage where her dark curly hair had been shaved away from the cut on her head.

"You're a cute looking mess," he said. The side of her face was scraped and there was a patch over one eye. But she was smiling at him, and words didn't matter a great deal. He took her good hand and squeezed it, bent down and kissed her softly on her good cheek, and on her lips. "Gosh," he whispered, aware then that his semantic approach must sound exceedingly vulgar to Sidney Copeland.

It was then that he saw the rest of them—Mrs. Winship, frail but apparently surprisingly fit after her attack of the day before, the white-clad nursing sister on the sofa beside her, and Caroline Winship.

He saw her with a shock that jolted him to the soles of his shoes. She was still in the yellow chair, but it had been moved. It was no longer backed up against the fireplace like a beleaguered throne. It was beside the desk, turned so that her back was toward the door. Miss Winship faced the window looking out onto the Square. She had her stick gripped in her hand, her head bent forward like some great, silently brooding figure from Michelangelo, passionately alive in spite of the heavy-lidded eyes, still glazed, that were fixed out of the window, not seeing him, or if she saw him ignoring him as if he were not there. Mary put her hand up, touched his lightly and shook her head. Until she did, he had not realized how he was staring at her aunt, and he turned away quickly.

Sidney Copeland was winding up a roll of bandage. "I think you'll be fairly comfortable, now." He managed to ignore Dan too. Only Mrs. Winship seemed interested in his being there. She smiled at him from her pillows on the sofa. He went over to her.

"I hope you're better," he said, and stepped back as the nurse executed an unobtrusive but neat movement that seemed somehow to prevent him from coming close to her patient.

Mary held her hand out to him with a quick smile. "Why don't you bring a chair over here by me, Dan," she said. "Or sit down here on the ottoman." She moved her sprained foot over to make room for him. It was reassurance McGrath badly needed. He felt awkward and ill at ease. Mary and her mother were the only ones who seemed to want him there, but Mary's wanting him was enough. He sat down by her feet and touched the taped ankle gently.

"Hurt?"

She shook her head. "No. It's all right now."

"What happened? Can you tell me?"

He glanced at her aunt in the yellow chair.

"It's quite all right, they all know," Mary said quickly. "It was stupid, that's all. I thought you were going over there to find him. I thought you knew. So I followed you out. I saw you speak to Copey, from Mason's window downstairs, and then I saw you at the top of the Square, and going through the garden. I was this side when everything happened. Only I didn't come in. I—I waited, and then I went over, by myself. For a long time I've—well, I've wanted to go back and go up those stairs. So I— I climbed over the barrier and went up. I was at the top before I realized that—that anybody was still there. He came up out of the back stairs. He ran when he saw me. He ran down and got in the street, and I started after him. I tripped on something and fell. I must have hit my head on the iron rail, because that's all I remember. I don't remember falling all the way down. That's where you found me, wasn't it?"

Dan nodded. "He . . ." He hesitated. It was a hard question to ask. "He didn't strike you, then? Honest?"

She shook her head. "Really. He seemed as startled as I was. I don't think he saw me at all—not to see who I was, I mean. Of course he wouldn't recognize me. But he just sort of gasped and cut and ran for it."

"You were a fool to go." Caroline Winship's voice was grating. "I told you to keep away from there. You might have been killed too."

"I'm sorry. I shouldn't have—"

"Be still!"

Caroline Winship raised her hand peremptorily. She pulled herself forward in the chair.

"What is that? Who are those men?"

She struck the floor with her stick. Her voice rose. "Who are those men!" she exclaimed again. Her free hand shot out, pointing in an imperative gesture through the window across the Square.

"What are they doing there? What are they doing in my house? What right have they—"

As she struggled to raise her heavy body upright, Dan moved across the room, and standing behind the yellow chair followed the intense staring gaze of the brilliant heavy-lidded eyes.

"An Englishman's house is his castle . . . all the winds of heaven may whistle through it, but the King cannot . . ." The words remembered from his schoolday history flashed ludicrously into his mind. He was astonished, looking out through this window for the first time, to see how close the ruins of Miss Winship's house were, and how clearly he could see the frail and delicate hanging staircase and the open balcony formed by the transverse hall, with no branches of yellowed leaves to obstruct the view. Something Mr. Pinkerton had said that first day flashed into his mind also: Miss Winship had bribed the gardener to prune away the branches that shut off her sight of the bombed house from the window where she always sat, eternally brooding.

It was like being in the front row of the balcony in a theater,

Dan thought suddenly, watching the balcony scene from *Romeo and Juliet,* with the pale sun spotlighting the stage, the dead leaves blown about on the ground by sharp gusts of wind, the disorderly impatient crowds in the pit, and the half-dozen men from the two cars pulled up in the road—the Capulets and Montagues in modern dress, armed, not with swords and pikes, but with pickaxes and crowbars.

Miss Caroline Winship's heavy voice beat angrily through the room. "Who are they? What are they doing? They're trying to steal my staircase and my mantels! Copeland!"

She turned toward the room, gesturing with her stick at the telephone. "Copeland—put me on to my solicitor!"

Sidney Copeland, startled, came across the room toward her.

"Don't excite yourself, Caroline. You'll—"

The rap on the door cut him sharply off. There was a short silence in the room. Miss Winship gripped the wing of the yellow chair with one hand. Her voice was again the hoarse cry of the beleaguered despot as she faced the door. "Who's there?"

Copeland took a step toward it before it opened and Inspector Bull came in. Dan McGrath, watching silently, had the curious impression that something else had come in with his stolid and burly figure—the dignity and authority of the English law.

Inspector Bull had a paper in his hand. "I have a warrant for the search of the premises at Number 22 Godolphin Square, Miss Winship," he said. "It is your privilege to be present while we make the search, if you wish to do so."

"No," Caroline Winship drew herself erect. "No."

Dan McGrath was hardly aware of the legal formalities, or even of little Mr. Pinkerton, like a small grey skiff trailing in the wash of the law's majestic craft. He was staring past Bull and past Mr. Pinkerton at the third man easing himself uncomfortably into the room behind them. He had on a raincoat, but his trousers legs were of tweed that was more oatmeal than brown in color, and his sandy greying hair was rumpled. It was lighter in Miss Winship's sitting room than it had been on the attic third floor, between the lift and Arthur Pegott's room; but even then Dan had the same instant impression of baggy tweeds, a slight build, an indefinable air of good breeding. The man was far from peering at him now with quietly amused interest, but he was the man Dan had seen up there with his hand on Pegott's door.

22

THE man came on into the room, diffident and hesitant, and Dan McGrath, still staring at him, was suddenly aware that the man was looking at him. He had a slightly shamefaced look, then, and a deprecatory and apologetic smile.

"I say, awfully sorry, my dear fellow," he murmured. "Not sporting, you know. Not sporting at all."

Caroline Winship's voice had sunk to a soft whisper, an iron threat in a velvet tongue.

"Get out of my house, Elliot."

"I have asked Mr. Elliot Winship to come here, Miss Winship," Bull said coolly.

Sidney Copeland stepped forward from where he had halted on his way to the door. He had an abrupt authority of his own. "It's my professional duty to warn you, Inspector, that Miss Winship is not a well woman. She has suffered a slight cerebral hemorrhage—a stroke—last night, as a result of finding her nephew killed in his bed. Any undue excitement and nervous strain at this time . . . I shall hold you personally responsible."

Miss Winship was still gripping her stick in one hand, the wing of the chair in the other, her hooded eyes alive and brilliant with passion, fixed on the man who was Scott Winship's brother. She moved them slowly to Copeland as he spoke. Her lips curled in a mirthless smile of contempt as she turned without a word, wrenching her chair forward. She sat there, her shoulders and head thrust forward, her vivid gaze making an almost tangible path through the window and across the garden to the house across the Square. Her face was suffused and dark with anger.

Bull turned to Louise Winship, sitting white as death itself on the sofa, the nurse beside her almost vulgarly alive in contrast to the woman leaning back, one transparent hand gripping her throat as if she also expected a recurrent attack of her own malady, waiting for it in fear and despair.

"Mrs. Winship," he said soberly. "You have never told anybody the truth about this matter."

A muffled hacking sound and the thud of heavy blows came through the window, falling like a hollow period punctuating his quiet accusation. A shuddering groan came from Caroline Winship's lips. "They're stealing my mantelpiece . . ." She lunged forward and threw up the window. The hacking sounds of the pickaxes came clearly across the Square.

"It's time for you to tell the truth now, Mrs. Winship." Bull looked steadily down at her. "When your husband left the farm in Kent, you knew he was not coming back—not for some time. Did you not, Mrs. Winship?"

Louise Winship gripped her throat more tightly with her frail bloodless hand, and bent her head forward in assent.

"More than that. You knew he was going to sell the picture. He had got your permission to sell it. Had he not?"

"Yes." She breathed the word rather than spoke it.

"You knew he had sold it and gone to Paris. That's why you waited in Kent until the day before the dealer was to come to take the picture. Because you thought your husband had the money, and had got safely to the Continent."

Through the open window the hack-crash-thud of the men across the Square stopped momentarily, and continued again with a new rhythm. Dan McGrath looked over there past the plane trees. The carved Adam mantelpiece was gone. It stood against the wall at the foot of the staircase going fantastically on up to the open sky. The fragile pink damask torn from the overmantel hung on the delicate ornamental stair rail, flapping in the breeze. A crowd of onlookers had materialized almost in a moment, standing along the road and on the benches in the garden. He recognized the maid Sarah and the day porter from Number 4. The rest seemed to have sprung up like mushrooms on the lawn after a warm rainy night. Two policemen in uniform stood on either side of the premises at Number 22. The workmen were hacking methodically at the plaster covering the solid chimney shaft.

"Why did you not tell your sister here that you had sold the picture, Mrs. Winship?"

Miss Caroline Winship was motionless in the yellow chair. "I—I couldn't."

A fit of coughing choked her. She clutched her handkerchief to her mouth.

"You were ill, the night you came from Kent. Your sister called in Mr. Sidney Copeland, a surgeon who had tended your husband."

Dan went across the room to Mary and took her hand. She looked up at him, her face pale, as Bull's slow and inexorable voice went on.

"These facts are recorded in Inspector Pulham's report and elaborated on in his private notes. You did come to Mrs. Winship, at eight-fifteen o'clock the night she arrived from Kent, did you not, Mr. Copeland? And while you were there, Mrs. Winship was seized with one of her asthmatic attacks?"

Copeland spoke reluctantly. "If I remember correctly, that is so. It was a long time ago."

"Too long," Caroline Winship said. Her gaze across the Square was unwavering. Her voice had a hollow quality of doom, above the hollow pick-pick-pick of iron points echoing across the trees.

"Too long for a woman to suffer," Bull said quietly. He turned back to Louise Winship. "You were married to Scott Winship from 22 Godolphin Square on the twenty-second of January 1925. The roses that you get—have got each year, except during the war—come on the sixteenth of October—which is the day you married him in 1924, secretly, in the Registry Office in Oxford. You wore three red roses. Scott Winship had no money to buy more. Mr. Elliot Winship here stood for his brother. He is the only person, presumably, who knew you were married to him then."

Elliot Winship flushed as she looked round at him. "Sorry, old girl. I'd really got to tell him, you know. Police, and all that.

Awkward, you know, withholding information, and all that sort of thing."

Dan McGrath could hear the voices of the men working across the Square, and the hack-crash, hack-crash—hack-crash, hack-crash like incidental discords, hardly heard at moments, sharply audible at others. He looked down at Mary, took her hand and held it tight—a taut and frightened orphan of a storm that should never have touched her life at all.

"It was also on the sixteenth October," Bull said, "that this announcement appeared in *The Times*." He took a faded newspaper clipping out, holding it in his hand. "This was also in Inspector Pulham's private papers—an entry he added almost ten years after everyone else at Scotland Yard had forgotten Scott Winship."

"I—I have always been sorry," Louise Winship whispered. "I've never forgiven myself."

"Nor have you ever been forgiven, Mrs. Winship," Bull said evenly. "I'm sorry to have to tell you that the flowers that have been sent you for so long—the few primroses that came on your birthday in April, and the three roses on your wedding day— were ordered to be sent to you on those days, and paid for, for twenty-five years in advance, on the day your husband bought his ticket to Paris. Confidential instructions with bank notes to cover the charges were posted in London on that day. The florist received them the next morning, October third, and the order was entered on his books that day."

The frail color that had risen to Louise Winship's cheeks drained out of them.

"You mean—he did not intend to come back to me? Oh, no, no!"

"Not exactly," Inspector Bull said. "The shop they were

ordered from was bombed during the blitz. They stopped coming then. They began again when the florist's daughter opened up the shop, and being an honest woman, carried on the obligations that she had records left for. It was Pegott who sent the roses the other day—on the wrong day. It was Pegott who told Sophie Barnes, the girl in the florist's shop, to change the address from Twenty-two Godolphin Square to Four Godolphin Square. He had—guessed by then that Scott Winship did not know your present address or that Number Twenty-two had been destroyed in the war."

The quality of the rhythmic sound coming from across the Square changed abruptly. It was no longer the hollow hack and thud of the falling plaster but the ringing metallic note of iron on harder substance. Dan looked over. The plaster was gone. Left was the blurred pink of the solid brick and mortar, and he heard the clank of the sledge hammer striking the chisels into it, picking the iron mortar away piece by piece—each resounding blow translated, quivering, through Caroline Winship's rigid body, tearing away the substance of her heart as it tore away the solid substance of her property.

"Pegott came here to join Miss Grimstead's staff with one thing in mind," Bull said. "His father was a stonemason, and he'd listened to his father's stories. He knew about Scott Winship, and he'd learned by eavesdropping about the picture Winship had sold for ten thousand pounds. In his father's ledger there's an entry for additional labor at Twenty-two Godolphin Square not included in a contract for repairs to the area and rear foundations. September twenty-eight, 1925, there's an entry 'Remove mantel and brick from hall fireplace chimney, first floor,' and on October third there's an entry 'Replace same.' The day before that second date was the day Scott Winship came up from Kent and took the American dealer to the house to view and buy the picture. Miss Caroline Winship was staying in Richmond. The servants were away. The house was closed while Pegott senior was making repairs to the foundations.

"Sophie Barnes thought Pegott, the valet, talked wildly about a fortune he was about to make. She thought he was fooling her, but she also thought he was going to marry her, so she listened. Pegott knew he couldn't hope to manage alone, especially with Miss Winship watching the house to see that her mantel and staircase weren't carried off by collectors. He went to see Mr. Elliot Winship on the pretext of selling him some of his father's moulds, but couldn't get to see him. He finally decided on Dalrymple-Hughes as a relative who might be able to persuade Miss Winship, I expect, to allow the search. Because Pegott was a cunning man, and he had put several things together. He believed that a picture worth ten thousand pounds had got walled up in the house there. He'd got a good deal of information, by prying and eavesdropping. He'd told Mr. McGrath his father always thought a mistake had been made—by which he meant his father had not thought Scott Winship had taken the picture away.

"Pegott was ready to act. When Mr. McGrath came here, he made the mistake—as others did, and natural under all the circumstances—of connecting him with the picture. But when Pegott found out from Mr. McGrath what that book about lost paintings was saying, he became frightened, or suspicious. He had taken the book from Mr. McGrath, and learned, or believed he had learned, that the picture was a fake. It was that noon that he lunched with Dalrymple-Hughes. I presume he then sold his 'interest' in the picture—namely, his information that the picture might be concealed, walled up in the masonry, in Twenty-two Godolphin Square—to Dalrymple-Hughes, who had drawn a cheque payable to Pegott for one hundred pounds, reducing his own balance to some three pounds.

"Whether Pegott thought Scott Winship had returned and was trying to get his picture again, I do not know—and whether Dalrymple-Hughes thought he had to act quickly or not at all, is only surmise. But he bought himself a sledge hammer and cold chisel yesterday afternoon. It was the chisel that Miss Mary Winship stumbled over on the stairs last night. It and the sledge hammer have been identified as resembling those sold yesterday to a man of his description. And that he was afraid, we know from his having bought bolts and put them on his doors. He brought the sledge hammer down to this flat with him, not, of course, as he is said to have told Miss Winship, for protection, which is absurd, but because he planned to get up early—he had set his aunt's alarm—go over to Number Twenty-two and go to work to find the picture. He was sure, from what Pegott had told him, and from what he had himself picked up around here, that the picture was there; and presumably he did not know that it was suspected to be a forgery. He had been brutally killed, of course, before the alarm went off to wake him."

"The picture is not a forgery," Miss Caroline Winship said coldly. She did not move her body or turn her head. "The picture is not a forgery."

"You have known all along that the picture really is in the house over there, Miss Winship," Bull said quietly. "You must have known it, of course. The senior Pegott received his fee from you. Inspector Pulham suspected that. He suspected, however, with nothing he could legally demand a search warrant for. No crime had been done in the disappearance of the picture.

You had paid back the dealer; you had closed the door. Pulham came to that conclusion after a number of years of watching the art dealers' sales, and collectors' and museums' acquisitions, here and abroad. You knew that, did you not, Miss Winship?"

"I am not a fool," Caroline Winship said steadily. She did not move until Louise Winship's horrified gasp. She moved her head then for an instant and shot her sister a single glance before she turned back to take up again her brooding vigil.

"Inspector Pulham," Bull went on slowly, "had Mr. Sidney Copeland's report on Scott Winship. He had serious head injuries from the war. The prognosis was unfavorable. Recurrent attacks of amnesia were to be expected. For a long time Pulham expected Scott Winship would return home, as he'd returned when he escaped from the military hospitals where he'd been a patient. Later, Pulham concluded Winship would come back when the five thousand pounds were gone—come back for the picture, to sell it again. It was Scott Winship's return that Pulham was waiting for after he retired from the Force, and up to the time he was killed on Home Guard duty in the blitz."

He took two steps to Miss Winship's chair and looked out over the garden at his men. As he looked back at her, and spoke to her, her gaze stayed, unwavering, on the house.

"It is Scott Winship's return over there, Miss Winship, that all the staff here, and your sister, the policemen who patrol the Square, Mr. Copeland, all of them, think you are waiting for, as you sit here, always, at this window."

"It is false," Caroline Winship said. She struck her stick violently on the floor. "False. That is not why I have sat here. My picture is there. It was *my* picture. It was the only valuable picture in the whole collection—and *my* father gave it to her! He had no right. I took care of my father. She was too weak and sickly to take care of him. I took care of Scott Winship, after the first war, when he ran away from the hospital and crept back, lost, his mind blank!"

She was rising, her cheeks darkly flushed and mottled, staring with a kind of dreadful agony across the Square. Dan McGrath saw that the workmen had gone through the brick. A gaping black hole in the pink blurred chimney column was opening. A man with a crowbar was prying loose a section of the solid wall. The sledge hammers rose and fell. The senior Pegott, he thought, with sudden irrelevance, put his bricks together to stay forever.

Caroline Winship's breath came in labored gasps.

"Yes," Inspector Bull said slowly. His voice was sombre. "I know. I know you took care of him when he was ill. But you've not sat here because of your picture, Miss Winship. It was not because of your picture—or the picture you thought should have belonged to you—that they'd got to tear you away from that staircase the morning the house was bombed out. It was because you were not at Richmond on October second. You were not at Richmond at all—and you were in that house when Scott Winship came there with the dealer, and later when he came back from the bank and told you he'd sold the picture, and that he and his wife were going to Paris to live. But Scott Winship did not get to Paris . . ."

The wall tore loose under the crowbar, a great square of brick, held together still by Pegott the stonemason's art, tearing loose from the chimney face, crashing down to the floor as the workmen jumped back. They moved in again to prize out the sheet metal backing that Dan McGrath could see there. It looked to him at first like some part of the furnace flue. He thought then that it could not be, by the way they were working at it.

Or by what he saw then in the rigid transfixed figure of Caroline Winship. She stood there with one hand on the window frame, gripping it so that her knuckles were white under the brown blotched skin. Her breath came in spasms as she watched as if in some horrible enchantment, her brilliant eyes glittering.

The sheet metal backing was coming out as the men prized it loose. It came forward, like an oven door falling open. The men moved back, in some fantastic slow motion, as if themselves seized by some weird enchantment. Dan McGrath stared, catching his breath, his face turning slowly white.

Lodged in the cavity that was exposed was a statue. It was not a picture. It was the statue of a man, kneeling, his torso bent forward, his head between his knees, bent forward kneeling, like some hideous abject worshipper of an evil god, transfixed and mummified in the act of some hideous contrition. But it was not a statue. It was a man. Or it had been a man. Dan could tell that too by the way the workmen and the policemen stood, and the way one of them, after a petrified instant, reached slowly for his cap and took it off, and the others followed one by one. And by the way they moved quickly back as the terrible kneeling figure there seemed to come to some fearful life, moving sideways out of its ghastly crypt, leaning, toppling, falling slowly out and down, down at their feet and onto the floor. Dan McGrath could see it there, the form and figure of a man, for an instant—and then, in an instant, shrunk, shrunk and collapsed into a dark and awful heap on the floor, decay and dissolution. Dust thou art, to dust returneth.

One of the men there not in workman's clothes moved then, after a long moment, reaching into the cavity that had been Scott Winship's tomb for twenty-four years—from his daughter's birth, through her childhood, through a war that had brought her to maturity, always believing he was alive and would one day come back to them. Out of it he brought a small flat rectangular object. As he held it, Dan saw something, dark and unshaped, barely more than an amorphous cloud, fall from it. The man was holding in his hand a frame, the frame empty, the picture that it had once held crumbled, disintegrated, a handful of shreds and dust fallen and dispersed.

He turned, looking in mute horror at Caroline Winship.

"He's mine," she whispered. "He's still mine. He belonged to me. The picture belonged to me." She beat her stick on the floor. "They were plotting to sell it. Even before they went to Kent they were plotting to sell it and go away, and leave me!"

It was like some awful recitation dredged, whispering, up from the bitterest depths of her heart. "That's why I closed the house. That's why I let them think I'd be at Richmond for the day. I knew they'd come. I was ready for them—for both of them —and *she* did not come!"

She wheeled round, her face livid, the heavy eyelids torn open from her brilliant gleaming eyes. Louise Winship shrank back in speechless terror before that glance.

"I hate her! She took him from me . . . *She* should be dead!"

Miss Caroline Winship threw up her arm, her stick poised. "She *shall*—"

Her thick body was convulsed, the stick fell from a clawing hand to the floor. She held herself erect, terrible for an instant with hatred and despair, and pitched forward. She lay there, her face purple and suffused, her hands clawing once before they were still.

23

D<small>AN</small> held Mary Winship, white-faced, close in his arms. He did not care to look around the room, in the silence there in which life seemed suspended.

Inspector Bull's voice was calm and grave.

"And you would have died, Mrs. Winship. You were meant to die when your husband died. You were meant again to die yesterday. Miss Grimstead's coming up and calling Copeland here was the only thing in the world that saved you. That, and her first stroke last night, after she'd killed Eric Dalrymple-Hughes to save herself, just as she'd done Pegott, and tried to do to Mr. Pinkerton, thinking he knew more than he did, or possibly mistaking him for Pegott."

He turned as Sidney Copeland came back from the room to which they had carried her.

"Your task is here, Mr. Copeland," he said evenly. "Not there. There's no pity needed for a murderess. This woman killed a man she was in love with because he married another woman, and then carried on a sadistic torture under the guise of kindness to that woman and her child—pretending she'd paid the dealer back out of her own pocket when there's no doubt she merely returned him the money she'd taken from Scott Winship when she killed him the night of October second—pretending that a letter had come from him in Monte Carlo when her sister was too ill to detect the forgery, and destroying it in a pretence of anger before anyone else could see it.

"There's no doubt Miss Winship has for years been administering poison to her half-sister Mrs. Winship—to bring on the supposed attack of asthma whenever the flowers that she herself had sent arrived, and every time her sister made up her mind that her husband would never return, and decided to have him declared dead so she could marry the man who'd stood faithfully by her year after year. It was nothing poisonous to anyone else in the house. It was something she could herself easily administer, when she pleased, to keep up the fiction in the minds of reputable medical men that it was a psychic disturbance, connected with the presumed presence of her husband. Miss Caroline Winship was playing on her faith and affection, trying to destroy her before her death even, in the minds of her daughter and the man who wanted to marry her. People get tired of neurotic women, always sick and worn out."

Louise Winship, stunned and scarcely breathing, kept her eyes blindly on him, as in a daze.

"We can find out what it was. The valet Pegott had a tin of mushrooms in his despatch case. I've wondered if he suspected this part of Miss Winship's design too."

Louise Winship shook her head. "I never eat mushrooms. They made me sick as a child. I've never touched them since."

"Then mushrooms they were," Bull said dryly. "The liquor from the tin in your broth would be all you'd need, Mrs. Winship. If your attacks hadn't always been connected with the fiction of your husband, your doctors would have had you in hospital finding out what it was—if your sister had allowed you to go. An allergy to mushrooms, or to anything of the sort, ma'am, would have made you deathly ill, in the way you were. And that's no doubt why during the war you weren't ill. Your sister was too busy worrying whether a bomb or the blast would wreck her house and expose her guilt, and tinned mushrooms were not easy to get. I imagine you'll be a well woman, now, ma'am. And you can thank Miss Grimstead's prying ways that you're still alive. Her and Dalrymple-Hughes. It was him hammering his bolts in the woodwork she heard and came up to investigate."

He turned to Copeland with an inquiring glance. The surgeon shook his head.

"There's no chance, Inspector. But if she could pull out, she'd be paralyzed for life."

Mary Winship held tight to Dan's hand. "I don't want her to live and suffer," she said quietly. Her face was still white, her eyes wide with shock. "I—I can't believe it. She was always kind to me."

Inspector Bull passed over without remark an error of omission in prognosis that Scotland Yard could hardly be expected to make but that there was no need to mention.

"I think you were the one person alive that she cared about, Miss Winship," he said gently. "She tried to send you away when she felt things were closing in, to keep you out of it. I expect she could have thought of you as her child."

Louise Winship sat up, breathing deeply, as if testing whether she could really breathe again, freely and without fear.

"It's very strange," she said unsteadily. "Once, a long time ago, I—I *knew* he was dead. I knew it very clearly. But then I'd forget. I told Caroline. She said it was because I wished him dead, so I could marry. I remember now the night we were bombed. She kept crying, 'They'll never find him.' Over and over again. And when the demolition people came, she sat at this window and didn't move, or eat, for days. One day she looked over there and said, 'God has saved my house for me. I'll build it up again.' She tried to get a license to rebuild."

She breathed a deep free breath again.

"We didn't mean to be wicked, to hurt her so. She *had* taken care of him. And he—when he was very ill, he *had* thought he was in love with her—before we met. It was cruel, but we couldn't help it. We were terribly in love."

She held out her hand, and Bull took the newspaper clipping out of his pocket and gave it to her.

"The King and Queen have returned from Sandringham."

"King George and Queen Mary," Louise Winship whispered. Bull watched her reading the old announcement.

"A marriage has been arranged and will soon take place between Scott William Winship, late of H. M. Guards, and Miss Caroline Winship, daughter of the late Colonel Elliot Philip Winship, D. S. O., of 22 Godolphin Square."

She closed her eyes for an instant. "It was the—the very day we were married. We didn't know, of course, that she'd got the announcement off to the press, and we were going to tell her the next day. We were terrified. But she found out. She pretended not to mind. She insisted we be properly married, at home, not to embarrass her. Then she took care of us. We had nothing but the picture. We couldn't bear it, eating her bread and living in her house. That's when we decided to sell the picture. We weren't sure it was genuine. Scott was almost frantic with delight when he got me on the phone and told me we'd got ten thousand pounds. But we were afraid to tell her. He was going to Paris and get us a flat. I thought the excitement had brought back his illness, when I didn't hear from him. I was afraid to tell Caroline. She was so kind to me, and so bitter because he'd left me."

Sidney Copeland went over to her. "Don't, my dear. It's through with, now. I was a fool, not to see."

For one moment it seemed to Dan McGrath that Mr. Sidney Copeland was very nearly human—until the surgeon happened to notice then, off in a corner, an almost forgotten man. Mr. Elliot Winship. He stiffened slightly.

"I don't see what brought you into all this."

Elliot Winship took his pipe out of his pocket and looked at it. He looked up at everyone then with a quiet deprecatory smile.

"Trying to help out, that's all," he said apologetically. "Made a frightful mess of it, I expect." He looked at Dan, shaking his head in genuine ruefulness. "Must really apologize, old boy. Swine, absolute swine. No lunch. Foul cocktail. Tepid stuff —horrible. Felt like an ass, a complete ass, trying to have you on. But, you see, I'd not done young Pegott in. I'd been in his room, too, but I'd just sat there waiting for the bounder to come in. Never thought of looking in the wardrobe. Never crossed my mind. Then Mrs. O'Neill said he'd been to see me about the ruddy moulds. And I'd known his father. Good man, Old Pegott. Jolly fine stonemason, always talking in riddles about missing valuables walled up somewhere. I expect he'd twigged. In part. Knew there might be something back of that metal screen. Heard about the blasted picture later. I always thought he was a bit addled, you know. Until Mary got the wind up about this other McGrath fellow that wrote the book, and all that."

Elliot Winship looked around at them a little more cheerfully.

"Well, put two and two together, then, and all that sort of thing. There was some plaster on his rug—sort of thing I'd notice, d'you see—and there was Caroline's wretched house staring me in the face. That's when *I* twigged. In part too, may I say. Thought I'd have a look at the place last night."

He smiled less happily then at his niece. "So sorry, old girl.

But you really had me bothered. Didn't mean to frighten you. I'd just got out of the clutches of the gendarmes—and my friend here . . ."

He glanced at Mr. Pinkerton, who, still white-faced himself and shattered, stood back against the wall, looking little like anyone's friend.

". . . and all I could think of was to make a run for it. Didn't know you'd tumbled down the stairs till I rang up good old Grimstead this morning. Thought I'd best see the Chief Inspector at once."

He took the square of oatmeal tweed out of his raincoat pocket and looked at it ruefully. "Only got two suits left, you know. Expect Mrs. O'Neill can see an Invisible Mender to patch me together again. If anyone can see an Invisible Mender— wonderful woman. But I *am* sorry, Mary, you know. I hope McGrath doesn't hold it against either of us. And you do look frightfully disreputable, my dear."

He smiled at her, and she looked at Dan.

"I'll string along still," said McGrath the magnanimous. "I guess she'll patch up as well as your coat."

Sidney Copeland cleared his throat.

"If I understand your idiom, Mr. McGrath," he said, "perhaps I'd better remind you that in England we like to know something about the young men our daughters marry—about them and their families, and their families' antecedents, if they've got—"

"Good old Copey." Elliot Winship interrupted him amiably. "Spoken like a true Heart of Druid Oak, old man. And as an expectant stepfather, he's right, you know, McGrath. Absolutely right. We've heard about these wolves with an easy grin.

233

Got to keep up our austerity standards, old chap. Now, how many murderers can you offer? Can't let down the bars, you know. You've got to measure up—"

"*Elliot!*"

Mrs. Winship's strength was coming back.

"Sorry, old girl. But it does rather occur to me that McGrath has a damned lot more reason to ask for our credentials than we've got to ask for his. If I were Mary I'd not stand back. I'd take him, no questions asked. Look at his face. God never made a counterfeit, you know. And Copey surely knows enough to know that McGrath had nothing whatsoever to do with his nationality at birth."

He smiled at Dan, and Dan grinned back. "Thanks, pal." He turned to Sidney Copeland. "But you're right, sir. The Mc-Graths don't mind being investigated. There's our Embassy. Or try your own consul in Baltimore. But after all, it's up to Mary, isn't it? Or is it? I forget I'm not at home."

"Yes, it is, Mr. McGrath." Louise Winship smiled at him. "It's up to Mary."

"She'll have to live in Baltimore, Marlyand. She'll have to learn how to cook if she doesn't know how. A pioneer woman, drawing the water and hewing the wood. When she can hobble around, that is. We don't work our women when they're lame. She won't have much money till I make it, but she'll—"

"Oh, don't, Dan, don't!" Mary pulled herself up with her one good hand onto her one good foot. "Please don't! I don't care if we starve. All I want is—"

"Good girl," Dan said. "Here, use this." He took out his handkerchief and wiped her face tenderly with it. "You're sweet, Mary. Maybe life won't be so tough, where you and I are going."

234

"I say," Elliot Winship murmured. "I'd rather like to go there myself. I could do with a joint of beef. I'm so fed up with offal."

24

Inspector Bull had gone. Dan could see him through the window, his burly figure moving through the ragged overgrown rhododendrons across to the house where the staircase curved gracefully up to the sky.

"Well, I think Mr. Pinkerton and I'll go along," he said.

He lifted Mary Winship's chin and kissed her gently.

"Get well quick, will you, honey? I'm tired of always having an audience around. It ruins my technique."

Mary smiled up at him. "I think it's quite—okay."

"Speak your own language, lady. You speak yours and I'll speak mine. Good-bye now. I'll be back."

A sort of dumb compassion wrinkled his lean earnest face as he looked down at her. "Don't think about it, Mary, sweet," he whispered. "Don't let it get you down, baby. It's—"

She buried her dark head quickly in his shoulder for a moment. "Oh, no! It's—it's horrible—but at least we know. There's nothing we can do. We don't have to worry and wonder, and be always waiting, any more. And Mother—Mother'll be well again."

"That's my girl." He held her tightly for an instant, and

then for the fourth time his audience made no difference to Mc-Grath of Baltimore.

Out in the hall Mr. Pinkerton stopped and took off his steel-rimmed, lozenge-shaped spectacles, and polished them with his torn handkerchief. They were unaccountably blurred. He blinked his eyes, put the spectacles back on, and looked timidly up at Dan McGrath.

"I'm very pleased, Dan," he said. "I'm really very pleased, about you and Mary. I'd really like to congratulate you . . ."

They shook hands solemnly.

"And I've just thought of something," Mr. Pinkerton said. "Do you recall?—she always told everybody Scott Winship was dead. Miss Caroline, I mean. She said it over and over again. Oh, dear, what great fools she must have thought us, not to believe her when she was telling the truth."

"Right," Dan said. "I thought of that, back in there. Let's forget it now, shall we?"

Mr. Pinkerton nodded vigorously. He was glad to forget it.

"Well," he said. His heart sank a little. "Well, I expect I should go back to my room."

It was so seldom that he felt the tremulous brush of the butterfly wings of romance rising above the terror and brutality of crime to erase the memory of it, and to flutter through his small grey heart leaving there a precious deposit of its radiant and iridescent dust, that he was loathe to let it go. He looked up at his new friend.

"Nuts," said McGrath. "You and I are going out and get some lunch and go to a movie. I guess the Winships'll be glad to get rid of both of us a while. And I know just the picture you'd like to see."

It was in Oxford Street near Marble Arch. They crossed

Park Lane after lunch at the Dorchester, where Mr. Pinkerton would no more have dared to go alone than he would have dared to call at Buckingham Palace at the sherry hour, and went into Hyde Park on their way to the Edgware Road. Small knots of listeners were clustered round the stands of the few hardy speakers already out. An occasional policeman strolled by, to protect the right of each and every one of them to say what he would, unmolested. Suddenly from the makeshift rostrum nearest the Marble Arch came a hoarse vibrant voice.

"The wicked *shall* be repaid—*and* the good!"

Mr. Pinkerton stopped dead, blinking, clutching at Dan's coat sleeve. They could not see the speaker, but they did not need to.

"Oh, dear!" Mr. Pinkerton said. "That means . . . Dear, dear. Miss Grimstead must have given him the sack."

"No," said Dan. "He quit. Sarah told me this morning. He presented Miss Grimstead with his compliments, and left. Not —in those words, however. Something Biblical, Sarah said, that she couldn't think of repeating."

"Goodness," said Mr. Pinkerton.

Nevertheless, he was somewhat relieved. He scurried past the knot of listeners round the former chef, keeping well on the off-shore side of Dan McGrath, trusting the chef would not see him or he the chef. While he had no reasonable doubt that the man was properly clothed, or the policeman would hardly allow him there in Hyde Park, in Mr. Pinkerton's mind he would be forever clad in a simple nightshirt, and Mr. Pinkerton had no desire to see it again, or those bare feet and horny toes.

He would, in fact, much rather see Miss Rita Hayworth. He knew, as he trotted along beside his friend McGrath, that that was what they were going to see at this cinema, because he had already been there twice. The queue of women formed outside the theatre dampened him for just a moment, as he was sure Dan was not the sort who'd queue up and stand in line, even for Miss Hayworth. Then his heart rose. The queue was not outside the theatre but outside the butcher's next door, where a large sign in the window said "Offal Today."

Dan McGrath stared. "You don't really eat the stuff? Or is that a critical comment on the dramatic offering presented next door?"

Mr. Pinkerton blinked at him. He was a little bewildered. "Awful, I mean?"

"Why, of course we eat it," Mr. Pinkerton said warmly. "A grilled kidney is very nice. And calves' liver. A young beef heart is nice too, when you can get it."

"Ah," Dan said. He grinned. "That's what you call them. I hope Mary's careful what she says to my father. He calls them something else, though not in public, or when my mother's around."

Mr. Pinkerton blinked again. Every time he thought he understood the Americans, something happened that convinced him he really had not yet reached that point.

Inspector Bull stood on the hanging balcony of the bombed house with Inspector Carson, in front of the gaping hole in the chimney face. All that was mortal of Scott Winship had gone. The dried and blackened canvas dust, that with a woman's passionate and embittered heart had been his death knell, sounded in the deserted house after the first way, waiting for a second then to rend the walls and send it echoing through the dying leaves to be heard again, was gone too. No one would ever know whether it was genuine or false, lost forgery or lost masterpiece crumbled irretrievably to flakes and shreds, some blown into nothing by the wind.

"He was wedged just in there, sir, with the picture propped up in front of him. Poor devil. His skull was smashed. And this sheet was fixed in to cover him from sight."

He took up the square of galvanized tin leaning against the bricks. "It's part of a furnace sheathing. She must have planned the whole thing out some time before and had this cut and brought to the house. She must have been strong as an ox to get him in here."

Bull nodded soberly. "Her father was paralyzed. She was used to lifting him about, I expect. She was a powerful woman. But this isn't heavy."

He took the sheet of metal from Carson's hands.

"No. And it was fixed in neatly behind the bricks to seal him in. I wouldn't be surprised if she'd not stood here with old Pegott while he laid the brick so he didn't have a look behind."

"I expect if he had done, he'd have joined Winship, and she'd have finished the brick work herself."

"Right, sir."

Inspector Carson bent down and picked up a dried black flake of the old canvas. "Too bad about this—if it was worth £10,000. The heat from the flue in winter and the damp in summer were too much for it, I expect." He let the fragment fall to the floor. "Well, I hope old Pulham's looking down on us. He'd like this."

Bull crossed over to Number 4. Miss Caroline Winship's room was closed, the door locked. Hope could live there again. It lived already in the sitting room of the flat where Mrs. Winship and Sidney Copeland were, and where Mary Winship waited for Dan McGrath.

He stopped last in Miss Myrtle Grimstead's office.

"I'm certainly glad I went upstairs, Inspector," Miss Grimstead was saying briskly. "I never believed Mrs. Winship was quite so seedy as she looked."

It was the most flagrant knowledge after the event, but what of that, Bull thought.

"And I shouldn't have gone up, Inspector, and insisted on ringing Mr. Copeland, as I did when I saw how very seedy she really was then, if I'd not heard scratching and hammering. I never suspected it was that Dalrymple-Hughes putting bolts on my newly decorated woodwork. I never would have thought Caroline Winship was not ringing the doctor on purpose. I thought she was too unstrung at her sister's distress. And I didn't find out what the noise I'd heard was, until I looked about again that night. I'm afraid I gave Mary and Mr. McGrath quite a turn, but I found out what had made the noise."

Miss Grimstead was managerially efficient and crisp about the whole thing.

"I shall report it to the Estate Managers," she said. "I think the Winships should be held responsible for the damage done. And I shall also request them for permission to require Mr. Pinkerton to find other lodgings. He's a great trial to me, Inspector Bull. *Besides* a loss of revenue. Do you realize he's inveigled them into permitting Mr. McGrath to live here without charge as long as he's in London? And with Mary all crocked up, heaven knows how long that will be. A week? Two weeks? Who can tell? When I inquired of Mr. Copeland after lunch, he as much as told me it was none of my business."

Inspector Bull, a patient and also a kindly man, chewed at the end of his tawny mustache.

"Well, Miss Grimstead," he said placidly, moving toward

the door. "If it hadn't been for Mr. Pinkerton, there might have been more trouble."

He smiled faintly, inwardly, and shook his head a little, thinking about it, and recalling that it was Pinkerton's remembering Miss Caroline Winship had called him "Mr. Pilkington" that had tilted the whole puzzle into place in his mind. It was Pilkington Crescent where Pegott's father the stonemason had lived.

"We should give him full marks for that."

Miss Grimstead raised her brows briefly.

"And another thing," Bull said. "I shouldn't give him away, and I'm telling you this in confidence, ma'am. But I shouldn't try to put him out of this house, if I were you. He owns it. He's the Pinkerton of Pinkerton Estates Ltd."

He opened the door. "Good day, ma'am," he said mildly. "I expect you'll not have any more trouble now for a bit. I hope not. Good-bye."

It was not often that Miss Grimstead was at a complete loss. She stared speechless, now, at the door that had closed behind the large cinnamon-brown figure of the inspector from New Scotland Yard. Miss Grimstead had been standing behind her desk. She now said "My God!" and sank down into her chair, still staring at the door. Suddenly she raised her hand and put it over her mouth.

"Pinkerton," she whispered. "Pinkerton of Pinkerton Estates Ltd." Rich. A bachelor. Not a bachelor, a widower. Widowers were simpler than bachelors. Every woman knew that.

With an unsteady hand Miss Grimstead reached down, unlocked and pulled open her lowest desk drawer. She took out the bottle of her restorative, a trifle of gin kept medicinally for emergencies—though never yet for one like this—poured a couple of inches into the glass she also kept there, and swallowed it no heel taps. She replaced the bottle and glass, closed the drawer and locked it again. After a few moments of meditation she reached out and pressed the bell for Sarah the maid.

When the girl came, Miss Grimstead was herself again, brisk and managerial and efficient, with two bright roses blooming in her cheeks—brighter than usual, actually, as Miss Grimstead customarily took a little water with her restorative.

"Sarah," she said. "We're going to move dear Mr. Pinkerton into Mr. Dalrymple-Hughes's flat. I think he'll be more comfy there."

It was her former favorite's flat. Off with the old, on with the new, Miss Grimstead thought to herself a little groggily. "And Sarah, don't forget to put a hot water bottle in his bed at night, dear. Gentlemen like to be warm and cozy. And clean towels twice a week, Sarah. I'll speak to the new valet. We mustn't keep Mr. Pinkerton waiting for his breakfast. And the lamb's kidney we saved for Colonel Mayhew—I'm sure Mr. Pinkerton would enjoy that, grilled on a nice piece of hot toast."

Sarah backed out of the door. "Cor! *Dear* Mr. Pinkerton. Ain't 'e goin' to be surprised." She set out on an open run to the kitchen to tell the staff.

Miss Grimstead, after further meditation, broke a hard and fast rule: she took a second drop of restorative. She then took the bill she had already started to make out for Mr. McGrath in the box room. She picked up her pen and dipped it in the pot of red ink on the desk in front of her. There was a small item of five pounds surcharge and service fees over and above the basic charge. She crossed it out. Then she thought again, crumpled the paper in her hand and dropped it in the trash basket.

"And isn't Mr. McGrath going to be surprised!" she thought. *"He* thinks Mr. Pinkerton is *pathetic."*

What was it Mr. McGrath had said to her about Mr. Pinkerton? She tried to remember.

"He's one sweet little guy," he had said.

"Well!" said Miss Grimstead. She sat smiling to herself. It was axiomatic, in any bright lexicon, that no lonely widower could successfully resist the blandishments of good food in his stomach and a hot water bottle in his bed. To say nothing of charm. Miss Grimstead pulled the silken thread, sweet with honey, from her mind's alert cocoon. A spider might have hers elsewhere, but one could hardly speak so of the manageress of Number 4 Godolphin Square. Miss Grimstead started deftly weaving her happy web.

Mr. Evan Pinkerton sat breathless and enchanted beside Daniel McGrath at the cinema in the Edgware Road, enthralled by Hollywood and love among the Americans.

www.ingramcontent.com/pod-product-compliance
Lightning Source LLC
Chambersburg PA
CBHW020800250626
47155CB00003B/1162